THE TURNING POINT

THE TURNING POINT

ONLY A LITTLE INTO THE FUTURE

W.J. BLACKWOOD

Matador
Unit E2 Airfield Business Park
Harrison Road, Market Harborough
Leicestershire LE16 7UL
Tel: 0116 279 2299
Email: books@troubador.co.uk
Web: www.troubador.co.uk/matador
Twitter: @matadorbooks

ISBN 978-1-80514-111-2

British Library Cataloguing in Publication Data.
A catalogue record for this book is available from the British Library.

Printed by TJ Books Ltd, Padstow, UK
Typeset in 11pt Adobe Garamond Pro by Troubador Publishing Ltd, Leicester, UK

Matador is an imprint of Troubador Publishing Ltd

1

JUDY

The Foundation saw their assumptions and adopted rules regarding the abduction of girls as perfectly validated. This was due to the perceived success that had come with the first few examples. Basing their approval on a small set of victims was a big mistake, however, and one which The Foundation would not normally have made. With Judy, they had made a major error as a result. In their plan, all the girls were to self-present in Los Angeles by applying for false ads seeking applicants for possible work, not obviously in acting, which would have been too suspect, but merely to try out for minor promotional material and advertisements. It was an early weakness. They had recognised this and sought to compensate by checking the girls' backgrounds, and this assured them that nobody was likely to come looking for them when they vanished, but it left other matters unexplored. This was the case with Judy. A first hint should have come when she showed the ability to actually perform in her commercial. That should have been the warning that there was potential trouble ahead. However, The Foundation was based on a need-to-know basis and this secrecy had sometimes permitted the premature acceptance of the imperfect because the guiding principles could never be questioned from below. And, by Judy, they fell as a result.

All that they had found out about her family was correct, but it was not a good guide as to how it had formed and shaped Judy. Now, this is generally true and that should have been recognised and allowed for by The Foundation. She had been surprisingly understanding of both parents when they went through escalating levels of immoderate behaviour before finally divorcing. She had one brother who was in jail in Illinois, but everyone knew the reason for that and sympathised and blamed Chicago. Her mother had stayed behind and remarried a drunk and had joined him in his recreation. They ran a liquor store which was being wiped out by a new twenty-four-hour supermarket. She recognised the mother as weak and eternally chasing fantasies but thought that she herself was not the same and decided that she had no need to be determined to change. Her father, in times of trouble, escaped. He had fled south to the heat where he managed a trailer park in Florida for snowbirds who could not afford the retirement villages. It was obvious to her that an element of this had been passed down to her, but she decided that in some circumstances it was the thing to do and that in her place in that obscure town on the edge of Michigan, facing at best the chance of a job of repetitive monotony for life, it was the appropriate response. She had come to LA because the changing fashion in the current place for taking flight to was slow to arrive in her corner. On arrival, she found it a tawdry, dangerous and divided place where she struggled to keep out of having to live in the bad neighbourhoods and could only afford to be a tourist in the good ones. She persisted through doggedness and had had a series of jobs not too much different from her previous prospects back home. She could just afford a ten-year-old car and an apartment shared with three other girls. It was in an area that was not quite a sink address but which was slipping over the edge. It was the three girls that were important to her. Men were not at all frequent in her life as she was very difficult to woo and treated them with amiable detachment when they thought that they should be taken seriously. Whether the seriousness was that of the self-regarding stud or a case of an all-round inflated ego, she would quietly laugh at them in a slightly patronising manner, and there was no need of further dismissing their attention. She had decided within a few weeks of arriving in town that this was not the life she was wanting and was constantly and actively planning her next escape. There were all kinds of schemes for this under review at any time: going back to college, changing jobs or changing cities. She was just determined that she was not going to resolve herself to things or get out of trouble under a man. What The Foundation had missed was that the dream of stardom, while it might have been the root of LA's appeal in the past, was not something that Judy gave a thought to. LA was just a big city in the sun where everybody led the Californian lifestyle as she viewed it from Michigan. She did not give Hollywood a thought, and it was only one of the girls she shared with who had seen the ad from Panomnes Productions and dared her to apply – which of course she had.

She worked long shifts in a chain restaurant which was not enough yet to supress her frothy attitude to her existence. So, when an invitation to Panomnes Productions arrived, she was transformed and thought that this was the way out she was seeking. She drove to the place with a friend from the apartment called Rachel, who was suspicious and deeply mistrustful of all good fortune arriving out of the blue. They found the place well out of town in the desert and were duly impressed by the size of it and the organisation on display. Such was Judy's showing at the trial that they called her back soon after and had her do a real commercial for a local chain of nail bars. The Foundation had reached that level of sophistication. The commercials were being done for real by then and not for dummy clients. This was another layer of avoiding distrust. Even Rachel was convinced.

Judy innocently babbled on about these developments afterwards, but it was in such a way that her friends accepted it as her good fortune as she never appeared to brag about it. However, she was from that moment, set up as the next Foundation target for disappearance.

2

THE MECHANICS OF VANISHING

Judy's intended fate was to vanish from view. To become a permanent missing person and a police file that would be visited less and less over the years until it was ignored completely. The business of abduction was a new one for The Foundation and it sought to put someone in management role over it. The man they chose was a Mr Said-Maartens. He was a man as close to being without background as any of his very few acquaintances had ever encountered. One once asked about his name and wondered if there could be any Middle Eastern or Dutch connections, as Said-Maartens spoke perfect Received Pronunciation. He could honestly answer them that he did not know. He had not asked either parent about their name; it had never occurred to him to do so. He was an only child, knew of no cousins and could have instigated a search out of curiosity, but curiosity was not a feature of Mr Said-Maartens.

He had started out in hotel management, was very able and ambitious and had become a manager at a very expensive hotel in London by his early thirties. He speculated, for he was never specifically told, that his talent in general customer service, arranging things for overseas guests and his guarantees of absolute discretion when the things he arranged were of a carnal nature had been noticed. He had been approached and offered the task of managing a very exclusive bijou hotel, the function of which was the entertainment of very important male guests by the most beautiful young women imaginable. The offer came from a body that referred to itself only as The Foundation. It came with over treble his salary. He accepted almost at once through greed combined with a strange unworldliness in one who had seen most of the unsavoury sides of human nature. It was a richly appointed establishment which appeared exactly as the kind of hotel where the prices are not ever mentioned and only listed on a discreet invoice conveyed to the customer almost with regret at the end of the stay. He did not know who he worked for and never thought of speculating about it. This lack of curiosity applied in all but one aspect of the running of his new place. His experience had ingrained in him the rigour of financial analysis of all parts of his hotels. He knew costings and revenue streams as second nature and lived by the dictates of the spreadsheet. He was not long in his new position when the complete absence of this aspect of his previous life was apparent. What he thought of as his responsibility was never mentioned, and unless, as he assumed, there was somebody higher up taking that on, then it seemed not to matter. So, he put together a spreadsheet of his own, entered all the income and outgoings as far as he knew them, or could guess them, and decided that the place was not close to making a profit and assumed that the continual loss of money bothered nobody above him.

He had been instructed to pay the income of the place to an account in an obscure Swiss bank. In matters of taxes, local and national, he did nothing, and no authorities ever approached his establishment. He was not tempted to fiddle, and neither were the other staff as they were all very well paid and knew, while never having been plainly told, of consequences beyond simple sacking should they attempt to cheat. A large part of his job was to send upwards, reports on the activities of the clientele. He came to imperfectly understand in time that the purpose of his establishment was to form part of a vast club among the influential in business and politics across the globe. His function, and that of an unknown number like him worldwide, was to provide an exact record of the sexual preferences of all its members. The membership of this club could be approached when favours were sought but always in the background, and never with any crudely expressed thought of blackmail.

Mr Said-Maartens had only been uncertainly aware of the number of such clubs before he was summoned to Cupertino Ca. to be in charge of the whole network and was of necessity introduced to their extent. He had consented as readily to the move to California as he had to his initial recruitment. In London, he had been provided with a free flat in an expensive street in Islington which seemed to go with the job and further boosted the value of his generous salary. In California, he was given more money yet, plus a secret sum paid into a trust for him in the Bahamas and a free house in Old Palo Alto. It had six bedrooms with the surplus accommodation tax also taken care of and a garage with space for four cars – it was by then, of course, illegal to fill all of them – and a large garden made almost completely private by screens of mature trees and flowering shrubs of proven indigenous origin. A Mexican came round to look after the garden and his wife was the lady who cleaned the house every day. The neighbours, who were too Californian for the normal American hospitality, found Said-Martens and his wife to be just another mysterious and secretive tenant of the place, and had nothing to do with them apart from once reporting them for lighting their log fire on a particularly cold couple of days in February. Said-Maartens would have lost points on his newly acquired State Social Credit balance, but The Foundation had the debit cancelled when he told them of it.

Mrs Said-Maartens had been a receptionist in one of the better hotels he had worked in. She was of limited intelligence but applied what she had to her job exclusively and was as discreet as her husband in dealing with the clients. She was humourless and obsessed with cleanliness. When Mr Said-Maartens was recruited to the establishment in London, he kept up the pretence that he was simply working in a very expensive small hotel. When they moved to California, he simply said he was moving to the headquarters of the chain of hotels, which was half true, and as it was merely an office with no women attached, the pretence became much easier. She passed her time in perfect fulfilment with a couple of women's clubs, shopping, and obsessively disinfecting bits of the house after the lady who cleaned had gone home.

In the office, Mr Said-Maartens had a staff of only around thirty to manage all the establishments across the world. They were from all over the world but with a sprinkling of what he took to be Americans, and even one who sounded English, although he never identified himself as such to Mr Said-Maartens when he had heard his accent. Why the office was in California he never found out, but it must have been convenient to somebody who was perhaps nearby. He again made the same decision about monetary concerns when he got out his amateur spreadsheet and, once he was more familiar with the finances of running other houses, he entered the data as best he could for a random selection of them. They all come out the same as his London house; none of them made a profit.

One day, he was warned to expect visitors the next day. Did that mean that some reprimand was to be delivered? His mind then launched out on one of its rare expeditions into speculation. If he made an accidental mistake through not knowing something he was supposed to know, then what would happen? There were whole areas that he knew he was not supposed to know about, but other matters that he was assumed to be the master of. The problem had always been that the boundary could never be discussed, and where it lay was forever uncertain. Drifting utterly unknowingly into a major disaster was always a possibility. The thought followed that he might then be got rid of in some perfectly plausible accident. A new name would be in his seat in days, he knew. In exactly the way that he had never met his own predecessor for any handover.

The office was going about its business quietly when he got there. Exactly at eleven o'clock, a middle-aged woman and a much younger man appeared; they were evidently his guests. In his large private office, he knew it was no good producing pleasantries such as enquiring after their journey, because he did not know if they had come only a few blocks or from the airport after an overnight flight and knew he would not be told. The younger man, who seemed not yet twenty-five, remained silent and only answered questions later. The woman was in her forties, was tall and had been slim but now had a slight overlay of middle-aged volume. She was dressed in a business suit of obvious outstanding tailoring and had her black hair swept back off her head and immaculately gathered at the back. She had to be described as handsome as she was not pretty, nor had ever been so, and her skin was very slightly coloured but not by the sun, and yet she had blue eyes. Her expression, until she spoke, was completely withdrawn and she seemed lost in private thought, but when she interrupted her internal processes to address somebody, her face for an instant took on a surprised look, as one who has just woken up. The face then became animated, and persuaded or explained or warned as was necessary but never engaged, and the eyes almost always roamed elsewhere than the person she was addressing. She spoke with a very slight Scandinavian accent as far as any could be noted but introduced herself as Ms Saldanha. Said-Maartens was not given and never found out any first name. The man was dark with perfectly groomed hair and only a hint of England in his voice. He too wore a costly lightweight suit and obviously tailored shirt. His face was soberly good-looking. They both gave him cards which

Said-Maartens knew were probably merely labels enabling him to get in touch with them and names to call them when he did. On the cards, the elder merely represented herself as Ms Saldanha, while the younger represented himself as a Mr David Johns.

Ms Saldanha at once laid out before Said-Maartens the story of a whole new aspect of the business which he had no idea existed. Ms Saldanha listed the essentials of a new project briefly and succinctly, covering the thing with more frankness than Said-Maartens had ever been led to expect from The Foundation which employed him. She started by talking about their aims in the private hospitality business being to gain leverage with all sorts of figures in politics and business but did not say what they did with that insight. As she knew that this was the first formal notice Said-Maartens had had of these motives, she offered the comment that he had probably worked that out for himself. Said-Maartens allowed himself a slight nod of his head and raised one eyebrow in recognition of this – he also indulged in a surge of internal self-congratulation on his conjecture about the establishments. Ms Saldanha returned an equally muted gesture of the slightest of smiles.

She outlined, again, as she was sure that Said-Maartens knew very well, that many customers developed a preference for certain types of women at their establishments. It was the next revelation that he was greatly troubled by, as Ms Saldanha continued her unfolding story with the presentation of a much more sinister extrapolation. Several clients had approached them through their local establishment managers to ask for a certain type of girl to be their own. She explained that, at first, they had assumed that it was the exclusive use that was being requested and had been prepared to negotiate suitably expensive terms for access like that. However, it had then emerged that what they wanted was simply a woman to be delivered to them as a piece of merchandise. They had assumed that as The Foundation was used to sourcing the best of staff that they would likewise be able to find women of any kind for them. She carefully defined the demand as one for respectable and well-educated girls and, while virginity had had to be impressed on them as not reasonable to ask for, they nonetheless had put a premium on it if it could be found.

Said-Maartens' mind went into a panic at this point.

Is she talking about some kind of sex slavery? How can they possible arrange that – what kind of organisation is this?

Ms Saldanha carried on and answered his unspoken questions.

"The Foundation was at first wary of such a proposition but then saw that it had the potential to deliver a very powerful threat to hang over the client, much more intimidating than the release of the details of sexual preferences ever would be."

She presented this as a matter of evaluated risks and not at all as anything springing from the humanity of the thing.

Said-Maartens managed to interrupt.

"Are you saying that we have agreed to go ahead with this service?" he asked, and attempted to make his voice sound as mundane as possible – almost as if he was anticipating a part in it, and deliberately using 'we' to reinforce that impression. The reply came in appreciative tones that showed that he had been accepted as genuine.

"Why yes, we decided to go ahead with it and have delivered several sample consignments, mainly to Middle Eastern clients already. You will understand that the demand so far has mostly been from there," and she added after the briefest of pauses, "It is often for European types and mostly for the all-American type of girl."

She spoke in a flat voice devoid of emotion and her face carried no sign of any either, and neither did that of the silent and younger dark man who had been attentive throughout.

Said-Maartens was now mentally paralysed but had to interrupt again.

"But… how is it that you, I mean, how is it all arranged – brought about? The details, I mean, and the dangers of the implication that…"

This confusion was taken as occasioned by mere surprise at the enormous amount of work that had gone into it which he did not know of yet.

"Well, as I'm sure again that you know, there has never been any difficulty recruiting excellent staff for our establishments through normal means of recruitment, given how much we pay. But with this new venture, there are great differences and obvious difficulties to be overcome. They must not be professional ladies and have no hint of sex in their grooming. They must be kept in an apparently normal process until the last minute, when we send them off to their destination. Their disappearance has then to be accounted for."

Said-Maartens had to interrupt again, although his head was in no less a confused horror at the huge leap of wickedness that was being described to him. He tried to see if there had been some misunderstanding on his behalf.

"And they are just sent off to some man somewhere… in the… in the Middle East, and they just go off quietly?"

This time, he knew he had betrayed himself and sounded like a disbelieving and outraged old woman, and choking back the rest of his response, he lapsed into a plainly reluctant silence.

The woman paused and frowned slightly. Her left eye twitched just perceptibly.

"We have a workable scheme set up to cover the whole process. I could remind you, Mr Said-Maartens, that when you oversaw our London office, you called in our outside help department to solve that little trouble with the blackmail by some nobody. They had him taken care of in a discreet way and the whole problem was solved very efficiently, and there was no connection with The Foundation at all. In fact, you did rather well on that occasion as I believe has been notified to you before this. So, the morality of the present situation can hardly trouble you – and besides, you must just think of the truly massive power this gives us over certain people in a very unstable and religion-plagued part of the world. We won't be able to pretend to accommodate their religious nonsense for ever, you understand."

Said-Maartens missed this last bit and only remembered the previously mentioned occasion vividly and knew that although he had called in the outside help, he had left the solution up to them. He had called for them to dispose of the tormentor but had only meant in his own head to stop this pest he had attracted and convince him to call off his immature blackmail attempt. When they resolved it by very discreetly killing the amateur extortionist, it had frightened him at the time, but he was not able to object or do anything about it. But now this action had been reflected back to him as his alone. At the time, he had even come to let any moral aspects of the affair be overwhelmed by the sense of awe that he allowed himself to indulge in at the ruthlessness and efficiency of the act. He came to think of it more and more only as a manifestation of the strength of the foundation he had joined. Then, in his way, he stopped considering it altogether, just as he had at first refused to analyse it responsibly. But now he started to appreciate it as part of the complex web of control that The Foundation had woven to protect itself at every level. In case of trouble, he was now seeing that all links from the murder would lead to him. This dread was made more substantial by being recognised as long established but ignored through his own lack of vision and ability to indulge in, and comfort himself with, amoral fantasies.

It silenced him and brought on a new kind of mental numbness. He stopped thinking altogether and, detecting and welcoming what she took for submission, the woman went on.

"And so, Mr Said-Maartens, we have a whole system of very effective cover-ups and front offices set up to deal with this. You do not need to concern yourself over those aspects – all has already been dealt with – although," and here she went into a slightly indulgent tone, almost as if trying to entice a child, "you will be shown all about it and how it works."

This shocked Said-Maartens back into paying attention, and he wondered, with a new panic altogether, why this woman saw the need to tell him about any of this.

His tormentor, for that was how Said-Maartens now saw her, continued in an almost affable voice.

"I'm sorry, Mr Said-Maartens, I'm anticipating myself here. Firstly, I should have said that The Foundation wants you to front this new export concern. We realise that you knew nothing of it until today and that it must seem all very sudden, but as I said, you will be shown all the set-up before we ask you to take the reins."

There was a pause during which the question about whether he would accept this offer was not asked and was not expected to be asked. Said-Maartens replied in a flat voice wanting any emotion and certainly expressing no reserved hostility.

"And what role exactly do you envisage for me?" he asked, because there was nothing else to say as he saw things.

"Well, what we have in line for you to do," Ms Saldanha went on with a hint of 'glad to have you aboard', US-style, in her voice, "is to take a management role in the whole thing. We want you to deal with the clients we notify to you. We want you to be their point of contact with us. Get to know them and see what exactly they have in mind. You can then liaise with a team we have – and don't worry here, all will be explained to you. As I say, you will liaise with our team to see if we can get a match for the client's request. We will provide a series of profiles and supply photos, video samples and passwords to get into their social media sites and that way the client can be sure that he is getting what he wants. He will be able to get a thorough idea of what she is like before he makes the purchase."

She paused again but Said-Maartens still said nothing, and his face betrayed less, as his mind was in the same state and had started on this news and saw at once that all traces would lead to him and not to any of them if a girl escaped and was found hysterical by a patrol who might prove to be beyond a pay-off.

"Of course, you will not be expected to handle everything yourself. And that is why I have brought David Johns here to meet you. David is the courier – of course, in time, we hope to need more and would like to put him in charge of a team of couriers, but for now David is our expert. He accompanies the girls to the target and deals with disguising the project until the last – when it is too late."

David hesitated until he was sure that Ms Saldanha's gaze was not on him but that Said-Maartens had looked up at him blankly and then beamed him an uncertain smile which acknowledged only that they were both in this thing together. Then, however, he only uttered loudly, "Hi," in a warm but slightly conspiratorial voice.

Ms Saldanha went on.

"You will be working with David, obviously. He will not have to base himself here, but he'll be in touch all the time and will call round to compare notes and develop techniques between trips."

David just broke a smile at Said-Maartens but nodded seriously and looked grimly competent.

"I won't go on about the set-up now, it will just confuse you. I want you to come down and see us in two days, and we can explain everything then and you can get a look over the place."

She handed Said-Maartens another card which bore the bland name Panomnes Productions and had an address near Los Angeles.

At the front desk, very brief formalities were observed and then they were gone.

•

Said-Maartens and his wife dined that evening on their terrace in the shade of a mimosa, and Mrs Said-Maartens had done everything correctly as usual. She always insisted that you could find any ingredients in California. Said-Maartens only sampled his meal but drank above his share of a bottle of thin mass-produced wine which bore the State Eco-Approval mark. When that was done, he remembered a case of stuff from a family vineyard in the hills behind Santa Cruz and went and fetched one and set about that in turn. He had always taken the same attitude to drink as he had to food, undiscriminating and never to excess. This evening, he was relying on it for help. His wife noted this but said nothing. After the meal, Said-Maartens remained on the terrace underneath the mimosa and drank steadily. He allowed himself to be borne along on the tide of previous panic which had overcome him in the office. He quickly took the unprecedented leap to considering getting out of this foundation. He reasoned that he had enough money set by now to disappear. Where he would disappear to had to be thought of because he knew it would have to be brought off well because if they found…

He had always covered this fear with a blanket of normality that reasoned that because everything in his existence was well ordered and normal then nothing like these imagined extreme responses could be possible. This led him in an invalid and circular fashion back to the position that the threats did not exist in the first place, and he was content with that. But now he had admitted to himself that he wanted to get out and that would involve disappearing, and therefore, the threats must be real. He kept desperation subdued by engaging in practical speculation about the mechanics of disappearing. A new identity would be needed but presumably there were ways of accomplishing that. Would he be able to stop expecting the blow to land every moment of his day after ten years, or would it be twenty or more years? There was his wife too. He would have to make up an impossibly involved pantomime to stop her contacting anyone from her past life. It would simply not be practical and if she found out, she would go into immediate hysterics and destroy everything at once. Perhaps he could leave her behind along with The Foundation. The panic returned and shifted to terror because he had caused this whole situation by always ignoring the obvious signs that this had not been a normal life for years now. He took a large gulp from his glass and stood up and took a few desperate and jerky steps across the veranda. He grabbed the rail and looked out over the garden. The sun was setting and there was a warm golden light illuminating obliquely the remains of his lawn and painting the west-facing trees. An unseen bird was filling the garden with a loud, metallic chirping and a plane droned faintly through the sky. There was the slight hum of traffic on El Camino Real in the distance. The unseen neighbours were also in their garden, and he could hear the murmur of unconcerned voices. He welcomed normality's attempt to resolve his desperation and symbolically breathed it in for a few minutes. He then turned back and lowered himself into his chair again. Said-Maartens forced his breathing to slow and his guts to unravel, and thought about what the source of all this disruption in his day was. He reasoned that these new girls that they had decided to send to the customers were in no way different from those in his London establishment. It was merely a difference in logistics concerning the delivery of the same service. That they did not actually know what they were going to was an aspect that he rationalised as a technicality. The Foundation must be taking the trouble to vet the customers and indeed to match them with suitable girls who would probably soon accept their situation. Arranged marriages worked well in parts of the globe, and these clients would all be very rich after all.

In this way, the alcohol eroded his objections or, rather, it helped him to chip away at the leavings of his moral sense. He took no more wine and went inside to watch sports on TV while constructing further the myth in his head and ending up imagining that these girls, whoever they were, would probably be better off in the long run. A power outage would have interrupted his viewing, but they had a generator permit and it cut in at once. He slept well before taking an early flight to Los Angeles the next morning.

He had been selected to take a major role in an enterprise that others may object to, but they did not know the full circumstances and could be ignored. It was for the greater good of The Foundation. In this way, he arrived in Los Angles a fully compliant figure. He was driven towards the hills through endless streets lined with tents made of scraps of discarded plastic sheets, and cardboard hovels which had recently greatly multiplied. There had been riots recently but they went under-reported in what filtered through to Said-Maartens. Against these, the State passed ever more restrictive laws on what it was permissible to think and had recently devised the effective idea of linking this to the Social Credit scheme. He looked out on the people on the sidewalks. None of them would understand and therefore did not need to know, whereas he did and was about to be honoured with all the details.

The car arrived in the desert past Pasadena at a huge white single-storey building. A modest sign before it indicated Panomnes Productions. It was surrounded by well-spaced pines and low-flowering scrub that contrived to look like an immense garden. Said-Maartens was escorted to the office, where Ms Saldanha was waiting for him alone. Ms Saldanha did her usual impression of suddenly awakening and indicated to Said-Maartens an area of seating with a view out over the sparse flowering scrub saturated by sunlight. She began an explanation of the scheme in a casual manner, and this alone, in Said-Maartens' new frame of mind, was enough to further reassure. She started by telling him that the whole idea had been customer led, as she put it, but had been impossible for them to put into effect until a method involving part of The Foundation housed in the present building had occurred to someone. The arrived-at solution had involved branching out into making short ads for the local TV market and this they had done solely to attract girls. Incredibly, there were still thousands of girls who persisted on coming to LA to get out of some forgotten corner of a fly-over state and to get an acting job. The Foundation put out ads for actors for promotional material in various likely web targets. They invited the better-looking of them to the office for an interview. They asked various personal questions in a form they gave them to fill in, which included details of referees, next-of-kin and their original address. They started the process by calling the names they had from their forms, mentioning the girl as having given them their contact details and requesting some contrived and trivial information to aid with the employment. When they got the answer that she could go to hell and that they did not even know where she was, or something similar, they promoted the girl up their list. They then sent somebody, often thousands of miles, to ask more questions in her hometown, and when they had confirmation that she was another hopeless piece of social jetsam who would not be missed, they were satisfied. Then they gave her some part in a commercial, which was often phoney. Finally, the trap was baited with a discussion about possible similar work abroad if she was interested in it. They almost always were. This suggestion was purely conversational and had no written record and was never committed to a phone call, text or email. It was therefore entirely deniable when anybody subsequently came looking – which they never did. Affairs were prosecuted by the courier, who was previously unknown to the girls. David contacted the girl untraceably by phone once only and arranged to meet up with her regarding foreign acting work. The small number of girls they had so far exported had all agreed, and David then did an outstanding sales job on them. He mentioned Panomnes Productions frequently only to establish his own reputation. He presented them with a contract with a fictitious production company in some completely different corner of the globe from their point of delivery. For any subsequent investigation, David himself left no documentation of his existence; his name never appeared on the false contracts, and he never gave any of the girls contact details for himself during the arranging of their abduction. It was always David who arranged every meeting personally with the girls at their previous meeting, and he was always sure they would turn up. If anyone would ever go so far as to connect him with the disappearance, then there was no forward connection between David and Panomnes Productions. They were doubly insulated.

Ms Saldanha worked some more on him, but Said-Maartens, however, was in little need of further reassurance. The staff in his establishments he had considered as volunteers for the role, whereas these girls would not be, but he wickedly submerged those doubts by reflecting about how voluntary, in effect, the life of a professional girl could really be. The girls were only delivered to the most moneyed of environments, and should any word of something seriously harmful to them ever emerge from the wholly sexual existence they lived, then the consignee had the threat of the revelation of the girl's provenance hanging over them. They were all in prominent enough positions politically for that to have weight. That none of the girls had complained of their fate was advanced as a final point which could be held to close the discussion. In fact, many had sent desperate messages to David, but he ignored them and eventually they went quiet as they became despairingly settled into life in a virtual prison. But Said-Maartens only saw that if a feckless daughter of a trailer park in Rustville, Pennsylvania should be involuntarily drawn into helping their purpose then it was, in effect, correct. He did not let the vison of any actual girl such as Judy enter his reckoning. He was building layer upon layer of comfort and complacency around the top of his stomach, where worries caused the acid to torment, and he was thoroughly content again. Judy did not exist.

Ms Saldanha wound things up and proposed a meeting with David and a tour of the building. She led the way down a broad corridor with dark blue carpeting and pale sky-blue walls. They entered an expensively appointed meeting room. There was a small bar in one corner, and the large window gave onto a small pond fed by a simple marble fountain. The overflow from the pond trickled off into the dry soil where a patch of thirsty flowers grew. Ms Saldanha very seriously explained that they had a dispensation from the environmental authority for the little stream wasting itself in the desert. Facing them and looking neither hostile nor welcoming was Mr David Johns, the courier.

3

DAVID

David was born for The Foundation. He was young and only then becoming entrusted with some serious duties, not because of any suspicion of disloyalty but simply due to worries that his abilities might not yet be a match for what was needed. So much about The Foundation was informal, but the membership were generally aware which side of the divide they were on. It was arranged not quite in the classic cellular structure employed in espionage, but as a vast, entangled web of stems and branches which touched occasionally and exchanged information in a limited and controlled fashion. Only a set of very high, distant and remote managers knew all the workings of any one branch, but any given one of them knew only limited details of any other branch. A very few knew everything and directed the almost living organism from a position so remote that they were all but invisible, their ultimate leader especially so. The Foundation presented itself to the world, or at least the parts it chose to present, not at all as an entity but as multiple aspects involving charities, lobby groups and even learning institutions. Secrecy at every exchange within The Foundation was enforced by a simple corporate ethos; one was introduced to all the business you were allowed to know, and what you were not told of you knew to ignore as, again, the threat of penalties was never mentioned but ever-present. None of this was discussed, and almost all the members and most employees kept to the party line through loyalty. David was a member and quite new. He was half English and half American. His father was a professor of climatology at a provincial English university. This effectively meant a professor of global warming, since he never ceased in a single-minded evangelising against it and did little academic work, and none that was not connected to it.

David's mother was an American of very similar views to his father. She was tall and spindly, dressed oddly and had a thin straggle of mousey hair that looked as if it was falling out. They produced David, and many acquaintances wondered at the method involved. David absorbed rather than had formally drummed into him that society's misguided ways had been punished by the curse of global warming which his father had preached in vain against and so none of it was any of their fault – a comfort like that which the assumption of Calvinistic predestination used to bring to many. As he grew up, his father made use of his contacts to have him taken aboard a major charity that had a strong element of global warming in its concerns. David's father enrolled him with the charity rather than considering college. He saw that the science was settled and that it would be much more useful if he was to join a body that chased the righteous vision.

This charity (unknown to the father) was one of the manifestations of The Foundation, and David spent several years in Africa, not much of it on helping the place, but identifying and highlighting the effects of global warming. David did the work without questioning for a moment the connections he was surreptitiously trained to find. These were then passed up the line and brought to perfection and they were then floated for the world to see and be horrified by. The results of his work were passed back to him in the bush, such that he could see how much he was contributing to the fight, and he did not question the worth of his work. He in turn passed this to his father, who was greatly pleased with the work of his son.

After a while in Africa, his abilities, especially in the promotion of his own work, were noticed. He was moved sideways into other work altogether. He was moved to the US, had his salary greatly increased and he was put on what seemed to David like administration work. In fact, they were evaluating what greater use they could make of him. They worked with him on the idea that a righteous cause may be served in many ways, and as he had not been untouched by this concept at home, he accepted it at once. They moved him to what was to become Said-Maartens' department in California while Said-Maartens was still in London, and he accepted this without question.

Now, David was a natural salesman. He needed to

persuade others not only of the validity of the message but of almost any message. This had been noticed. He would habitually promote the most trivial aspects of his life as the only way to do things. He never posed as one who was taking a superior stance in having devised any of these things but merely as somebody who wanted to spread the benefits of what he had found to all. There are such people. They knew that they would need somebody, and possibly ultimately several couriers and conmen who would pull the girls towards their fate. David was summoned by Ms Saldanha and was introduced to the whole concept. It was presented to him as a logical extension of their establishments, and the need was put to him as far more vital in providing leverage with those who were working against The Foundation. This was all much as Said-Maartens would later hear it, but to David it was framed much more as an appeal to his loyalty and for him to selflessly come forward and take up further very difficult duties in The Foundation. They were ready, as with Said-Maartens later, to discount concerns about the girls' fates, but David had the concept of the inevitable casualties of society woven into his head. He assumed rather than reasoned that he would not be to blame but that it was a sin occasioned by a flawed society, the very society against which The Foundation was making war. After they had once again gone on to thoroughly establish the appropriateness of the means serving the end, they thought to themselves that his apparent compulsion to sell things to others would serve as the means towards the means.

When Said-Maartens was introduced to the scheme, David had already moved several girls to their new destiny.

He had very successfully applied his compulsion to talk up the mirage they were being enticed with and had seen them off at the airport, to be met at the other side by an immaculately uniformed chauffeur holding up a card with their name printed on it. They were then sedately driven off to their fate, never to be seen again. Yet even at this early stage in his new post, unformed questions were present; not then any challenge to his worldview, but they were there already in the basement of his consciousness.

4

THE ENTRAPMENT

David had prepared a full presentation on Judy and lights were lowered, and at once the image of the face of a young woman who appeared in her early twenties filled the screen. She was introduced as Judy Ruono. David had seen the image many times, but still he left it there for a while in silence before he started the rest of the presentation. Her colouring was a kind of off-blonde, as if infantile pure blonde curls had not quite transitioned to a real shade on maturing and straightening. The face was a curious amalgam; it was basically oval, and she possessed a certain beauty with a touch of the severe and daunting type favoured in models, although this was submerged and overwhelmed in an impression of naïve prettiness. The naïvety seemed to make her completely unaware of the austere beauty and even possibly the basic prettiness, although something surely gave her a foundation of confidence. This confidence was uncertainly projected in this picture, and in all the images which followed, by a fixed smile showing a crescent of perfect teeth. The eyes, however, took part in this in a more obscure way. They welcomed and even entreated the world to notice her, but they gave a hint – not that they had any fear of what they had encountered so far in life – but that they did not know what else might be there that they had not been able to imagine. This caused what sexuality the picture projected to be half formed or altogether doubtful, depending on how men perceived it.

Image followed image; she had already taken part in two promotional shorts both filmed in the studio, the second of which, for a nail bar, had been genuine and had aired on a local cable channel. David showed several stills from these and then broke off to show them complete on another screen. It was obvious that she was too talented to qualify for the main current mode of celebrity – the near random and fickle elevation of the ordinary that reassures the mob that a lack of outstanding ability is exactly what is needed.

David had himself travelled to her point of origin, which was in a small town in Michigan. His next meticulous page was a map of the Upper Peninsula of Michigan, with the town highlighted by a red circle. In a failing motel, left over from a previous era, he had stayed for a week while making very oblique enquiries after her family… David had contrived a meeting in a bar with Judy's mother, where, after a long lead-in, he got her to introduce the topic of her daughter and elicited the sought-after verdict that, "Judy can go to hell because she has run off to LA and left her poor mother behind because she didn't give a damn for me."

The assurance that nobody was likely to come looking for Judy Ruono was all that was required.

David went meticulously on with the revelations of his investigations. He had looked in detail at her current circumstances. Again, he had a Google Street Map image of her building on a page of his presentation. He had somehow secured full access to two social media sites that she used. He had extracted a series of pages from them which revealed a girl who skimmed along the surface of life. At times, she posted comments that were humorous and honest, and always the jokes were on the froth of contemporary existence and never relied on any simplified clichés of shallow cynicism that so many display as a defence against the accusation of naïvety.

David had made sure that there were no current attachments in her life. There seemed to be few references to such in her postings or, strangely, in any past ones either. David was therefore happy that there was nobody to miss her. His presentation was finished, and Ms Saldanha left the room, telling David to give Said-Maartens complete details of how he planned to move in on her and everything he would do between then and getting her to the airport for export.

David began a detailed explanation of a scheme planned in detail. He emphasised that he had no demonstrable links with The Foundation or Panomnes Productions. He would approach Judy Ruono by calling her and arranging to meet somewhere. It would always be done that way. He would never appear before any of her friends. He would say that somebody at Panomnes Productions had given him her name as a likely candidate for a part in a whole series of commercials being planned in London that needed an American girl. He had sent her work for approval, and they had loved her. He would give her his card which had a false name and bore the logo of a non-existent agency. The address was a temporary office that could be hired by the day and would be activated if need be. When she bit, it would then be a simple matter of getting her quickly away. There would be no trace of David at Panomnes Productions and if anybody enquired after her, they would rightly claim that she had suddenly left them after her one commercial and there would be deliberately accessible records of attempts by them to contact her, then nothing. As with the previous shipments, David would secure a passport for her which would be a phantom, with no record of it ever being issued. After she had been shipped out, he would arrange for a steady then slowly fading stream of posts from her, describing life in London and mentioning a non-existent agency and all manner of new non-existent friends. He then announced that he was looking forward to working with him on this new project, as if they were both employed by a supermarket chain on a promotional push.

With the thing rapidly dealt with and time on their hands, David offered a further tour of the place. They went to a large hallway where several corridors met. Here were assembled dozens of mini-exhibits concerning the nature of the work of the place. There was everything from simple posters through display stands showing stills and quotes to screens playing a selection of the material they had made. It was all material of the most compassionate and unimpeachable nature. There was a group being shown around at that moment who looked earnest to the point of anguish as their guide assumed weary familiarity with the inequalities of this world. They had done work for bodies from local lobby groups through state promotions right up to publicity work for the UN. A poster session highlighted the fate of a population of snakes threatened by an industrial development along the Bay coast, not far from Said-Maartens' office, and a loop playing in a corner was explaining that the effect of global warming in a corner of W. Africa was driving nationalist emotions and therefore instability and conflicts.

On the way back, David summarised:

"Of course, there is much more going on here – for instance, we produce many of our blogs, and there are other activities which I'm not allowed to visit."

He said this with the intention of underlining their presumed importance and without betraying any sense that he might feel slighted by being thus excluded. He then equated his position to Said-Maartens' own, with the intention of flattering him, by saying that many were not allowed to see the commercial section, but it was obviously appropriate for Said-Maartens to have access. The flattery was completely successful and Said-Maartens again felt contentment with his role boosted by this.

*

The next day, David was on his way to a diner which was not remotely a diner in the traditional sense but paid homage to a place that had itself been a reinvention of the concept – such was LA. He had called Judy and presented himself, as on the previous occasions, as an agent with only an association with

Panomnes Productions who had seen some of her work and would like to meet her and discuss a possible project. For this, he called himself Greg Luce, and as with the other girls, he had had business cards with his name and the logo of his fictitious agency printed and had a rent-by-the-day office lined up in case she needed to be convinced of his authenticity. It referred to a website which had been set up months ago for the Greg Luce Agency. The name had been given to him and along with it, a passport from the same source as Judy's. He was driving to a first meeting with her through the golden-grey traffic haze of a Los Angeles morning. The image of Judy in the commercial moved through his mind. She had performed its inane routines in a credible way and delivered its trite message in a natural voice that rose above the level of the content being projected. She managed to convey to her possible audience that she was aching to do something more than this commercial but would meanwhile be professional enough to do it better than it deserved. She really was up to doing at least this kind of work and, although he knew nothing about acting, he thought idly that she would need to change at least her surname before she could make any progress in this business. Then he checked himself with a return of reality; advancement as an actor was not what was being planned. The feeling suddenly came to him that he knew something of her already, and that had not happened with his last consignments. He had concluded there was nothing in them to know, no matter how long he might be around them.

He entered the diner and walked slowly up the length of the place, inspecting booths until he spotted her. As the moving images of her commercials were so much more than the still portraits, so her real presence stood in relation to these moving images. She seemed to leap out at him as she laughed at something a friend in the booth with her had said. Instantly, without speaking to her or even having her notice him, extra layers and aspects and complications of her nature were obvious. David was astonished and stopped in the aisle, staring at her as if baffled. Despite all the images and movies, he had come into collision with something totally unexpected and, in addition to that, something that he had never before encountered. She was dressed in blue jeans and some sort of top that David could not define but she was recognisably stylish. He noticed that there were no tattoos visible and remembered that this had been another complaint from the clients about the first consignments. They did not want the goods covered in graffiti.

She had no idea what he looked like and glanced at him staring at her and threw him a smiling but disparaging look that still seemed to be not unkind. This panicked him and he had to at once adopt the role of Greg Luce and go right up to the booth, but even as he went those last few paces, he had already started to understand that this would not work. He went instantly into his persuasive frame of mind, which, he had discovered, was facilitated by the adoption of his new name. So, it really was Greg Luce, a basically competent salesman, who stretched out his hand to her.

"Judy? Hi – I know you from your pictures and all that great work you've been doing over at Panomnes Productions. Greg Luce – we spoke – can I join you?" he asked, indicating the vacant side of the booth.

"Sure," she answered, suppressing a giggle over the look she had just given him. On sitting, he came face to face also with the friend and only then gave her a thought. This friend should not have been here by all the laws of these inductions. She was dark and pretty but had a hard and cynical air and shot him an untrusting look. His flat mid-Atlantic tones she was suspicious of. For a second, he was thrown off his stride. To gain time, he ordered coffee for them. In the time it took for the waitress to withdraw, he had decided to limit this session and avoid all specific information until he could get her alone. The friend was introduced as Rachel, who said nothing and just stared inimically back at him.

"She thinks you are out to con me and came along to look after me," said Judy lightly, in a perfectly enunciated and slightly old-fashioned mid-west accent.

This was doubly not what was wanted – not only a witness but a hostile one. David launched into the act which he had thought out long before and that had been altered to adapt it to the questions that his previous consignments had asked. He presented himself as an independent agent who worked very loosely with Panomnes Productions and who had seen her work and thought she would be ideal for something that a client of his was wanting. He had presumed to show them her commercial, and they were interested and would like to see her in their London office for further tests and possible work. He hoped that Judy would not mind him showing her work around, he added, sounding genuinely apologetic.

"Hey, I don't object to you spreading the word, but how come the guys at Panomnes didn't call me themselves?" she asked him, not showing any suspicion but in a half-amused way.

"They're not into promoting people. A friend there showed me your stuff – he shouldn't have done it, but he owes me a favour and I thought of this client… and here we are!"

She leant forward on the table and, treating him like a friend up to some harmless trick, she stared at him with her still-smiling blue eyes and raised an index finger and tapped him lightly on the nose in time to her words as she announced, "You're up to something, Mr Luce – if that's your real name – so who are these guys in London that are so interested in me?"

She looked at Rachel as if to say that she wasn't as soft as she made out, but the dark one shot back a look with a twitch of her mouth that was intended to prompt several more questions that she had previously convinced her to ask.

A sudden desperate inspiration came to David. He broke all the established cautions and invented, and then announced before the dangerous third party, the name of the non-existent agency to satisfy her.

"Well, us agents make our money bringing people together, but I can easily tell you – it's the 'Gartfoil Agency'."

This name, which came from some unconscious recess of his mind, was so strange that it almost might have been acceptable as irony, although this was lost on Judy, who just thought it sounded suitably foreign. Once he had started at his inventions, he found himself going much further.

"They've got an office in San Francisco and if you like, I can give them a call to see if you could speak to London – would that ease your mind?"

Judy raised herself and held herself straight up with her hands of the bench and looked stern at last.

"OK then, let's hear them – and... and... and I want to speak with them!"

She turned to the dark one, who looked a bit more reassured.

David called Said-Maartins's office and, while it was still ringing, said, "The Gartfoil Agency?"

When it answered, he asked to be put through to him. Then he started a desperate improvisation.

"Hello, this is Greg Luce, the agent who called you about a Miss Judy Ruono. I'm sure you will remember."

There was a silence while Said-Maartens tried to work out what was happening. David continued.

"Look, I don't have the number of your London office, but Miss Ruono would like to discuss some details with them before she goes over there – would that be possible?"

Said-Maartens asked how she could possibly call London, and David answered as if there had been some misunderstanding

"Well, just your London establishment – where you used to work!"

Said-Maartens realised what was needed and said that he would need some minutes to brief the large well-dressed lady who was now in charge of the place, and would call her right away and tell her to keep the number engaged until she knew how to answer. David cut the call abruptly.

"I know more about what their head office needs than they do!"

He then went on about irrelevant and invented details for a minute or two to allow the line to be taken and then invited Judy to call. He read out the numbers of what was plainly an international number and let her call it. It was engaged and she tried a few more times till the fat well-dressed lady announced in a very plumy English voice, "The Gartfoil Agency, how can we help you?"

Judy was surprised and beamed apologetically at David – then she was silent.

"Ask her about how I recommended you for the job," urged David.

"I'm sorry but can you tell me if there is a possible job for me over there – Judy Ruono? Maybe Mr Greg Luce has spoken to you about me?"

The fat well-dressed lady played her part to perfection and paused for a moment as one who has so many other matters of a similar nature to consider, and then said, "Ah yes – for the cosmetics job. But we usually only speak with your agent, Mr Luce, at this stage…"

Judy silently handed her phone to David in shock and delight.

The fat well-dressed lady asked David if she had played her part correctly.

"Yes – thank you, absolutely perfect. Thank you again," and finished the call.

He handed the phone back to Judy and did not ask if she was satisfied now but just made a pointless remark about how late it must be in London. The con had worked, and her withheld faith was granted in full. She felt part of something significant that went beyond the US, for, like many Americans of limited experience, she could not really conceive of the existence of foreign parts. David made light of her doubts and said in an indulgent way, "Well, now that that's all over, I think we have everything tied up, and the next stage is for me to get some details together and possibly to plan the trip... does that sound OK?"

She merely nodded her head, but the friend still looked grim.

5

THE ENTANGLEMENT

On the way back from the restaurant, David found that he was driving aimlessly. David's mind was under assault by this vision of Judy – that he had told her too much and that Ms Saldanha should know and that her friend Rachel would be demanding further checks on him and that she was increasingly enchanting and that her mocking and untrusting laughter was somehow without hostility and that she was even more attractive when she was in that mood. She was the first person he had met whose life was entirely unguided by a set of ideas that lead to an orthodoxy in all matters. She was an independent being and he was bewildered how such a stupid creature, one who had been given no introduction to the ideas that underpinned him, could successfully face and surmount all that life had dealt her so far, wearing a smile of one kind or another most of the time. He could feel the structure of his worldview start to crack and give way.

He steadied the turmoil in his head by latching onto the one practical thing he had to do, which was to call Ms Saldanha and request a meeting at once. She appreciated the danger of what he had revealed and summoned him to Panomnes Productions right away. Ms Saldanha did not react well to what was revealed to her. That he had improvised cleverly, and that Said-Maartens had played his part so well did not compensate for his invention of The Gartfoil Agency. If he was going to tell a shipment the details of her fantasy agency, then a false website at least should have been instigated. She at once spotted thse danger that the girl would look it up on the net. She called somebody, and a middle-aged woman of very dull and sober appearance, dressed even more severely than Ms Saldanha, joined them a few moments afterwards. They were assured that they had plenty of library material to quickly put together a false website. When she heard that it was required instantly, she paused and thought a moment and then said that she could bypass any delays and mount it on their own server under one of their web addresses, such that it would show up on a search and look like a normal independent site. She took David's email address and said she would notify him of the site soon. He was still at the meeting with Ms Saldanha when she sent it to him. At Ms Saldanha's suggestion, he called Judy to pass it to her. She had already, as anticipated, tried to access the agency at the suggestion of her chaperone but had come up with nothing and was newly suspicious. David said he would email the URL to her, which he did, and Judy was able to confound the eternally suspicious Rachel and even further advance herself towards believing in David. Ms Saldanha concluded that, if David was very thorough in his post-abduction cover-up texts to the girl's friend, she was content for the project not to be aborted.

Driving back, he dwelled on the sting of having been reprimanded. He was prolonging his torment quite deliberately because he was frightened of where his thoughts would turn should he curse the Saldanha woman and recklessly resolve to silence her by breaking the rules in ever cleverer and well-thought-out ways in future. He knew but had not admitted to himself yet that if he emptied his head of the matter, then Judy would come leaping into his thoughts. He would be overwhelmed with delight in recalling her gestures and interpreting all the many ways she smiled or even laughed with her eyes. He would also have to endure the waves of self-disgust that would come when he remembered brief looks of newly established trust in him which had darted affectingly up at him from raised eyes in a still-downturned face. He had known all along that a false website was needed as a precaution for the London destination. Then, as a self-revelation, he saw that the failure to set up the site had possibly been an unconscious way of being able to demonstrate that it was all nonsense. That there was no such agency. He wanted to be able to tell her that it had all been a tremendous joke. She was not going anywhere, and he had just been duping her for reasons he had not yet made up. He wanted to give the meeting a way of being seen that way by her, and plausibly by him. It did not occur to him that she would be enraged by such a savage jest that could have no other purpose but to humiliate and disappoint her. But he wanted anything that would displace the terrible intent of their whole encounter.

In his apartment, he lay down on a couch and simply stayed there with the same thoughts going around in his head. Through into the early hours of the morning, he stared at the light pollution of suburbia which showed him where his unblinded window was. He was still wide awake and more aware of himself than he had ever been in his life. Some time before dawn, when he was not even dozing but had attained a strange state of semi-trance, it came on him very simply. Judy then surged forward as the only possible way to go. She was his fate. He was at once released, and sat up. He was almost unbearably content with life and very tired. He knew that he had created a mass of troubles for himself and recognised that he would have to work very hard solving them and would most likely fail. That was put to one side until the morning, and he went to bed, lay down on top of it in all his clothes and went at once into a deep sleep until early afternoon.

6

THE DIVERSION OF THE SHIPMENT

What was set out for him to do in the following few days had now to be changed into what he wanted to do. He was going to steal Judy from The Foundation. He would steal her away to somewhere safe where The Foundation would never find them. He was like Said-Maartens and instinctively suspected rather than objectively knew that he would need to disappear very effectively to ensure that nothing happened to them. As a spur to the task of working out how it was going to be done, he called Judy and arranged to take her out to dinner in a few days' time. She altered the day to accommodate her schedule at the bar she was then working nights in but accepted. He then had only three days to convince Ms Saldanha that he was doing his job as he should do and to simultaneously plan a whole other scheme and sell it to Judy.

This was not just the impracticality of the befuddled mind of infatuated youth but the totally unreasonable approach of one who has been brought up insulated by an orthodoxy and, later in life, whose only contact with women had been with those similarly steeped in an only slightly altered version of that same approach to all things in life. He was hopelessly behind his years in dealing with women – indeed in dealing with humanity in general.

The first thing that he did was to go to see Ms Saldanha and arrange for the rush supply of a passport. He was assured that it would pass examination when she flew. The Foundation had all manner of contacts. He was promised the passport a few days after his dinner date. He would keep it himself and present it to her at the last minute at the airport. But he had nothing yet, apart from an utterly impractical infatuation with Judy and the resolution not to be a party to her forced removal. These had allowed that first night's sleep, but he had more sleepless nights to come. He found himself substituting one abduction for another but this time with him accompanying her. It was some time before the full implications of this scheme came crashing over him in waves of panic. The prospect of being ready in a few days to explain to her that there was no job in London, his part in the terrible deception and where she was really destined seemed improbable even to David. To then declare that he knew he wanted to be with her, when he knew so little of her, was even more unlikely, but not to one so incredibly unworldly as David.

He resolved to leave her thinking that she was off to a new job but that he would say that he was accompanying her for purely business reasons. They would then go somewhere else entirely where all would be explained, by means not at all anticipated by him yet, and she would be won around not least by his forthright moral stance. Displaced completely by this mental disorder was any thought that he was just as wrong to have taken part in the sending of the first shipments. However, this too would be rationalised in turn.

He had first to decide where they would go. He had also to consider how he would earn his living. Judy, he knew, had taken a long series of any jobs available, so that question did not trouble him. Despite all his new infatuation, he was dismissive, and had no ambitions for her that matched her own, which of course he had no idea about. She could be a waitress, or a shop girl, and it would all contribute something. The question of his own progress in life did not trouble him too much either because, although he could make no specific guesses on what might be on offer in the future, he had long seen himself as being a valuable member of an unquestioning and righteous elite and took that idea of himself forward in his speculations, and did not anticipate that he would be of little use to humanity and was of a type valued only by The Foundation. With regards to that foundation, he knew he would have to dip out of their sight for a while, but he failed to see how necessary, but almost impossible, it would be to keep himself hidden for ever after. He thought they might at worst attempt to lure him back or perhaps disrupt his new life in some way. He saw nothing worse in looking forward. He thought of the imagined reaction Judy would have to having to leave the US for an uncertain future. He needed somewhere where he knew somebody local that was also remote, where they could hide for a while during which he would convince Judy. The only people he knew abroad were from his former charity that he knew now was all part of The Foundation, and so he would be able to trust none of them. This led his thoughts to the only one in the charity that he knew of who had rebelled. This was Richards, a fellow Englishman, who had been with David on a project in Tanzania. He had just started to see the connections upwards from the charity to The Foundation and had had the good sense not to challenge them over it but simply to walk away. It was not approved of, but as he had been told nothing of any other activities, and never introduced to The Foundation, he was allowed to go. David could remember challenging him as to the wisdom of what he was doing. Richards had argued only very obliquely in defence of his reasons for going but, looking back now, David could understand what he was hinting at for the first time. He had taken with him, for a bride as it turned out, a new and junior assistant who was Icelandic. They had gone back there and settled on the bleak north coast. Richards had taken Icelandic citizenship and they had both secured posts running a nature reserve. David thought that he might contact him. He knew that this was unwise but decided to simply announce that he would be along to visit him with a girlfriend as they were planning to tour Iceland. When they got there, he would explain all and hoped that Richards would understand. He saw this as a very probable outcome due to the reason he was fleeing being so much stronger than the suspicions that had driven Richards away, also the presence of Judy being a parallel to his wife, as David saw things. The danger that he would be putting them in was not given a thought, as he saw the north coast of Iceland as hidden away from the world. He did not yet recognise the lengths The Foundation had at its command to find people, and the measures they could take when they did. He emailed Richards on his personal account and announced that he was coming to Iceland as a tourist and would be there the very next week. He had a reply almost at once, and David was very fortunate indeed as he was effusive in his reception of the news. He spoke of David as a great friend from the past, which he was not really, and was eager to meet Judy and wanted to show them around Iceland. He said he would be in Reykjavik at that time and would come to the airport to meet them. He asked for phone numbers such that they could text and coordinate the meeting. David was overwhelmed by this reception and saw it as a sanctioning of his whole flight. He saw it as Richards approving of a story he did not even know. He illogically decided that when they got to the airport, the reaction of Richards would be an enormous help to him in telling Judy the whole story.

David started a storm of texts to Judy. In them, it was very easy to be inventive and to have them sound convincing and sincere as the fictitious job in London had been wholly replaced by the vision of them living together with all questions of the past, The Foundation and his potential part in her kidnapping being somehow resolved.

"See you for dinner, Thursday, as arranged. I have so much to discuss with you about the job in London – it is looking great."

"Agency has requested that the timing needs to be in advance – can you be ready to go next week? Will discuss Thursday."

"There is so much to be arranged with the agency regarding possible follow-up contracts that I will be coming with you!"

"No – I will be in a hotel just for a few days and you will be in an apartment they have for their new models in Kensington – for Kensington, read Beverly Hills!" He then went on to make up all sorts of details, but he had no idea if they were likely or not.

"Bring your own make-up as they want to see what your own vision of you is before they apply the stuff the client has supplied."

"Have you any special dietary requirements? Mrs Cooper wants to know – that's the one who oversees the welfare of the models on a day-to-day basis."

"Don't worry about London – sure, it's a big city but between Mrs Cooper and me, we can show you around and make sure you get used to the place – and the accent!"

To all of this, he received no negative responses at all. Judy was entirely convinced by the bombardment of lies that appeared on her phone. She showed a lot of them to her self-appointed chaperone, Rachel, and she too was slowly won round in those few days and agreed that this was something she should go for.

David decided to wait to book the flights until after the dinner, not to make sure of Judy, but to allow for no possibility of discovery by Ms Saldanha. On the day before the date, he went dutifully to Ms Saldanha and at an unduly prolonged meeting assured her repeatedly that things were going well in the matter of this latest consignment. He was told to keep in close touch with Said-Maartens and he went home and composed a lengthy email to him on his Foundation account, detailing everything. He told him an arrival time taken from an examination of airline schedules at a remote, stifling and fly-infested regional airport in the Middle East. He cautioned that he should, as was procedure, instruct the party receiving the consignment to be presentable. He expected arrival next week – possibly on Wednesday – but he would advise of exact times soon. This was taken correctly by Said-Maartens to mean that as the arrival would be in a particularly alarming location, the need for the lackey, who would be waiting to take the girl away, to be immaculately uniformed and to drive an expensive car was higher than ever. Said-Maartens duly passed on to the client the estimated time of delivery and the cautionary instruction about the driver to minimise the possibility that the delivery might finally work out that nothing good was likely to happen to her in a place like this and belatedly take a fit of hysteria in public such that her passing might be noted.

Thus was David well organised and almost ready when he went to dinner with Judy. He had booked a place to impress at Newport Beach with a terrace overlooking the harbour. Preparing for the dinner, Judy stood naked before her mirror and critiqued, not thoroughly, what was revealed. She congratulated herself on all that she saw and did not recognise the slight bulging of her abdomen which would have gone unremarked even by almost all of womankind, but which was intolerable to the world of modelling. She recognised that she was pretty, as that had been a major prop to her self-esteem through the various troubles that were behind her, but she did not notice her best feature, which was the mischievous sparkle of humour that played about her face much of the time. She did not consider that her face lacked the austere, almost alien, and aggressive stare that is demanded in that area of work. She dressed in a perfect dark red dress that she had bought from a second-hand top-label shop called 'Previously Treasured'. It was not too high in the hemline and neither did it reveal other than the slightest of inducements at the other end. During all her contemplation and assessment, the thought of David as a man was never considered. She only wanted to make herself seem appropriate to her great new branching out. She was difficult to hit on and hard to impress, and David had certainly failed in the latter and had not been even perceived to be attempting the former.

David simply drove to the restaurant, and his car was valet parked. He got there first and was shown to a table at the back of the place, which was done out almost successfully as a rural French brasserie. When asked if he would have a drink while he waited, he ordered Coke and felt the waiter's disapproval. He had not long to wait before Judy arrived. She came into the reception area and looked around to see if he was present. She was stunning and elegant, and all heads turned who noticed her. Her make-up was restrained and her hair perfect. She saw him at the back and was starting towards him when a waiter rushed up to accompany her. She walked entirely at ease and not intimidated by the air of the place; indeed, she responded to it with the flash of mischief and a restrained little smile that suggested that she was considering pulling the tablecloths from under the settings as she passed. David stood up as she approached, not from any knowledge of manners but because he was overwhelmed and simply wanted a full view of her. If he was smitten before, he was totally lost from that point on.

The menu was like the décor – a barely passable imitation but neither of them noticed. The prices were well above what might be encountered even in the Dordogne in August, but only Judy noticed that and took it as a token of the standard of life that was ahead of her. She was easily persuaded to a glass of champagne while they waited for the first course, and when wine was suggested, David was unable to even consider a choice, but Judy was determined that wine there would be and went down past the long list of French mysteries and at last spotted a bottle of local Zinfandel which one of the girls had brought home for somebody's birthday, and they ordered that. The meal proceeded faultlessly for David. He was transformed to one even younger than his years. The conditioning of The Foundation was dissolved away by what were the effects of a teenage infatuation. She was delighted with the evening and treated it as the first stage of the unexpected undertaking ahead of her. She at last started to notice the signs in David's every move and utterance but just reacted by pretending not to take any of it seriously. She kept him at arm's length with her typical funny irrelevances which pretended to misunderstand his meaning and thereby deflect his intentions without causing any hurt. He saw what she was doing and yet found every sally more endearing than the last. How could he respect a girl who threw herself at him, and he did not think that there was a middle ground he might hope for somewhere between open surrender and the treatment he was getting now. He tried to direct his habitual ability to sell things to serve his own cause but found it did not work.

He had very little material in his past life to work with and certainly nothing in his present existence to sell to her. He fell into a state of happy confusion, with unconnected and brief utterances his contribution to the occasion. He was, however, deeply happy and thoroughly content with himself entirely because of his moral turnaround in respect of Judy – that was still enough for him.

In this way, the dinner passed, and both were content with the occasion; David because he was more in love than ever and Judy just because she was happy. David settled the bill with his bottomless Foundation card and ran Judy back to her place. His last words were to be ready for the airport in, at most, three or four days. She would hear from him tomorrow on the details. When he got back to his apartment, David found a package had been delivered by a courier. In it, he found Judy's passport. He looked at her picture and went to bed deeply content.

The next day, he applied himself. After a deliberate call to Said-Maartens to check up on the exact name and location of the remote Middle Eastern destination that Judy was destined for, he booked a one-way ticket from LA for the Friday coming. David did this with his Foundation card. He sent emails to Ms Saldanha and Said-Maartens saying that all The Foundation paperwork had been completed for the anticipated shipment. He then sent a separate email to Said-Maartens to tell him what time his representative had to be at the airport. These obscure and coded emails were largely an old precaution as by then there was no chance of The Foundation being subsequently investigated and only the very slightest risk that their emails would somehow be intercepted as they had available the latest in encryption methods. He kept up a repetition of essentially the same message, by way of reassurance, right up to almost the flight time. He then booked two tickets one-way from LA to Reykjavik via New York for the same day and texted his friend when to expect them. They were to leave around two hours before the first leg of Judy's destined journey to enslavement. This he did on his own card. He then similarly spent the time until Friday almost constantly texting Judy about when he would pick her up and all manner of gentle and sensitive anticipations of the days ahead.

7

THE FLIGHT INTO CONFUSION

On the Friday morning, David called to pick up Judy on the rather dangerous street where her building stood. The plastic tents were now starting to encroach further around the corner of the block less than a hundred yards away. She emerged from the communal door even more elegantly turned out than seemed possible on her severely reined-in budget. She was also visibly elated and not concerned to hide it. She besieged him with endless questions about London and he lied adequately and painted again for her, in more vivid colours, a picture of a new life of money and opportunity in the most wonderful city in the world. She knew almost as little about travel and geography as the first consignments but questioned that their first flight was to New York. David explained that they were only staging through there and that it was a very long way to go. He had seven hours to work out something to tell her when she questioned the destination of their connecting flight. She was disappointed when told that there would be no time to go downtown and see the city but brightened when she realised that the seats were bigger and the catering was free because David had upgraded them, and her only previous flight had been to LA on a budget airline. Just before they left, he texted Said-Maartens and Ms Saldanha to say that the consignment had been delivered to the airport. All he would consult his phone for from that time forward was for news from the friend in Reykjavik; Foundation emails were now consigned to his past.

However, two events had combined to destroy his flimsy new world. The first was that he had never before used the airline on which he was pretending to ship Judy to the Middle East, and the booking procedure had asked for his email address. He had, without thinking, put in his Foundation one because he was using his Foundation credit card on ostensibly Foundation business. The second was that a plane, of the same airline, due to leave at almost the same time, had gone technical with a warning light when taxiing out and they had substituted Judy's intended aircraft while they scrambled about to get a replacement. Meanwhile, they announced that the flight had been delayed and their system, upon having this fact entered against the flight, emailed all on the passenger list to announce this. Said-Maartens had received his text about the consignment being delivered but was being very conscientious and noted that it was almost three hours until the flight was scheduled to leave. He was delighted to find a flaw in David's work and when he had no definite text to say she had taken off, he went into the airport flight list and discovered that there was the delay beyond the normal departure time. He had not the imagination to decide that anything was wrong but merely that David was lax. He at once communicated what he had found to Ms Saldanha. She by nature saw all sorts of possibilities in what had been revealed. She emailed David and got no reply. She at once went into his email account – to which she had full access as it came through Foundation servers – and saw proof in the airline delay message that he knew the flight had been delayed but had not told them. She was puzzled and called finance to look at his credit card account, and they confirmed that he had paid for the flight. She was relieved at this but as the day went on with no further word from him, she became anxious again. Like all other staff, David had to do all his banking through a Foundation bank. He knew this but had not thought through the implications as in his loyal past he had never needed to. Ms Saldanha called finance again and told them to contact the bank and see if there were any personal transactions lately that stood out. It was in this way that she learnt that David and Judy were on their way to Iceland.

She saw immediately what had happened; that David had defected because of this girl and was going to ground. The confirming signs: the look in his eyes when he showed them her ad and the seemingly irrelevant way he would snap back in her defence over trivial comments against her – all this and other tiny betrayals came to mind, and she knew they had been buried in her mind and receiving no attention. David had been trusted in a position where he knew too much and recently promoted to a level where he knew far too much.

If he went to the press, she doubted that they could be kept silent for ever. By nature, most of the fourth estate were now very sympathetic to everything The Foundation promoted and would not give David's story credence, but eventually it would come out and a huge and probably ultimately unsuccessful attempt would need to be made to counter it. The simplest solution would be to have David eliminated in some way, and she called the official department for such things. There, her decision was accepted without question. Iceland puzzled her until she looked into personnel records of who he had worked with in the past. There she discovered his friend who had been allowed to leave after becoming involved with a girl from Iceland. She did more burrowing in records and soon had full details of what he was up to now and where he lived.

On the plane, Judy's mood became even more euphoric as she consumed airline wine with lunch and continued with it afterwards. She had a window seat and David pointed out various locations as they passed beneath them with the aid of the little map on the screens above their heads. He spotted the Mississippi himself and was childishly proud of himself when he indicated its long ribbon of light to her. She paid due attention to his efforts but was disappointed that they would not cross Michigan. She seemed to be at last trusting of him, but he saw that her mood was due to what she now saw as a great adventure that really was happening, that and the airline wine, and nothing to do with his presence. Yet they had become friends and the mood as they crossed flyover-land was light and a touch joyful. For David, that was enough, and he was too terribly inexperienced to be able to foresee her rage at what must happen at Reykjavik. Somewhere over Ohio she fell asleep and only wakened on the approach to New York. Their plane was late, and David alerted the crew that they had only a short time to get the connecting flight. When they disembarked, a courier was waiting for them, holding a card with their names on it, and rushed them to the boarding gate for Reykjavik. When Judy spotted where they were going, she was placated by being told that it was just another stopping-off point on the way to London. As night was coming, she wondered if they would have beds on board. David confirmed that they sort of would. For Judy, the new plane was obviously foreign and had notices and announcements in English and some other language. A dinner soon arrived and more wine on request and she was entirely convinced by these fascinating new events that her life really was changing. She was fascinated by the concept of sleeping on a plane and when they dimmed the lights, she lowered her business-class seat and fell into a contented sleep. He looked over her shape under the thin airline blanket and felt no surge of lust but regarded her entirely as an exquisitely beautiful form. Beyond her, the window revealed a bleak corner of Labrador in a perpetual grey twilight. There were patches of snow and countless still frozen lakes. He wanted to fly for ever and cross endless tracts of tundra or storm-flecked glimpses of an unendurably cold ocean, while warm and content next to his Judy in the almost murmuring engine noise of the dim plane's night.

He could not sleep but put himself, so late in the day, to working out what would happen when they arrived. Or rather, the impossibility of resolving that problem and the desperate imminence of the event caused him to change reality for himself. He thought rightly that she had become much more trusting of him on this flight and then impossibly extrapolated this to certainly imply that she would react well to being effectively kidnapped and, with perhaps only a little consideration, would be resigned to being with him. She need not fall in love right away; indeed, he did not expect that, but she would surely come around and a wonderful life together would open before them. As to the non-existence of the modelling job and the reality of where she had really been bound, it was only a question of presenting it correctly and of announcing that he was her saviour. She would welcome this news too, he decided. He would do it at the airport with his friend present. That would help. They would stop for a coffee, and he would reveal all, with his friend possibly backing it up as the kind of thing he had always suspected The Foundation as capable of – or at least confirming its existence. In fact, he could maybe put a call though to Said-Maartens and ask him to just this once, and for the sake of him and Judy, confirm what he had told her. And being in public and with his friend there, she might be reluctant to overreact while she was being told the whole story.

Later, when they were roused for an early breakfast, she appeared refreshed and rose smiling and was plainly still on her great adventure. After they landed, she was anxious about having to disembark, but he told her it was just a precaution. They went through arrivals and were queueing for passport clearance when David looked beyond the immigration booth across a baggage reclaim area to the open doorway where people were waiting to greet them. He made out his friend, but his guts turned over when he saw standing behind him what was evidently an Icelandic policeman, but also a large grey-uniformed representative of the UN International Environment Protection Force. His mind was again returned to reality, and he knew that The Foundation had put them onto him. They would extradite him for some fabricated lapse of eco-duty – he had known this tactic used before in Africa to curtail an officious local who was giving them difficulties and would not be drawn into the web. David could see that if he went through immigration, his adventure was over. He had to flee to keep Judy. He fell out of the line and retreated towards the gate, explaining to Judy that there must have been some error as they should never have been made to disembark after all. He found a staff member and drew him to one side and concocted a story that circumstances often allows us to invent and desperation compelled him to convey convincingly. He said that they had been bound for Iceland but that he had just this moment learnt by text that he must be in the UK that day. He begged that they be allowed to reboard the flight, which he knew was just staging through on its way to Glasgow. Then, in a parallel to JFK, they were rapidly taken through back passages to departures where they had to go through security again and David had to discreetly buy tickets. Soon they were back on the same plane and in the same two seats. She looked upon the whole episode only as a sign that he wasn't the seasoned traveller he pretended to be.

When they did not appear at arrivals, the Icelandic policeman, who was totally out of sympathy with his imposed partner, managed to take a long time to check with the airport as to where they were, but the UN representative was more prompt in calling through about the non-appearance. Nevertheless, they had taken off for Glasgow before that call was made.

On boarding the plane, Judy again noticed the destination. David explained that Glasgow was in the UK and that she should not worry. But she persisted with the puzzle, and he dug another hole for himself with the lie that they were a couple of days early and that he wanted to be able to show her some of his home country and he apologised for not telling her. The idea came to him of visiting his parents. He had not been to see them for years and called them increasingly rarely because he found it impossible to tell them about the change in his duties and was completely unable to explain his contribution to the cause. They could drive down over a couple of days and he promised separate hotel rooms and no unwanted approaches. She came right back and converted this to 'no approaches at all' and then lightened again and went back to enjoying her adventure with this new addition to it.

8

ARRIVAL

At Glasgow, he was very anxious but could not see beyond immigration and knew he had no more tricks to pull. However, they emerged onto the concourse and nobody paid them any attention. He knew someone would turn up here looking for them at any minute and went immediately to the row of car hire booths to get them a vehicle. It was just after noon that they picked up the car on a bright, cool and blustery day, with sudden brief showers obliterating the sun from time to time. They threw their bags in the back of the car and David paused before the controls while Judy just looked around her at the strange surroundings. She was not tired and had not even noticed that the time was askew. It was cold by southern Californian standards but not by those of Michigan in winter, and she put down the window and drew in breaths of cool mountain-scented air from the northwest wind. She was delighting in small things; sitting on the wrong side of the car, all the odd licence plates – the look of everything was different from America – and there were low green hills in the distance, which by their greenness alone reminded her a little of Michigan. David had never had to deal with a stick shift before and played around with the controls and then lurched forward into an empty corner of the car park, trying to master the clutch. He kept glancing around, looking for some co-opted official car approaching. He was embarrassed also at appearing a fool before Judy, but this was not troubling her; indeed, if anything was likely to endear him to her, it was this display of incompetence, and she giggled without malice every time the car dashed forward or stalled. In the end, goaded by a sense of obvious exposure while conspicuously lurching around in the car park, David set out very uncertainly. Judy had no idea where they were or where they were going and was happy enough with that.

She trusted that they could drive to London and therefore assumed they were in England, although she had no idea where this England was. David had little more idea. He had never been to Scotland before. His knowledge of geography was very poor and had been largely missed out of his minimal education. He saw signs for Glasgow and assumed that Glasgow was north of the airport and took the other direction as it was more likely to go south towards London. He motored on and finding himself trapped in a filter lane was fired off the motorway and onto a road that promised the Erskine Bridge. It mattered nothing to him as he was now lost. He worked again on explaining it all to Judy. He now decided that that would surely be possible after two or three days of touring around enjoying themselves. That would for sure bring them together so that it would not be seen as such a bizarre tale. In this way, he postponed the disaster yet again and returned to living happily in the present. He ventured a glance over to Judy and she was also lost in the present and obviously entranced as they crossed a huge bridge high above an empty river with low green terraced hills before them, still streaming mist as a shower cleared, and higher sunlit mountains now visible in the distance. They went on through some brief areas of grim public housing for which Judy forgave England, because it was not nearly as bad as some bits of LA, and David did not notice, as he was concentrating hard on repeatedly varying speed limits, bus lanes and endless directional signs that made nothing any clearer. There were also huge billboards among the dwindling adverts urging the populace to righteously accept higher fuel taxes and commending, for their economy, the windmills which blighted the surrounding hills. They came to a roundabout which David had approached on the left but ended up turning to the right as he was confused by the layout. Horns were sounded. After he had recovered, they were out on a country road with tourist-orientated signs promising that they were headed for a more acceptable part of Scotland. He persisted with an existence placed entirely in the present. They followed various signs and went up the east shore of Loch Lomond. They had a late lunch in a hotel by the water's edge. Afterwards, in the sunshine, they climbed up though a birch wood of newly sprouted leaves of a dazzling green. There were primroses on the banks of a stream of transparent water which ran down a continuous series of little falls. For a time, they had to shelter from a quick shower by a large overhanging boulder which had tadpoles and little froglets spasmodically exploring a pool that had formed at its foot. They laughed together at the sight. Judy's foreign adventure got better and better, and David's romantic delusions grew hugely more real to him.

At this point, we must return to the airport where, arriving just after Judy and David, two young men parked their car outside the terminal, ignoring all the restrictions. They were dressed quite formally and the impression they conveyed was one of being seriously humourless and unprepared to engage with the world. Otherwise, they were perfectly plain and immemorable. They made for the car hire desks. By activating a latent air of extreme aggression when their enquiries elicited a flicker of recognition, they got a result and, without having to ask for names, ran back outside and made for the pick-up car park. They were just in time to see David leave, his car the only one in motion, and they took a chance and followed. On the motorway, they overtook him along with everyone else and took a discreet photo of the two of them and sent it off to Ms Saldanha. When it was confirmed that they had the right target, they slowly fell back and followed on at as great a distance as they could risk. They skilfully followed them to the hotel, passing it by and parking behind a screen of pines where they could watch for him departing. Then, on what they knew was a road without junctions, they stayed well behind. When Judy and David went into the forest, they passed their car and continued for miles until they got to the meeting with the main road. There they again parked behind a hedge and waited. They congratulated themselves on doing this after being alerted when the plane had left Reykjavik and having a long way to drive to the airport. They were the new in-house men. The Foundation no longer subcontracted such things to the criminal world.

When David and Judy eventually appeared and turned the car north, they slowly pulled out and followed them, again as far behind as possible. But David had a feeling. He was constantly surveying the cars in his rear-view mirror and then two of them, between his pursuers and him, both slowed to turn up a farm track, which left their car more visible on straighter stretches. And they revealed themselves by their next manoeuvre, which was to dart forward with noticeable acceleration and then slow down to take station again as far behind as they dared. Memory plays tricks but David's memory dredged up images of this very grey car from earlier in the day. He panicked and sped up then slowed again. The car stayed far behind them, as if on a long tow rope. He foresaw the Reykjavik situation all over again and some bureaucratic fudge would follow in which Judy would be told that all was somehow cancelled and sent back to LA and he would be demoted and sent to the charity in Africa or somewhere even worse. He drove on. It was early evening and Judy was sitting very contented, watching the strange countryside slip past, when she roused herself and suggested finding somewhere for the night – but instantly repeated her caution about separate rooms. David acknowledged her with a grunt; his eyes were still flitting back and forth between the road and the mirror. They went on for several miles in silence before David saw a sign for a turning to the left. There was a large old-fashioned advertisement for a hotel propped up on a farm trailer in the field by the junction. He approached it fast then braked hard and swerved left into the narrow road that wound up a hill in front of them. The one who was monitoring the roads on the map on his phone saw that it was a loop off the bigger road and had no other way out. He told the driver to accelerate past the junction and to park at the point where the roads rejoined. There they paused for a couple of hours before retracing their path. David saw the grey car speed past the junction, did not consider the tactics that the two men were using and relaxed at once. They went up round a right-angled bend into a small and neat village of basically one long, straight street. As David took the right-angled bend too quickly and strayed onto the other side of the road briefly, a man walking up the hill noted his carelessness, paused and raised one eyebrow before walking on.

He was wearing a wax jacket of great age, an unpressed checked shirt, brown corduroy trousers and an old pair of walking boots. James Torquil Graham was the great-great-grandson of a famous member of the local gentry. They had had estates in the area, but these were long since lost and the roof of the family castle had fallen in over a century ago. He had been to school in the village but was sent away to private school when he became eleven. He was in his thirties, had a physique that was formed in sport and the army and was now maintained by physical labour. He grew riotous brown hair that seemed meant to be red and had a face that was more attractive to women than men seemed to feel was deserved. He subsequently trained as a lawyer and practised in Edinburgh before deciding to go native and return to the village when he fell heir to a shadow of the family estates. That was only a short while ago but since then the government's relentless efforts to put him out of his meagre business had brought a slightly anxious cast to his features. For some reason best known to the man at the time, he had been married young, a very good-looking but snobbish and domineering daughter of an arriviste millionaire. The marriage had gone downhill almost from the start and his decision to depart for a life of poverty very rapidly finished it. He lived in a house which he was restoring on a small and odd-shaped piece of land that was the remains of three or four farms. The bulk of the lands and the farmhouses had been sold. It was not far out of the village and lay between it and the forests that stretched away to the west. He had some trees of his own, mostly hardwood, some grazing land, a little arable and a collection of outhouses spread all over the holding. He was trying to grow a range of crops but finding no money in it and was ever on the lookout for some trendy and expensive vegetable that he could grow and sell to the likes of his ex-wife. He kept sheep of his own and rented out some land for fattening others' stock. He sold firewood and did some contracting work in the forest in winter. He possessed an advanced draining machine which he had bought from Germany, and he hired it and himself out when he could. He had done modestly well at first but was now beset by more and more new regulations which seemed to have no other purpose than limiting his income. He was known throughout the area and was liked almost everywhere. His budget was stretched, and he was wary of drinking his troubles away, but tonight was a night for the bar.

There was one shop and one hotel in the place, and David pulled in at the hotel and without a thought parked where the car was visible to anyone passing. Judy got out of the car at once and ran over the edge of the car park, which was on top of a hill with vast views over a flat plain between two ranges of completely dissimilar hills. It stretched as far to the east as could be seen. She then hurried with ludicrous half-skipping steps back across the car park and looked up and down the only street. No traffic passed and she could see only the lone figure of James Graham still making his way up the hill towards the hotel. This was smaller than any small-town America she had been in and was as out of this world as Judy had ever encountered. She thought ahead to the evening in this almost deserted place and thought that there surely had to be somebody else around. They went up to the hotel just as James Graham was also approaching. As they went in the narrow front door, James waited behind them until they had negotiated the door and its restoring spring. David went first with the bags and ungallantly left the door to swing back on Judy. James reached forward and pushed it open again for her.

"Why, thank you," said a distracted Judy, shooting him a backward smile.

Hearing the accent, he resisted the temptation to drawl back an imitation *you're welcome.*

He instead simply said in his Scottish version of received pronunciation, "Not at all."

Inside, the place was tiny and they found themselves in a short corridor with several small rooms on either side. There was nobody visible and no sign of a reception desk. James Graham went the short way towards the bar, but David called after him to ask where they could check in.

"I'll see about that right away," he answered over his shoulder, and veered off to the left. He came back into view and called back with mock outrage to an unseen figure, "You're surely not going to greet guests like that, Shona," before he vanished into the bar. The owner's daughter, in paint-smeared shirt and jeans, appeared in turn carrying the hotel register which she perched on a side table while she had them enter their details. David was confused and appeared awkward and shy. Judy engaged with her and was greatly reassured to find someone like this seemingly content in this corner. The hotel became even more acceptable when she found that herself and David were on separate floors.

On the way down to eat, she informed David with great seriousness that she had seen a whole five people visiting the shop across the road from her window. He did not react. At dinner, in a very small dining room, he was unusually quiet, but Judy was going to have a good time regardless. The same girl reappeared to serve them. Judy ordered wine and then consumed most of it herself. There were two other couples who were guests, and they provided a vivid contrast to the estranged pair that Judy and David looked that night. The silences persisted through the meal, and David tried to keep up a string of obviously contrived, awkward and irrelevant comments that Judy ignored. After a while, and sufficient wine, she started a conversation with the other two couples about their day and could not but tell them of how far they had come. Both couples were English, and one was from

London, so Judy asked them all sorts of silly questions about the place, but as she was American, they endured it and tried to explain that it was much bigger than she imagined but not really like L.A. She was not tired at all, but a great weariness was beginning in David. If having a wonderful time on their three-day road trip was winning her round, it was starting to produce a desperation in him. He consoled and excused himself that this was due to the jet lag as it had not been so bad at lunch.

After the meal, David was desperate to suggest something to do and with an absurd forced cheerfulness proposed that as it was still light, they should take a look at the village.

"I've seen about all there is to see of this place from my window before we came down," replied Judy, and led the very short way down two steps into the bar.

It was Friday night, and the place was full. There were young and old, men and women, and the small bar was loud with conversation alone. The barman, who was the owner, was soon helped by his daughter in a third incarnation that evening. Judy pushed David, who was Greg to her, towards the bar to get some more drinks.

"I'll have some wine again," she instructed. He had no idea what to order for himself. He was tired and confused and did not drink. He had no idea what they called any of the offerings and latched onto a Coke as the only thing he recognised. The owner, seeing his confusion, offered him a bottle of their house red and two glasses if that would suit them.

"That'll be just fine, sir," came Judy's voice over his shoulder, and the decision was taken from him. He returned with a bottle of some kind of Australian red which Judy gulped and declared great. There were no seats left and they crammed themselves in at a corner of the bar. The two English couples appeared – there was nowhere else to go. Judy started up her exploration of the concept of London again. Then she recognised James Graham in a group near them and went the few paces across to them and thanked him for his help when they arrived. She was introduced as 'part of an American couple' – with a nod back to Greg still in his corner – 'that he happened to come in the front door with earlier'.

"Oh no," corrected Judy, "he's not American but I don't know what he is – I think he was English back in the day."

The group were discussing official threats to the firewood business and Judy immediately added that she believed that things back home in Michigan were going the same way.

"'Cos that's where I'm from – Michigan – I'm just in LA for now."

Greg, in his corner, clutching his untouched glass of wine, was completely lost. He was growing more and more weary and when the tourists tried to engage him in conversation by asking him where he was from as they could not place his accent, he confessed to his origins in the small provincial town with its redbrick university but said that he had spent a lot of time in Africa and was now in the US. He announced this as if he was unsure of the facts and might just be making it up for them. His ability to sell things, which was the nearest he came to a social skill, deserted him as he had nothing to sell – not even himself. In Judy's group, the conversation turned more political, but James Graham noticed that she was not following a lot of it and, as it was by then imprudent to discuss anything political except among trusted friends, turned the conversation back to her by asking if they were on holiday. Before she replied, he introduced the company and shuffled up some and removed himself to perch on the edge of the stone fire surround to make room for Judy. They were at a small table by the fire under a huge bull's head mounted on the wall high above them. There was a couple around Judy's age, a woman of closer to James' age and a – very old to Judy's eyes – man who was called Roddy and had whiskers. Judy told them her whole story in every detail. She did not omit to add that it was on the basis of separate rooms, just so there wouldn't be any misunderstandings. The whole group fell silent for a moment when she had finished in the face of this torrent of candour. There was an air of disbelief which Judy caught on their faces.

"Jeez, just a minute and I'll get Greg over and he will explain everything to you," said Judy with a slightly forced cheerfulness – not resentful but slightly unnerved.

David was at once dragged over into their company and presented with something to sell and a party to sell it to. He went over the story as it had been presented to Judy and sold it to the company anew as he had previously sold it to Judy. His abilities, however, deserted him somewhat and he excused himself by claiming jet lag, but his listeners were still not convinced. Greg fell into a resigned silence; overcome with the retelling of all that he would soon have to reveal as a lie – and this in the time that he had assigned for laying the groundwork for his own absolution.

Judy became impatient and told him to go off to bed if he was so tired. As drinks were getting low, Judy ordered

Greg to the bar to refill everybody. He went eagerly, happy to have a role. They stayed there for the rest of the evening, with David semi-detached and leaning on the wall behind the older man. They discussed accents and David's lack of any detectable one. They asked how Judy was enjoying Scotland and she answered with real enthusiasm, although she had not known that she was in anywhere called Scotland until then. The older whiskered man seemed to have been a policeman, although there was some confusion there. She therefore simplistically linked him to James once she discovered that he had been a lawyer. Judy had several drinks too many for a night with jet lag. The wine, though, did have one effect on her; she started to betray a fascination with James. He noticed it and was flattered, although he told himself he wasn't. David hovered just outside of most of the exchanges and had given up sipping at his wine, hiding it away on a shelf by the side of the fire. From his elevated viewpoint, David noticed what was happening. He was employing his newly acquired social sensitivity which took effect when Judy's feelings were in question.

And in this way, the evening went on. There were increasing shouted bits of conversation exchanged with those along the bar and the other tables. Individuals would come up to them and have brief, quiet discussions with James or the old man, Roddy. Politics was back in the air and although Judy did not follow it, David understood some of it and was astonished that they should be criticising things that were obvious and settled. It did not shock but simply perplexed him. A fat man propped up at the corner of the bar shouted to the owner in frustration, "Are there any elections coming up that you've heard of at all, Ian? I was thinking I might have missed something about them in the news."

"That's plenty, Sandy – you've been told before."

But Sandy was not to be quietened.

"What you need to ask yourself is '*Cui bono*' – d'ye hear, '*Cui bono*' – that's what you need to be asking yourself to explain all this shite we are having to put up with. And there's Mr Graham over there, who will tell you what that means." He pointed over to their table while the owner tried to quieten the man.

"Come on, Sandy, you know fine that I cannae be having that kind of stuff in the bar. Can you no just stay off it while you're under my roof?" pleaded the owner from behind the bar.

James drank up quickly at this and turned to Judy to explain that he usually went home before the night got too rowdy as it did nobody any good in the present climate. The others understood this already. Judy also made a point of agreeing with him and drank up in preparation for leaving, as the jet lag was starting a feeling of pleasant fatigue and light-headedness and she was out of her depth with the politics. Greg overheard this as the bar had gone quiet after the exchange. Irrationally anticipating some agreement between these two that did not exist, an inspiration came to him, as he had drunk hardly anything, but he knew that none of them ought to drive.

"How far you got to go, because I could give you a ride if you like?"

James was surprised but then confessed it was about two miles and accepted the offer, although the return walk on a light night like this one was something he deeply enjoyed. He got up and Judy spoiled David's plan by announcing that she would come too.

"Good, I'll show you a little of what I'm trying to do over there then."

They went slowly out through the crowd, with multiple leave-takings by James. Once out the bar, he paused, turned back and put his head around the door.

"Who benefits?" he announced to the still-quiet crowd.

9

THE ATTACK

They went out into the luminous late evening. The sun had set but there was a pale blue sky shading almost to green on the northern horizon and it was now quite cold. Judy thought of going back for a jacket but hurried over to the car while David and James followed. David stood by the driver's door, which faced away from the hotel, and pulled out his keys while James took up position on the passenger side and Judy significantly followed to the same side and waited impatiently, shivering by the rear door.

There was perhaps a vanishingly short, whining crescendo before the first shot, apparent in a vastly decelerated perception, passed through the rear door on the driver's side with a surprisingly low tearing sound as if to signify that such a penetration was no trouble whatever. It then ripped and tore its way along the line of the front seatbacks before encountering the opposite door pillar, which it almost severed with a metallic screech. It passed between Judy and James at a deflected angle and, robbed of much momentum, it ricocheted off the tarmac and now, with its trajectory rendered chaotic, it tumbled over on itself making a strange whooping noise before thrashing through a hedge and audibly clattering to a halt below it in the yard of the hotel. James knew what it had been and grabbed Judy's hand then pulled her violently towards the hedge while roaring, "Run!" Judy could not but follow and almost fell as she was dragged after him but, in that time, she too knew what had happened and her legs began to actively propel her. David did not yet know. No complete idea had time to form, but a vague notion came to him that the car had let him down in some catastrophically mechanical way and that James' reaction was related to it. The second shot was higher but still off to the left and penetrated the passenger window before exiting through the opposite door and thudding into the bank at the base of the hedge. David at last began to appreciate the situation and moved around the back of the car but was only slowly accelerating, as if he might still be wrong in his new appreciation of the situation. James bellowed for him to move himself as he dragged Judy through the hedge and they both tumbled down a short bank to land in a heap in the hotel yard. A third shot was compensated too far to the right and went past David's head with surprisingly little noise but as a terrifying physical pressure wave hurtling past his ear. He attempted no more thought but launched himself after the other two through the hedge and landed between them. The two of them were at once on their feet and following James, who had started off across the yard, stooping slightly for the first few paces as their heads were still in the line of fire and two or three more shots could be heard thudding into the building just above them. He then straightened and ran out of the yard and ducked down a little hidden path beside a garage. They went on silently at a jogging trot, with James looking sharply behind them at times. They went through low unused paths remembered from James' childhood and across gardens well below the houses above them on the main street, all the time putting distance between themselves and the firing position. They came to a drop before a small gully with a stream at the bottom, almost hidden in the approaching night. James turned to them.

"Right – briefly – whoever did this is that way, so we must go this way." He pointed in the opposite direction. "We must keep off the road and away from any lights. We must keep hidden and get to my place, which will offer a refuge… for the moment," he added softly and apprehensively. "You're going to get wet – we will follow this stream under the road and into the woods – right?" he asked, not expecting an answer. Judy was still wide-eyed with shock. David started a disordered babble about getting to the hotel to call the police, but James interrupted him by scrambling down the bank and taking Judy with him. David followed. They had to duck low to get through the culvert under the road, and then continued with the small watercourse in its sheltering gully. When they were clear of the village, James led the way up and across a corner of a field at the same jogging trot. They crossed a fence and vanished into a wood. The light was fading further, and it was even darker among the conifers, but James jogged on with the other two following but stumbling on the uneven ground and projecting tree roots. They came to a track and, with a glance up and down it, James started along it at the same unbroken pace. Judy kept up but David fell behind. James arrived at a gate at the end of the wood and stood and listened. In the gloom, there was a steading visible among small, cluttered fields. David caught up with them and tripped and fell against the gate, which made a soft clunking sound against its latch. A barking came from the steading and James called out a dog's name: Teribus. A border collie bitch came darting up the track to them and jumped up to James as he came through the gate. She backed off a little and lowered to the ground with an almost silent growl as the other two came through. James quietened her and she caught the lack of light-hearted reassurance in his voice and noted instead its curt tone, taking the message on board. She followed them to the house and now considered herself on duty. They went through the back door and into his living room. James drew the curtain before putting on the light. He then went back to the door – the dog knew better than to come further than a porch area where she slept – and took her head in his hands and told her to go outside and be on guard. She trotted solemnly out into the little fields and concealed herself.

On returning to the living room, he found Judy leaning against a wall with the same wide-eyed look. David had collapsed into a chair and was staring at the floor, still panting. The room was cluttered with good furniture which was from his family and that he had rescued from the divorce. It was reasonably tidy, and a wood fire was set in the fireplace. James let the silence persist and leant down and lit the fire. He got up and crossed the room and sat on a plain high-backed chair and looked at them with open suspicion. David started to quietly protest as before and slowly raised his gaze from the carpet. James held up a hand to silence him.

"Before I call the police, I want an explanation of this from you two. Who is trying to wipe you out and why?"

He wondered if both were the targets but kept that to himself.

"Those were some kind of high-velocity rounds, and you wouldn't have got ten paces towards the hotel. Aye, and if the shooter had been a little more accurate, or I had not been in the Territorials to know what was happening, I don't think any of us would be here."

Then he added for Judy's benefit, "The National Guard."

"Now the politics of this place are fairly far gone in error and ill intent, but they are not so bad that I should expect this when coming home from the pub in a forgotten corner like this." He went on in a slow and insistent half-shout. "So I want to be told why I have just come this near to destruction. Because one of you knows, I am certain!"

David stopped his muttering and hung his head again even before James' question was finished. He was determined not to recognise the nature and origin of the beast that was stalking them and tried to make sense of what this would mean for the project to win round Judy and explain everything to her. He began to envisage how this violent interruption might be used as illustrative of how much he was rescuing her from, while illogically failing to recognise that this would also make him immeasurably more reprehensible. His thoughts got no further as, a few silent seconds after James' challenge, Judy broke her silence. She broke it at some volume with a determined but restrained hysteria in her voice that was not unrelated to James' own delivery of the triggering question.

"I don't give a damn who tried to shoot us, I just want out of here. I want back to the airport for the next plane to London. You people are all crazy, and I want out."

She turned to Greg.

"Get back up to the hotel and get that car going – I don't care what shape it's in, I want to go back to the airport. If there are no flights 'til the morning, I will sleep on a bench."

David did not respond but kept his head down and had his dreams dispersed before they could properly be formulated. Judy screamed that he was a useless son of a bitch and that she would go herself if he gave her the keys. She then spun round on James.

"It's all your goddamn fault – why don't you call the cops? What's the number and I'll do it myself. And you must have transport yourself – you should take me to the airport out of all this craziness. Then we won't have to schlep through all that wilderness again. You can take us straight there – it's not far. I just want out of this. Tell the cops we went to London – Greg, give him the address. They can get us there if they want. It's all the same goddamn country, right?"

She collapsed down on a couch and broke into a kind of angry sobbing. James went over and sat beside her and pulled her head gently onto his shoulder, and she allowed him to do so. David went even deeper into dejection at the sight and stayed silent. James now knew that whatever was behind this saga that had precipitated itself into his existence was known to David alone. He rose and announced that he would call the police but that they should stay with him until they had questioned them. After that, they could go where they wanted, and he would give them a lift back to the airport.

The police had become a multiple-choice service in the last few years. Assaults to the populace were well down the list after reporting racist incidents and the breaking of environmental laws. He narrated exactly what had happened and was listened to with a bureaucratic formalism that betrayed no concern. He put down his phone. He was suddenly full of foreboding but did not know why. He sat next to Judy, who was more composed now that he was paying attention to her. He looked over at David, who still had his head lowered.

"You know that when they come, they will ask you what you know of this."

There was again no response.

"Sit up and look at me and tell me why they shot at us," he demanded in his voice from court days.

David looked up at him with a strange look of hopeless defiance. He simply could not tell him what had happened, because it was still a terrible speculation that he kept dismissing every time it surfaced. He had also decided that anything from him could only be delivered after he had explained it all to Judy. The shots had some other explanation; he would resolve things with Judy and be forgiven and they would be together thereafter.

"I don't know any more than you do," he enunciated very slowly to try to give it the sound of truth.

Judy, who had righted herself and dried her eyes, suddenly came to life.

"Yea and maybe it is the Gartfoil Agency who are playing hardball for some reason – just tell us what you know, Greg."

He looked at her with adoring desperation and lowered his head again. But then he had a further inspiration. He looked up again.

"Maybe it was a case of mistaken identity. They thought we were somebody else," he announced, as if he had made a significant discovery.

James dismissed him with a wave of his arm.

"Right," he announced, "I'm going to need some help here. I'm going to get the man you met tonight in the Cross Keys down."

And then half to himself, "I don't know how I'll explain his presence to the police, but I think I'll have time to think about that before they condescend to turn up."

He called the pub and asked to speak to Roddy. He did not use pleasantries but simply dictated, "I don't care what state you are in for driving but I want you at my place right away. Come by the Baldrynan road through my woods. It's a fine night and the moon is up, so you maybe won't need lights once you are off the main road – understood? I've left my gate open and Teribus will be there, so be ready and call to her." As an afterthought, he asked if he could induce as many others as possible to leave the pub and drive around the village at random for a few minutes at the same time.

They sat in silence for a time, with James having given up on getting anything out of Greg and going over and over in his mind what exactly he was withholding. Judy was fixating on getting to London, where her dream was still alive. David kept his head lowered and fantasised schemes for the future that were more and more removed from reality.

The dog set up a barking and James went to the door and watched Roddy come across the garden, with Teribus escorting him before turning back to her hiding place. He was taken quickly inside and shown the couple sitting there, much changed since his last meeting with them in the bar. He greeted them hesitantly and received a very distant response from Judy and none from David, who never even looked up. Roddy looked at James for an explanation and he led him swiftly into the kitchen. Then, as an afterthought, he went back in and warned David, "Don't you leave this place – d'you hear? Stay there."

David still did not look up.

Back in the kitchen, they sat down on opposite sides of the table. James took a deep breath and ran both his hands through his hair as if he was able to feel the strange intelligence inside his head that he was about to convey. He then told Roddy the story from the time of them leaving the pub until that minute. Roddy looked oddly at James, who recognised the expression and countered it immediately.

"Aye – well, I'm not going mad, and I've got that pair of transatlantic houseguests out there to bear out my story."

"But nobody heard any shots in the pub, and those along at the kitchen end all night – surely they would have heard something."

"They were using a silencer, I'm certain – but they seemed a long way away – maybe from somewhere in the woods above the church."

Roderick McIvor was retired now and had moved out to that backwater several years before. His hair was white and what was left of it was a monk-like fringe around a dome of skull. He wore a generous beard of the same colour in compensation. He had been in the police in Glasgow but had left them prematurely and set up as a private investigator with varied and limited success. He had grown disillusioned with his police work and had left after allowing someone to get away with a murder that he decided, could happily have been carried out years before with a resultant great decrease in the misery of humanity. His private work had been even less engaging than his police work, but he kept it going for the little money it yielded. By then, he was getting very few jobs.

He sat for a moment looking up at James from time to time as if about to ask something but said nothing. He was reining in a boyish surge of excitement at being on the fringe of a case that could possibly have come from the pages of a crime novel when all his other work, bar the case he had had to walk away from, would never have featured in any fiction. They would have been far too mundane and sordid for the public taste, which imagines the criminal world to be filled with those of complex and able but flawed minds, rather than almost entirely by the mentally ill-equipped for life.

"And you say that the boy knows why this happened, but the girl has no more idea than we do?"

James went over his conversation with David again.

Roddy decided to dive in. "Would you mind if I had a go?" he asked, and nodded through to the living room.

"That's what you're here for."

They both went back in to find the pair exactly as they had left them. He went and sat next to David.

"Lift your head and look at me, son – I want to ask you about this shooting carry-on."

David raised his head to confront this Santa Claus vision who had called him son.

"I've told Mr Graham there already that I don't know who was shooting and I don't know why."

James noted the use of his surname and decided David was attempting to ingratiate himself.

"Now it may be in the near future that we will all be shooting at each other, but it has not come to that yet and if this… this… lunacy of history can be abandoned then we won't, but this far, we have avoided that state of affairs. So, you must concede that nothing like that ever happened to anybody around here before and yet as soon as my friend here steps out into the street in your company, somebody aims some very professional shots at him for some reason. You must be able to see why we think you may be able at least to hint at why this should have occurred."

"If you think it is my fault then I apologise for that, but I have to tell you that I've no idea what I'm apologising for," and that illogical slip rather gave away his state of mind.

Roddy gave up and went back to the kitchen with James.

"Well, that was not very successful," he admitted. "We will wait and see what the police manage – mind you, they are such an utter waste of time these days that they will probably get no farther than we have."

He paused and then went on.

"But the uniforms may just frighten that oddity out there

into revealing what he knows. And – I'm like you. I don't think the lassie knows a thing. But – if they ever get here – they will just protect their masters – ah, the Gramscian march through the institutions has well—"

He broke off there as he saw the look of disapproval cross James' face. He liked Roddy but always cut him short when he went on a rant, as he thought that this kind of polarisation was the country's worst problem.

James could see that Roddy's presence would not only be a possible problem when the police came but it would also be hard to justify, and he decided not to try but to send him away.

"We will almost certainly have to go back up to the Cross Keys when they turn up. Hang about there for us."

Roddy hurried off and it was just in time because the police turned up about ten minutes later.

They were two very young and incredibly hard-faced specimens with powerful physiques. They were a product of the policy of positive discrimination whereby recruits from certain postcodes were granted more favourable entry barriers. They were hung around with all the modern accessories and restraints; sprays, batons, cuffs of various kinds and a taser. To these had been added their newly acquired guns. They had a hostile and slightly aggressive manner from the outset and interviewed the three of them in turn in the kitchen while the other two stayed by the fire. They asked the same unimaginative questions mechanically of each one and were disappointed to get the same consistent response from them. Only James' description gave them more details on his guess about the type of weapon used and where the shooter might have been hidden. However, they showed no interest at all in this. They seemed to have finished with them and were starting to pack up their little-used notebooks when they called Greg over. They asked him if it was his car they were standing by when the shots had been fired. David had told them already that it was a hire car, but they evidently had not listened. They asked him the registration and he had to protest that it was a hire car for a third time as a reason why he did not know it. They stated that it was probably a traffic offence not to know the registration of a car that you were driving. They then left the threat hanging and told David that they wanted him to come with them up to the village. James went to the door with them. As they turned down the path towards the police vehicle, something disturbed some sheep in a nearby field and Teribus started barking in the darkness.

"I hope your licence to keep livestock is up to date and all your practices are fully compliant with it. I think we will have to alert the Farming Control Authority," the younger policeman stated, looking out into the night in the direction of the bleating.

After they had left his place, James went quickly indoors and called Roddy, who reported that he was parked across the road from the Cross Keys. James knew exactly where he was – he would be mostly hidden behind beech hedge. He told him that the police would be there soon with David alone and asked him to keep as good an eye on what happened as possible. Roddy cut short James' obvious closing of the conversation.

"Aye, well, that is what has been puzzling me. There is no car where you said you were at the back of the pub car park.

There are a few left nearer the road but none back there. You did mean beyond the approach to the back of the pub in line with the function hall?"

There was a silence from the other side. Roddy had to ask him if he was still there.

"Are you sure of that?" A car of some description is not sitting there? It is a hire car so the reg. will be new."

"There is no kind of car at all where you said you were. I took a prowl around when I got here and there is no broken glass or marks on the concrete that I could see, not that I'm an expert on bullet impacts. Wait – I need to go now, they're here. I'll call back."

The police car swung off the road and parked almost exactly on the spot they had been discussing. They all got out and the two police stood while David took in the car's absence.

They got straight to the point, and the only slightly more intelligent-looking of them stepped in front of David.

"Right – there's nae car here. There's nae broken glass or any marks in the car park. We checked in the pub earlier and nobody heard anything. So, we will be doing you for wasting police time. We've got your name and address here, but where will you be staying when you are here?"

David dumbly raised an arm and indicated the hotel.

He then protested that his car must have been stolen.

"If there ever was a car," was the response. "And we weren't called out for a stolen car – and if it is a hire car, you'll need to contact them probably. Anyway, we're no here for a stolen car."

They then got back in their car and were gone. David was

left in the middle of a silent and seemingly deserted village. His mind was now swamped by events and he had suspended attempts to rationalise them. He wandered slowly towards the hotel but desperately needed to be with Judy but had no idea how to get to James' place. Just then a car door slammed, and Santa Claus approached him, beckoning him to his car. He allowed himself to be led and asked if they could go back to James' farm.

In the car, Roddy called James as promised.

"I haven't quizzed him yet about what they said to him, but they have let him go and I have him here in the car."

David sat silent, letting things flow around him, not content to do so but having no choice.

"Bring him back up here then. But – I thought that whoever did this is maybe still around. Take the longest way here that you can – go well out of the village to try to make sure that there is nobody following you. If they know he is at my place, we might be in for a repeat performance. Oh – and the police have been every bit as useless as you said they would be!"

Roddy, in his twelve-year-old Renault, took the instruction very seriously. He got back to the house by a very roundabout route. Inside, James and Roddy sat around the kitchen table while David went into the living room to find Judy on the floor by the fire. She was putting on fresh wood and hardly acknowledged his entrance. He tried to draw her to him by telling her the whole story of the disappearance of the car and his treatment by the police. The first she had already been told by James and the second she did not care about. She resorted to a brooding and suspicious silence, and he retreated again into utter despair. James and Roddy joined them and asked again to be told everything that the police had said.

In the kitchen earlier, James had confided in Roddy that he was unhappy about having them at his place and that he was going to put them in a tourist chalet that he had been trying to build in his spare time. It was almost finished, but the rules covering such ventures had changed and there were a dozen meaningless new regulations to comply with which were holding it up. He was going to make an excuse to them, then get them out of the house. When the story of the car and the police was finished, he revealed what he had decided in a grave voice that would not be contradicted.

"Listen, you two – I haven't the accommodation for you here, but I want you to stay out of the way until we can find out something about what is happening tomorrow. So, I'll take you up to a tourist cabin I have in the woods. It is very comfortable and I've put together a bag with some bedding – separate rooms – and some food for the morning. We can just walk up there, it is no distance. I'll stay with you tonight." They went quietly. Roddy wanted to accompany them, but James ordered him away, saying that he wanted his car to be sitting normally outside his house.

"Tomorrow, we will both try to draw whoever they are out to follow us." With that prospect, Roddy left satisfied.

James led them away from the back door of the house as soon as Roddy had gone. If they had already found his place, he wanted them preoccupied with trying to see if Roddy was smuggling them away. They went in a straight line between two dry stone walls and further hidden by the house from the normal approach road until they entered the woods. There was still bright moonlight, and although James had brought some flashlights, he did not use them until the track was well into the forest, and they trudged on in silence. Judy was wearing an old duffel coat of James' that he had given her for the cold. The chalet had a large frontage with a huge picture window, and all the other rooms were in the rear of the building. When they got there, they went in the back door and James complained of the cold and offered to light the wood stove, but both were exhausted for their different reasons and asked for the bedding. Judy made up her bed and David just made a heap and crawled under it. James was careful to put lights on only at the back of the house. He then took his bedding into the large front room and made up his bed on a couch by moonlight. He was going to get into it and was wondering whether to shut the curtains or not when Judy came round the door into the room. She was shivering and was tightly wound round by a blanket.

James thought that all sorts of complications were about to cloud his judgement, but all she did was hold his arm tightly and whisper into his ear.

"It was that son of a bitch they were trying to shoot!"

James answered her quietly and insistently.

"Then you have to tell me why you think that."

"I'm sorry – I don't have anything, but I just know it."

She disappeared back to her room and went to sleep at once.

10

DAVID'S DEATH

When Ms Saldanha had discerned what was going on, she passed it rapidly to the Internal Safety Department. She had a name and a contact number in New York. Ms Saldanha sketched what they were sure had happened and Internal Safety moved instantly. They tried to intercept him in Iceland, but David had ruined that plan. They would have taken David back to LA but Judy could just have been left in limbo with no further communications and no trace of David or the promised agency. She would have been left wondering if she had dreamed the whole episode.

Now the team at the airport had gone a little too far in attempting to make up for the embarrassment at Reykjavik. Shooting at the target in the presence of the delivery and a stranger was thought recklessly excessive. Severe cautions had been issued and only very limited recognition of the speedy removal of the vehicle had been allowed. (It had been taken to a lock-up in a nearby town and afterwards recycled into a cube of scrap.) This disappearance of the evidence had managed to save them, with the aid of a particularly bureaucratic police force of very limited imagination and overriding laziness. They were told to get David and do it right, with no trace of the event being possible. Judy, they were told to ignore. If she got back to LA, Greg's identity was false, the modelling agency did not exist, and David would be gone. Nobody would listen to her.

Around dawn, which is very early in those latitudes in late May, James wakened and quickly dressed. He went silently to the back door and went out, closing it with the least click behind him. He took Teribus, bidden to silence. The grass was covered with frost and the morning was calm and cloud-free, with the sun just starting to send beams through in places below the trees. He let Teribus range all around the chalet without any reaction from her and was reassured. He took her into the forest and climbed up to a little bare hill with views over the surrounding trees. He could see a lot of the approach road and several forestry tracks. Nothing was moving and in the still air there was complete silence. He went back to the chalet and left Teribus on guard. Once again, she trotted off to conceal herself. James went back to the couch and, intending to simply doze, fell into a deep sleep.

Although he thought he had gone and returned with

sufficient stealth, David had heard him on both occasions. He was ending a night of turmoil verging on madness when the fatigue of the long terror-ended day overwhelmed him only temporarily. He awoke time and time again from brief nightmare-haunted dozes in a sweat which soon turned to shivering fits when he threw off his coverings in the cold bedroom. He gathered his damp bedclothes about him and trying time and again to digest the events of the last day, he would fall into another disturbed doze, overcome by his body until his mind would again urge him to waken in a more agitated state than the last time. He had been one of a righteous elect for all his short number of days. He had never done a thing towards any end that could possibly advance the general good in Africa, and since then he had veered far away from any such part until he was truly doing the Devil's work. Yet it had been presented to him as an honour and privilege to be doing such duties because it was assumed, in every communication he had with those above him, that he was now doing such tremendous good in unorthodox ways that it was not possible just yet for him to fully comprehend it. Somewhere just before dawn he returned to an approximation of logic and decided that all his problems came from his decision to betray The Foundation over Judy. He thus took his only brief diversion towards the truth that night. He decided that Judy had few feelings for him and that she had never pretended to have any. He passed on directly to what he would do about things now that he had come to his senses again, and that is where he resumed his nocturnal dash into fantasy. He could not imagine that Ms Saldanha was behind the shooting. He would present events as an unannounced change of the schedule that he would confess he would have been better to let her and Mr Said-Maartens know about. He would admit that it had all got very confused and complicated since they arrived in Scotland but never make mention of seeing the UN Environment Force waiting for him at Reykjavik. A very short time, and another less frenetic doze, later, he had convinced himself that that is how Ms Saldanha was seeing things as well. He then considered. In the light of what he had just decided about himself, he thought that the recent events were the result of some mix-up between his case and some other one that was unfolding at the same time. Evidently, some other operative was betraying The Foundation in a much more drastic manner. His little lapse occurred at the same time as a vastly greater treachery. He recognised that in such circumstances, The Foundation had to take grave measures. He reflected that they ought to take more careful steps to avoid mixing cases up when such action was to be taken. He dozed again and this time quite serenely, but excitement woke him again. He saw that all he had to do was seek out whoever was after him and explain things. Indeed, he thought that maybe their error had been pointed out to them and they were keen only to get him away from all this. He heard James come back in, gave him a few minutes and dressed himself. He slipped out into the morning and wondered at the cold and the dusting of ice on the grass. Teribus ran towards him but recognised him and did not make a sound. She sniffed at him a little as if to confirm recognition and then retreated to her guard post. David hesitated a minute to look around him and try to be certain which was the track they had come by last night.

Judy had spent a much quieter night after her declaration to James. It was all she knew with certainty. Jet lag and cold had woken her early. It was too cold to stay in bed and she got up and started to dress. It was around the same time, just after James had come back. Perhaps she had heard the door click closed in her sleep. She put on James' duffel coat, even indoors, and stood there for a moment wondering about going through to James. She went to the bathroom but could not contemplate washing when she discovered only very cold water. She returned to her room and was by her window and heard the back door close and saw David's encounter with the dog before he decided which track to take and marched off like one with a purpose. Judy saw all this and knew that she had to follow. There was no time to get James and convince him further. She had to go after David because she was suddenly sure that he was about to reveal himself, although she could not even guess at what she was about to see. She let him disappear into the forest and went out into the morning. Teribus gave her the same inspection and Judy bent and hugged the dog. She then crossed in front of the chalet and entered the track back to the house.

David stepped on rapidly downhill along the way they had come last night. He had reasoned that whoever was looking for him would certainly come to the house and that he would recognise their grey car, which had followed him the day before. If they were not at the house, then he would have to work out how to get back to the hotel, because he knew that they would certainly be waiting for him there. He would then explain everything to them. He anticipated that they would be relieved to get him and that he would possibly strike a deal with them by promising that he would not reveal their error in trying to shoot him. He smiled to himself at this thought. Judy hurried on behind him, at times losing sight of him and half running to catch a glimpse of him striding downhill at a bend in the track. Coming near the house, the trees fell away and there were the outhouses and a yard. Judy stayed back and went just off the side of the road in the trees, where she still had a view of the house. David gave it no attention but looked briefly around to confirm that there was no car present. He then looked about him to determine the way back to town. He was unsure but happened upon the direct track and set off as before. It again entered woodland and when he had gone out of sight, Judy hurried after him. He was already hidden by a bend in the track, and she ran for a bit and came too rapidly round a twist in the track that rounded a steep bank to her left. She was confronted with the sight of David stopped only a little way in front of her, and beyond him, by not much more, the grey car was sitting in his way. She came to an audibly sharp stop and dislodged some stones in her effort to scramble up to the left and stay hidden, but there was no cover as the bank was bare and sloped too steeply upwards. David did not hear her, although he could have done but his attention was all for the car. He started slowly forward and was relieved to see the passenger door open and the one who had been in charge of the road map the day before stepping out. He was even smarter in appearance than at the airport, as they had spent the night in a hotel. He resented the early start, was completely out of sympathy with the wilderness and hated David as the cause of the trouble over their previous over-enthusiastic approach.

None of this showed on his face, which maintained the same seeming detachment from all that went on around him. He started slowly forward towards David, and David reciprocated and advanced, addressing him loudly in a voice filled with an absurd relief.

"I've found you guys at last! There has been some terrible mix-up – you can tell Ms Saldanha that there is nothing to worry about."

He halted and held out his hand and the map-reader approached.

"Can we go somewhere and talk and I'll expl—."

That was as far as he got because the map-reader, who had not extended his hand and had the same disturbingly blank face, all of which failed even in this last second to signal anything to David, delivered a supremely swift and energetic ball-crunching kick to David's groin. David crumpled to the ground without a sound and was dealt two or three more similar kicks to his stomach. He started to retch but there was nothing to come up. He tried to look up and signal to the figure above him, as he could not speak between the retching and the involuntary gulps of air he was taking, but got a final kick in the face. The driver got out and ran towards them.

"That's enough – we don't want the bastard bleeding all over the car."

The pair of them hefted David to his feet and half dragged him to the car, where they hurled him onto the back seat. They then instinctively looked around and saw Judy. A look between them was enough to establish that they would ignore her. It was orders.

Judy saw all of this and heard every word and was

motionless with fright. The car began to move towards her and there was nowhere to run or hide. She stood there consciously trying not to wet herself as it drove past her. The driver glanced at her. It only went as far as the house to turn and a moment later it approached again around the bend of the track. Judy had staggered only a few paces from her previous position. She was perfectly visible, as indeed she had been when it first passed, but dredged some terminal courage from the depths of her being and resolved that if she was going to be taken as well, she would at least make a lot of noise and trouble in the process. But the car simply slowly moved past her. The two in the front seat did not even look her way, but David had tried to straighten himself to be able to look out. He threw her a fleeting and desperate look from a face twisted with pain at the effort to sit up, and there was blood coming from his mouth. What he signalled was a pretence that this was all some unfortunate mistake. This was followed in an instant by a desperately longing look that betrayed its own futility, and the awareness that he would never see her again.

Judy stepped hesitantly into the middle of the track as she watched them go. The track was not straight, and she soon lost sight of them and stood alone in silence among the trees as the last faint engine noise died away. She felt she had encountered as great an evil as she ever had in her life and had yet been passed by. She turned back towards the house for no other reason than it was the opposite way to the one the car had taken. A bird began to call an assured little song from the trees. Then there came the confirmation of her feeling that they wanted to harm only Greg. Her thoughts then tumbled after each other in an illogical stream as she bypassed the house in the sunshine and headed up the track towards the chalet again. Why had he sought them out, as now seemed obvious to her, and why had he called out to them? He had shouted that there had been a mix-up and to tell a Mrs Salad or something. The whole trip to London was off. Were the guys who did this to Greg the ones who had tried to shoot them? She never had got around to asking for her insurance ticket home. Why did he talk with them – what the fuck was going on? She saw the scenes of a life in London which had been sustaining her vanish. She felt stupid, humiliated and betrayed in ways that she knew she was unable even to work out – which brought a sense of disgrace as well. She went on up the track and the stream was again heard. Several birds were now singing. What was all that getting on and off the plane at that other place about? How could anybody be so stupid as to get off a plane in the wrong goddamn country? Why had they not gone straight to London? All that crap he had been telling her about a few days' holiday to begin with must have been bullshit. How had she swallowed all of that? Did he come to this Hicksville to meet those guys – and why would he aim to get in contact when they beat him up?

Teribus came running around a corner and bounded up at her. She bent down and drew the beast to her and hugged then released her. Teribus ran around her, her tail in a frenzy and barking with joy. James came round the corner in turn. He had eventually awakened and found them both missing and came after them. Waving her arms and repeatedly pointing down through the trees, Judy started an incoherent babble before he could speak.

"They took him – they took Greg. Crazy bastard was

actually looking for them. He called out to them – I followed him down here. He went out on his own to look for these sons of bitches. They didn't beat on him, it was all kicks. One in the crotch and he folded. Then more kicks – the one who was driving got out and told him to stop. Then they threw him on the back seat and just drove off with him – no, they were cool as anything – they went on up to your place to turn and then came back. They really went cruising slowly up there just to turn, cool as hell – they saw me again when they came back down. Can you believe these guys – they didn't even try to hide. Oh – I got the plates – I got the plates!"

But that was all she could manage, and she went silent and began to quietly sob. James pulled her towards him and looked anxiously around them.

"There's no need to worry – they don't want either of us," but he knew he was saying this on no evidence whatever.

She stood there and started to shiver. James again put his arm around her and led her down to the house. He put her in front of the fire and lit it. He took away his duffel coat and brought her a large tartan blanket which she wrapped around herself. She stopped sobbing and warmed slowly and just stared in front of her, resigned to being in a strange country among people she had not met until the night before and a seemingly insignificant part of some great drama that she understood nothing of. He made her ham and eggs with coffee and toast and brought it to her on a tray. She smiled at him as at least a well-meaning manifestation of her new world and, being suddenly very hungry, she began to eat but broke off and asked for a pen and paper. She wrote down the registration she had remembered and handed it to James.

"Are you going to call the cops?"

"Well, I'm going to call my cop at any rate," James replied, staring blankly at the number she had written. "There would be no point in calling the real cops – you said he went looking for them after all – and a kick in the balls is hardly going to excite them when they have already shrugged off a shooting!"

He called Roddy and told him to please come round right now. As an afterthought, he asked him to call by the Cross Keys and get their luggage from Shona and tell her that they would not be staying another night. His parting comment was that there was no need anymore to be careful about what route he took.

Roddy arrived before Judy had even finished her toast. James took her tray away and the two of them sat down opposite her and asked her to tell them what had happened that morning. She went through it all in a calm and deliberate manner, trying to tell them it all exactly as it had been.

"It just doesn't make any sense," was Roddy's judgement.

"It don't make any sense to me neither," she responded wearily.

They went on to her background in LA for anything to illuminate events. She told them about Panomnes Productions. She went into her small shoulder bag which contained all her papers and produced a card for the man in charge of the studio where it had been done. Then she went through the whole story about Greg again. She mentioned the diversion to Reykjavik – which name she had to read uncertainly from a boarding pass she still had. She went on through Glasgow, the car and their ending up in this corner and her suspicion that it was all deliberate. She dug out her fictitious contract and Greg's false card and gave them to Roddy. Then she dug out her passport and handed it over. She then thought about the Gartfoil Agency and produced her phone and the text that Greg had sent with the URL.

She looked as if she might start to cry again but suddenly pulled herself together. She took her bag, which Roddy had retrieved from the hotel.

"Can I go freshen up at all? There was no hot water in your holiday shack."

James showed her where his bathroom was, and she dug out her toiletries from the bag. She left them to their mystery.

Roddy went into David's case and searched. There was a passport but no phone. Some spare business cards but no copies of any correspondence. James indicated a table in the corner of the room where his PC was, and they sat around it.

"Let us see what we can make of this – by the power for everybody to become informed, if used with caution."

He started with Judy's contribution and copied in 'The Gartfoil Agency'. Nothing came up. It did not exist. Ms Saldanha had taken the site down as her very first move when she heard of David's defection. They tried all sorts of likely similar-sounding names and came up with no modelling agencies. He then went through her list of phone contacts and found 'The Gartfoil Agency' listed there. He called it. The fat well-dressed lady recited the number and asked if she could help him. He said he had a message for a Judy Ruono who was coming to work there.

"I'm sure you must have the wrong number – this is a private residence."

They then tried putting Greg Luce in and got several

hits but none of them remotely acting agencies in LA. They took the Greg Luce card and tried the number. It did not ring out but just came back as unrecognised. They tried his website but got 404. Ms Saldanha had caught up with all of this as well. They put the address into Google and got the place on Google Street View. It was a small vacant shop-like premises in a seedy suburban group of similar shops. They zoomed and checked the number. It was correct. They then took the name of some other businesses around it and got their numbers on their entries on the net. They looked up Panomnes Productions and got a hit at last. It was presented as a huge production company in the business of making everything from short publicity videos to major productions, stopping short of fully-fledged movies. They checked the name Judy had given them and it was there, as they made a point of listing all their staff with any sort of responsibility. The number given on the card tallied as well. They sat back, relieved that at least one aspect of the story they had been given seemed real.

At that moment, Judy reappeared in a pair of expensive-looking jeans and a classically designed winter sweater. They watched her advance to the fire and followed her and sat around it with her. They looked anxious from trying to think how they would break the news about Greg. She misinterpreted their expressions."I couldn't find a hair dryer, so there can't be a woman living here with you," she announced teasingly, to their relief. Their faces lightened but they still sat silent.

"I've been thinking about Greg in there – and I'm not gonna let him bug me. I don't know what the hell he was up to, but it looks to me that it wasn't legit – but I figure he did not mean me any harm as I know he had feelings for me. But I didn't encourage him – I put him down every time he would come on to me. Not that he came on strong; in fact, it was all very nerdy."

The two of them still sat there looking at her.

"Well – that's all I got. All I got to say on him. I tried and tried to think what has been going on, but I still got nothing."

She sat back on her chair, combed her damp hair a few times and then lapsed into her previous resigned state of surrendering to events.

James and Roddy then gently told her all that they had found out. That Greg's agency did not seem to exist and even Greg was a phony, and the agency in London definitely did not exist and that there was no modelling job waiting for her.

"Well, I had that more or less figured out," she said with a sad little laugh. "But where were we going?"

But they then decided there was nothing more could be done until California was out of bed. Roddy had a hunch which he said he was reluctant to reveal and said he was off home and would see them later. He decided that they would all meet in the pub around six.

James offered Judy the chance of dozing at the fire or helping him with what he remembered were called 'the chores' on American farms.

She accepted and, wearing again his duffel coat over the sweater and clad in a pair of Wellingtons that were filled out by several pairs of socks, she went out with him. It was a cold, bright day with the odd shower of small pattering pellets of snow between long sunny breaks. They inspected the sheep and lambs. They were a special Swiss breed and James had them lambing late in the spring. One had not yet given birth and James led it into a stall in an outhouse and having guessed correctly that the lamb was due, helped bring it into the world and presented it to the mother to lick it. They left them there for the night in view of the weather.

"Well, that was a first for me," admitted Judy when it was over.

He saw that he knew nothing of her background and discreetly quizzed her as they went around the place. He learnt almost all there was to learn as she did not feel any reason not to be frank.

He showed her some ducks he kept in a pond he had made by damming the stream, but they were mostly sulking from the cold in the little nest boxes he had built. They went past a large, harrowed field, ready to be planted with his latest idea in trendy produce – a rare form of Siberian kale reputed to be even more heath-giving than normal. She betrayed doubt by her look, and he responded to her realism by admitting that the price he hoped for was only a reflection of what a certain kind of person was prepared to delude themselves into believing it was worth. She laughed at that.

He took her to some old sheds that he had stacked high with seasoning firewood and his hydraulic splitter and a three-blade adjustable saw table that he had cobbled together himself. They visited the German draining machine, in its own little shed, which he explained at length until he saw he was boring her. Then he took her on a short excursion to the top of a small hill and showed her the view of his whole place, the forest around, the long plain to the east and the high, dominating mountain to the west, which still had a smooth cap of snow. All this was completely removed from Judy's experience of life.

On their way back, one shower turned completely to snow as they came to the house. She took off the Wellingtons and the duffel coat and went up to the fire and put fresh logs on and poked it into life before curling up in an armchair as before. She drifted off into a perfectly contented doze. James cleaned himself up and put on a tweed jacket and corduroys like a country gent. He came back into the living room and roused her.

"Come on – the best way to get over jet lag is to keep going!"

She stretched and then rose up quickly and was instantly alert.

"And I don't know if you can cook but I can in a limited fashion – though I don't feel like it tonight, so we will eat at the Cross Keys."

She wrapped up again and they went out to a thin covering of snow which the lowering sun had still not managed to melt.

"Ach – we will take the car. I'll leave it there and we'll get back somehow."

It seemed perfectly normal to her that she would return there.

As they entered the bar, Roddy at once almost seized James and took him into a corner. James just had time to give Judy some money and point her at the bar, which suited her fine. Such a girl is always welcome, and several remembered her from the previous night. Roddy instantly launched into a hushed but frantic report.

"I may be a fossil and out of step with everything in the modern polis, but I still have one contact I can trust. I called him this afternoon and learnt two things; the passport of Miss Judy Greta Ruono is a genuine US issue but that of Mr Gregory Luce is not – it's a very good fake."

James went to respond but Roddy stopped him.

"And the number which your friend wrote down belongs to a JCB registered in Shetland – so she was either careless or whoever did this is well organised."

"I've tried her quite a few times on this and she says she is sure of it – she had plenty of time to see it and then see it again when they came back from turning the car at my place," James answered distractedly, but with a quiet certainty.

They talked no more of it and went to the bar, where Judy presented them with what they had been drinking last night. They had just started them when the owner came up to Roddy and addressed him, almost whispering, in his capacity as honorary policeman for the place.

"Here, Roddy, after all that carry-on you had everybody going through last night, I went outside when everyone had gone to see if there was any sign of them all coming back again. But the only thing to see was a boy at a wee red car just back from the kitchen door, and the mirror was hanging off and one of the windows had been put in with the glass all over the seats. He was busy trying to rig up the mirror but when he saw me, he just got in smartish – aye, right on top of all the bits of window – and roared off."

Roddy and James just looked at him tensely.

"I was going to call the polis, but these days, what would be the point? And when everybody got back, nobody had missed it anyway. I swept up the glass I could see. So, what all that was I'm just going to keep quiet about."

"What kind of car was it?"

"Buggered if I noticed – it was a wee yin – red – and new-looking."

Now James had not noticed the colour of it in the terror of the moment and wanted to make doubly certain. They took Judy away from the bar, where she was still being welcomed as an exotic surprise, and they retreated to the same table in a corner as they had last night.

"What kind of car was it that you and Greg had from the airport, Judy?" James asked in very slow formal tones, which seemed farcical to Judy.

"And what's that got to do with anything?" she laughed back at him. "Hell, I didn't notice the badge on the thing. It was small – one of those compact little things. It was a red one, though, if that is any help to you," she concluded in a silly assumed voice, deliberately playing the dumb female to mock his strange question.

James glanced at Roddy and moved things on by telling Judy that Greg's passport was false and that he most certainly was not who he claimed.

"Well, that's no big surprise – you had to figure something like that with what's been going on," she said flatly, and then brightened.

"How did you find that out?"

Roddy just waved modestly and touched his nose. She was not stupid and reflected that these were people you would want on your side.

"Right then – more business to complete before we eat

and try to forget about all this for a while. I'm going to the car for my laptop."

Roddy started drinking while he was out, and Judy winked at him and began on her wine – she was letting the last few days start to pass from her already.

James returned and they noted that California should already be about their business. All they had on Greg was his card. They put the address of the office into Google Earth again and zoomed into Street View. It found the same empty shop front but this time they zoomed closer and saw a poster in the window advertising possible short-term lets. It gave a number and James wanted to call it. He gave his phone to Judy to sound more natural and she called the number. A weary-sounding secretarial junior answered.

"Hi, I'd like to enquire about the let on Wisely Boulevard – 2454 Wisely Boulevard?"

The other end paused and seemed unable to think what their connection was to this address. After consulting somebody else, she came back and sounded newly eager.

"You want to rent this property?" she asked.

"No – but I'd like to ask if you have rented it out to a Mr Greg Luce Agency recently."

There were more mumbled exchanges on the other end.

"You with the cops or something?"

"No – not exactly, it's just—"

"I'm sorry, we can't discuss these things like this." And she hung up.

"I just knew that was going to happen."

"So, your friend Mr Luce is not real and neither is his business – but why?" Roddy asked slowly.

They got Judy to recite her story again, which she did reluctantly but showed no impatience with them. She finished and they sat quietly thinking everything over when she exploded.

"I know what will prove it to you." She was half standing up and almost yelling and drawing the attention of the whole bar. She sat down again and went on, only slightly quieter.

"My video – my clip of it. I forgot about my video. That will show you things were true enough before that son of a bitch Luce came along. The ad I did before he came on the scene for the outfit in LA," she exclaimed, as if they should know what she meant.

They just looked blankly back at her.

"The ad I made was real. It aired on a local TV channel." She then added with great significance, "And a friend of mine posted it!"

She wasted no more time on them but grabbed James' laptop and very quickly took them to 'her ad'. She spun the machine round until the screen could face them, and there was Judy for about fifteen seconds or so speaking to them from her other life a long way away and pushing Suzy's Nail Bars.

"And do the people who made this know about Greg Luce or whoever he is?" asked James.

"No – I don't think so. He never claimed to have anything to do with them."

Judy rifled through her purse and came up with a Panomnes Productions card with the name of the producer who had made her decoy production.

"Well, at least we have something solid here – let's see where it gets us," and James called the number.

He got straight through to the man in question and very carefully asked if he had worked with a Judy Ruono, as he had heard she was about to do some work in London and wanted to ask him to confirm one or two things about her work. The voice on the other end denied any knowledge of the name and suggested that he might have the wrong number. James covered his phone and shot a look of appeal to Judy. She at once seized the phone and pleaded with the other end.

"Is that Mr Eisenman – sure it is, I remember your voice – but don't you remember me? Judy Ruono. The Suzy's Nail Bar ad a couple of months ago. You made it."

Mr Eisenman became slightly more cooperative and asked to be passed back to James. He announced that he could not answer such appeals without authority but that they may be able to help him but said he would need to pass it to his boss. He asked for James' mobile number and said that somebody would call back soon.

"There you are," announced Judy with relief. "At least something checks out."

Eisenman was well briefed on recognising when he was out of his depth and passed responsibility at once upstairs to Ms Saldanha.

They all three of them sat back with some satisfaction at last and looked around. It did not take long for James' phone to ring. Ms Saldanha asked to confirm his name. She then excused herself but knew he would understand that their studio had a policy of not discussing its clients in this informal way. She was very friendly and even warm about it and was sure he would understand.

"Right, we are getting somewhere here, but I think we

have a long way to go before we can connect any of it to Mr Luce!"

James then suggested they go through to eat now.

They did not think more about Greg that night, far less about Ms Saldanha. To them, he had become quite simply an unknown. But had they known the events of that day which were evolving not far from the pub, they would have been severely shaken but still no further forward in their attempt to see any pattern to events.

After the two suits vanished down the track with David in the back seat of their car, they went only a little distance. They had time to spare as they wanted to wait for near darkness before they went on to an old, flooded quarry they had marked out for the purpose. While still in the countryside, they went up a side road and, inviting him to relieve himself in the interests of not fouling the car, they helped him to hobble behind a hedge. All the time, he was mumbling about Ms Saldanha. They were not even pretending to listen. He tried to piss but found his penis was covered in dried blood, and most of the pink stream went down his trousers. When he hobbled back, they coshed him over the back of the head, and he fell unconscious. They then bound and gagged him and bundled him into the boot, where they had to fold his arms and legs tight to get him to fit. They then went into town and left him in an underground car park until evening. When they returned, they were high on cocaine. They took him out of town into bare hills. The quarry was high and exposed and they could see easily if there was anybody around. It was dusk before they got there. They took him out and he had a kind of consciousness and was just managing to groan and squint around him as they dumped him on the ground. They then put him in a body bag. He was convulsively twitching a lot, and this annoyed them. They zipped him up along with several boulders and struggled to the edge, where they tipped him, still technically alive, over the edge into the dark water. The shock of the water breaking his fall brought him briefly fully awake. There he tasted his own blood again, and the intense cold of the water filling his bag was also sensible to him. He floated briefly and then slowly sank into the depths. He knew what was happening. As the water reached his head, the body went through some convulsive attempts to hold onto life, but his brain surrendered itself, overwhelmed by the riddle of the violence that was crowning the now utterly unfathomable sequences of his life. The two men watched the last of the bubbles surface, and the map-reader indulged in a strange, quiet giggle to himself – then they took off their false number plates and went off slowly down an exposed hill with no lights on until they gained the main road.

At around the same time, dinner at the Cross Keys passed in a great babble of speculations about who Greg was and what had happened to Judy's job. Latterly, it developed into a more exclusive exchange between Judy and James. Roddy fully recognised what was developing but constantly returned them to the mystery to hand. But he had to recognise that they were not interested at that moment. Before he went, he ensured that things would not cool.

"I'll be round again in the morning, and we will be able to

really get started then," he stated in determination, with just a hint of apprehension that he might be kept out of things.

"Aye... yes... come round right enough. Let's see what we come up with then."

Judy leapt up and gave him a big hug and, due to wine, got very emotional about how they were all so great in helping her. He broke away with an embarrassed wave and was gone through the front door.

Judy sat down again and grew serious. The talk of settling the dinner bill had brought a very mundane dilemma back for attention. She had about thirty dollars at most in her purse and a credit card that she knew would not stand any strain. She went from exuberance to near tears and confessed to James the situation and said how sorry she was.

"Well, I sort of thought that was the situation," he said, as if he was pleased to discover that it was.

"I was just on one big dumb goddamn adventure with my good pal Greg. I was kidding myself big time – but I swear I didn't know it. Good old Greg or whoever you are – and wherever you've gotten to." She raised her glass to a corner of the room.

"Look – you're perfectly welcome to stay at my place until we can—" He stopped himself, as he found he did not want to think of her going home.

He went to pay the bill and asked if they wanted anything for the lodging that was never taken up. The owner waived it. He had already excised their names from the register in the continued belief that this was something he knew he wanted no part of.

James decided to drive and risk it. Judy slipped back into

an agreeable contentment where no troubles broke in and was happy to watch the forest roll past in the headlights.

At James' place, they hurried into the living room from the cold of the hallway. James put on two table lights and set about the embers of the fire, placing a couple of kindlers where they immediately took light. He piled three lengths of beech on top and turned to see Judy shivering. He went to the settee where the tartan blanket from that morning had been left and advanced to wrap it about her. He reached around her shoulders and her upturned face was inches away, and he closed the gap and gently kissed her. Momentarily, she returned the contact but then pushed him slowly but certainly away, with a hand on each of his shoulders.

"No, no, mister – that is not how things are," she corrected him gently. So many obvious reactions raced through his mind. That she was ten years younger than him, that he still knew little about her and that she had been intruded into his life by a potentially dangerous and as yet totally obscure incident.

"I'm sorry – that should never…" He trailed off into silence and tried to look apologetic but conveyed instead a soft longing and respect bordering on reverence.

Judy did not mistake his aspect and was close to giving in to it but turned away and half attacked, half teased him instead.

"If this is how you see me paying for the help… and… and… the accommodation, then I'm awful let down by you. I can't get my way back to the hotel, but your holiday shack will do for the night, and I'll get right away in the morning."

"No, please don't do that… it's very cold and—"

"I'll take the dog – can I take her? She knows the way and I know she will look after me," she said absurdly, with just a hint of irreverence breaking through the apparent determination.

"And I'll just have to stand the cold. I'm a Yooper and it didn't kill me last night."

"No, again, please – you can stay here. I have a room. We will be well apart."

He thought he had just seen the teasing below her surface but did not trust that he had and was left in embarrassed confusion. He went forward more tentatively and put the blanket around her again and very gingerly pushed her back into her chair before the now-catching fire.

"I won't try to… there will be no more of that, believe me… I didn't… let me get us nightcaps."

She had to try hard to hide her amusement at his confusion and the old-fashioned name for booze.

He came back with two large malts from a bottle he had been saving for he did not know what. She gulped too quickly at it and choked briefly and then appreciated its smoothness and sipped away in front of the fire. Peace was restored and they started again an almost frantic briefing of each other on their histories. He went over again in detail what he had covered at the meal. But this time he did not roll out the standard stories of his past that most of us have rehearsed for retelling without any thought. He covered his Territorial days but not the stories of amusing incidents and tales of hazards about which he permitted himself a measure of boastfulness, but instead reflected on the practical usefulness of the whole concept of part-time soldiers and pointless military customs, and wondered what good they would be if they had ever been really needed. He reviewed his time in the law in the same vein, recalling not his standard stories of cases won and personalities defeated but why he had quit and how he could no longer become concerned that Alpha Supply was in breach of their contract with Omega Manufacturing. He touched on his marriage but only to wonder at himself having been willing to enter into a relationship with somebody he did not really know, which, even then, was as much analysis of the interlude as he could assemble.

All Judy had in reply was her great adventure in going to LA. In that, she was easily able to match his disillusionment. She went over the long series of what she considered temporary jobs but confessed that she did not know what exactly was her grand dream that they were tiding her over for. She repeated that she had not gone to LA for Hollywood and the habitual delusion of stardom despite the short ad she had shown them in the bar. She again willingly exposed her silliness when she repeated that she had not been one hundred percent certain that Hollywood was even in LA. It was all a long way from Hancock, Michigan. She described the place for the sake of something to anchor herself with but soon exhausted its attractions. She hesitated and then remembered that she had not explained her surname. It was Finnish and the bit that was left had originally been Ruonovaara, but she thought that they had chopped it off to sound more American. She did not know when this had happened, but it was before her grandma's time anyway. She declared herself a genuine Yooper from Keweenaw – and from the Copper Island side of the waterway as well but saw it meant nothing to James. He did ask what a Yooper was, and she had to explain Yooper as being from UP, for Upper Peninsula, and the world grew larger in her head when she saw that there was no reason why he should know. She had little else to give up to match what she was hearing and was surprised that someone older than her and so experienced in life should consider telling somebody like her all this stuff. She did not want to give any more details of her family other than the sketchy outline she had already provided. Judy would be judged on herself alone and was mature enough not to be ashamed of them but was able to recognise that another might not bring her measure of understanding and forgiveness to them as she had learnt to do. She would do it in time. Other than that, there were only memories of schooldays to trade with his grand revelations, and that just underlined her youth. Nevertheless, she rolled out a few of the more picturesque ones but censored them of any personal details and left a picture only of picnics on the Lake Superior shore in summer and tales of the winter cold and snow – they were nearly in Canada, she explained.

All the time James was contributing, he reminded himself that Judy was far too young and remote to be telling any of his history to, but on he went on anyway, through a long series of hesitant and wondering rambles. At last, when in reply, she came to these shallow and evidently formulaic and less-than-candid stories from schooldays, he decided that he was stupid to have wasted such honesty on her and did not reflect that, after her LA stories, this was essentially all she had from life. He also did not think that she might prefer to keep hidden the usual naivety and obtuseness of youth or details of her family with which he might condemn her by association if they were disclosed.

When the whisky was done and the logs were subsiding into embers, their exchanges at last slowed down. When she started to nod, he showed her to a room and said good night.

11

MS SALDANHA REVIEWS THE CASE

In LA, Ms Saldanha knew only that a James Graham had been enquiring about Judy but that he had been effectively cut short in his prying. She had dismissed Judy from her consideration and now only wondered that she had seemingly got herself a champion so early instead of wandering around the UK, harmless to The Foundation through appearing as a delusional and incoherent stranger. Following quickly after that, she had had to field the ongoing probe that had penetrated as far as Panomnes Productions but, beyond admiring the persistence of this Mr Graham, she was not further troubled. The Foundation was secure. Then there intruded an aspect of this affair which she had not thought of at all. The customer in the Middle East who had arranged a grand reception for Judy at the airport as instructed, before she was to be hurried away to captivity, had been puzzled but not excessively disappointed when his staff had come back from the airport to report a no-show. He had tried David's number and got nowhere. The payment was on receipt of goods and so, not being at all impulsive, he resolved to sit quietly for a time to think. This man knew what The Foundation was up to with the girls they offered to supply. He knew they sought leverage, but this meant little to him, and he wondered at their stupidity in believing that it would give them any hold over him. In his world, the revelation of arranging for a western sexual plaything would occasion little condemnation. Nobody that mattered to him would think it odd for a man in his position, and most would envy him. However, in the world of The Foundation, the placing of a hand on a thigh twenty years ago had been vigorously promoted to be adequate reason to dispose of any politician they did not favour. They had come to believe, at least partially, in their own endeavours and had blinded themselves to the fact that it was all meaningless outside the woke bubble they sought to inflate. Indeed, the client in the sands saw that it might have given him leverage over The Foundation rather than the other way around. After sitting on things for a couple of days, he called Said-Maartens and complained about the non-delivery of the consignment they had promised. His last word before accepting Said-Maartens' assurance that things would be investigated was to state, with what to a lesser mind might have seemed like irrelevance, that he had had no delivery and had nothing in his possession to show that he had ever contemplated doing any business with The Foundation.

Said-Maartens immediately alerted Ms Saldanha and

played her back the routine recording of the client's call. She saw that her obsession with the affair had been wrongly directed up until now and that the part she had ignored had come back to threaten them more certainly than any possible squeals from David. As something to do to sound in control, she ordered him to LA the next day for a meeting to resolve the matter. Then she thought up a reason for him to come only afterwards and decided he would oversee getting Judy back and redirected to her original destination. She then sent upwards a message far above her head, outlining what had happened and appealing for some safe way that this might be accomplished, for she knew that this was more than the kind of middle-management decisions she was meant to handle. The reply from on high was not delayed, and instructed her to find out the situation over there before they could decide what they could possibly do about it. Mrs Saldanha assigned Said-Maartens the first task in repossessing Judy, that of being her selected investigative envoy.

12

RODDY'S INITIATIVE

In the morning, Judy woke and went for a long shower and attended very carefully to her hair with a dryer which she had found after all. She went back to her room and heard James making breakfast. She dressed and again presented herself very skilfully in what was approaching the last of her outfits from the Previously Treasured shop. She pecked him on the cheek to say good morning and she had barely started her coffee when the sound of Roddy's car was heard outside. He came right in and was not wearing his habitual jeans and woollen shirt but had changed into a slightly shabby suit which James had never seen him in before. He was carrying a huge whiteboard and a stand for it. It was covered by a bedsheet. He set this up in a corner of the room with only a brief greeting and went quickly outside to his car and returned with a huge paper flip chart and yet another stand. The trappings of his past life had more significance for him than he pretended. James had no time for this and had lots to do that day but decided to show patience for the morning at least. It was still cold and a steady light rain had started that was soaking everything, and so he lit the fire again and he and Judy settled down for the show. Roddy remained very formal and was making a deliberate effort to avoid even the slightest inquisitive look towards James about the course of true lust on the previous evening. However, after many glances, he was attuned enough to discern that almost certainly nothing of the kind had occurred. In balance, he was relieved for the moment for his adopted children.

Roddy had blank sheets on his flip charts but, on the whiteboard, after the sheet had been pulled aside, he had several boxes and arrows. He had three columns of boxes with arrows pointing downwards from one box to the next within the column. They were:

GREG LUCE/not real name > WHO IS HE? > WHAT IS HIS INTEREST IN JUDY? Professional/Romantic/Other more sinister?

LONDON AGENCY/not real> HOW DID GL ARRANGE CALL FROM US?/ Had help of some kind? > NO TRACE OF WHO SO FAR?

JOURNEY>LA-NY-Reykjavik/Glasgow > WHY SO INVOLVED? > LAST LAP IMPROVISED AT SHORT NOTICE > ALL SUBSEQUENT TO GLASGOW AIRPORT COMPLETELY UNPLANNED

There then followed an arrow turning up from the foot of this column to the start of a third one which was headed:

SHOOTER > HOW DID HE KNOW WHERE THEY WERE? > HOW WAS HE ALREADY IN PLACE TO REACT SO QUICKLY? > HOW ARE THEY SO WELL ORGANISED? > ARE POLICE PROTECTING THEM?
WORDWIDE PRODUCTIONS > ONLY TRACEABLE FEATURE > INVOLVED OR ONLY INCIDENTAL?> ANY CONNECTION TO GL?
GL KIDNAP > WHY WAS HE LOOKING FOR HIS KIDNAPPERS? > WAS HE EXPECTING THEM? > IS HE STILL ALIVE AND IF NOT, AGAIN WHY WAS HE SEEKING HIS KILLERS? > WAS IT THE SAME MAN/ MEN WHO DID THE SHOOTING?

Roddy intended to demonstrate that they were now in the hands of a professional, and as they read and reread his various boxes, James and Judy were convinced that they were.

"It's all a bit of a cliché from the cop shows but it helps to concentrate the mind to see things in black and white," announced Roddy as he stood ready with felt tips before the large blank flip chart.

"All this has been mentioned before and most of it comes of necessity from Judy, but I want to go through it once more, and it's going to be down to you again." He looked seriously at Judy, who looked solemnly back at him.

"You're going to have to be patient!"

They started with the first column and went through her dealings with Greg from the first call to her.

"He claimed he had contact with Panomnes Productions and that was where he had noticed me from – but Panomnes have nothing to do with this – he never said he was working for them or anything like that. He never mentioned them after the first call and that was just so he wouldn't sound like some total weirdo."

"Let's stick to the boxes here," insisted Roddy.

"Did he ever let any hint of his history drop during your meetings or your flight – or even in the car on the way here?"

"Nothing – nothing that I can think of. It was all about the present or the future. Not much about him – it was mostly about me," said Judy, and with the speculation of his death listed in one of the boxes, she did not know whether to feel serious or still furious over this fact.

Roddy went back to basics.

"Did he sound American to your ears, because his accent did not sound like anybody from anywhere in the UK – or the English-speaking world – to us. But he did have some distinctly English turns of phrase and even idioms that he came away with – but no hint of any regional speech."

James nodded thoughtfully.

"No, like I said before, he didn't sound like he was from the States," insisted Judy.

Roddy wrote on his flip chart: GL – Origin England/ Home Counties? History since late teens? Foreign and lately US where accent picked up but not long enough to adopt in detail. GL alias very carefully constructed with false background and false passport – this takes money and influence. Who did this and who wiped out all trace of him so soon after he left the States?

Roddy looked up at them.

"We couldn't find his website, but Judy has looked at it – right?"

"Sure, I checked it out – I wanted to see who he was... who he claimed to be before I went anywhere. There was a lot of crap there I don't remember but it looked genuine enough."

"So, somebody took it down – probably while they were on the plane – or my guess is while they were actually here."

"How do we know he did not do all that himself?" asked James.

"Why would he? He must have known that Judy had looked at his website and nothing had changed. It's not to prevent Judy having access; it's to stop other people – like us – from seeing it. And why – it was to help make Greg Luce vanish altogether."

"And the Gartfoil Agency had to disappear at the same time – well, it never existed but the website did for a time. And it was probably taken down by the same hand at the same time as the Greg Luce website," said James, slowly and quietly.

"And both sites were there to sucker me into this whole damned mess, whatever it is."

"So, all this has Greg Luce as a bit less important than we had been thinking," Roddy said hesitantly, and then started to write up the whiteboard and rub out some boxes to bring them up to date.

They all were silent for a time then Roddy assured Judy quite sensitively that they all accepted that she had given no encouragement to Greg but that he would like to know when Greg had made his feelings clear to her.

"Well, not when we met the first couple of times but just before we left, when we were preparing for the trip, he did hit on me a little. On the plane, though, he was more persistent but all the time he was kind of pathetic – I sort of felt sorry for him. He was easy to put off and never came on too strong at all – nothing like it."

Roddy looked significantly at James, but James did not follow the implication and just gazed blankly back at him.

Roddy moved things along to their journey to Scotland.

"We have it from Judy that the events in Iceland were chaotic. All we know is that at Reykjavik something put Greg into some sort of panic, and he had to instantly extend his flights. If there had been a plane for anywhere on earth leaving before the Glasgow flight, I am guessing he would have taken it. So, his last destination was pure accident – I am fairly certain we can assume that."

He paused and James looked doubtful, but Judy gave him a brief shrug and held up her hands palm upwards in a gesture that said it sounded good to her.

"But that's about as much sense as I can make of the journey. Was Iceland the destination or was a longer stopover planned? Like I said, I think it was a complete accident that they ended up in the same country that he was supposed to be taking her to but which he obviously wasn't – and even if he really was heading for the UK and I have mistaken what happened in Iceland, then why did it suddenly not matter when they got to London? Why could he feel relaxed about inserting a mini-tour of Scotland into the timetable without apparently contacting anybody about it?"

"He didn't use his phone on the last plane and not in the

car or when we were going around that day. I just thought what the hell, and was for going along for the ride by then. I just knew he was all done trying for one hotel room."

"So Greg and Judy arrive at Glasgow Airport completely unplanned and yet within just over twelve hours somebody has been organised to trail them and try to eliminate Mr Luce – and to do it in no subtle a way. The police don't want to know about it. The car is disappeared, and nobody sees anything except us – well, Ian at the pub saw somebody removing it but nobody has approached him at all, and you know him – he's never going to get on his hind legs and pester them. They have nobody at the back of the Cross Keys looking for bullet impacts, far less doing intensive crawls over the bottle yard chasing spent cases."

Roddy paused. "There is one last thing we have got – only one link into this mess that actually works and that is—"

But Judy interrupted him and silently held up her phone.

"The number that was supposed to be for the Gartfoil Agency in London," she announced, a little in awe of the fact and hesitant due to only just having recalled it.

"The girl has it, James," said Roddy, half shouting in his eagerness.

"And I'm telling you now that I'm off to London tomorrow to find out all I can about this number. I have already discovered where it is," he tapped his nose once more in his farcically conspiratorial way, "but that's not good enough – there is nothing beats nosing around on the ground."

James went to speak but Roddy cut him short.

"Not even Street View on your machine – I've done that already and it gets us no further forward."

James objected to the expense and the fuss, but Judy was quietly pleased that her mystery was being taken very seriously. James then changed his approach and offered some cash to Roddy for fares or to try to get all three of them on the same flights.

"No to the first – I'm not quite totally beggared by this modern world, and no to the second as I think the last thing on earth we want is for Judy – or even you, James – to be seen anywhere near that address."

Roddy left soon after as he needed to be away about three o'clock in the morning to make the first flight and would not be back until late in the evening. He made them promise to wait up for him and assured them that he would come straight to James' place after he got off the plane. Just as he was getting in his car, he shouted back that they may not recognise him when he got back.

She did not even let James return to the fire but observed that it was dry with just the least glimpse of the sun coming through.

"Where's the big coat with the toggles and my swampers? Let's take Teribus and get outside and get things done."

They went everywhere on the farm that afternoon and did many jobs. Judy took on a number of dirty and cold tasks. She cleared the logs and floating debris that had invaded the duck pond from the stream that had overflowed into it overnight and threw cold turnips, which chilled her hands to numbness, into a trailer to take to the sheep. She helped saw and split three lots of firewood and they took them in his little truck to the village and delivered them. Her presence was noted by the customers as the American girl from the Cross

Keys. Back at the farm, they went off up a track through the woods to where it opened out into James' bit of hill pasture. He wanted to see what new grass had appeared, as the rare sheep would soon be put out up there. They walked around the fence to inspect it and paused at the summit point while he pointed out and named every hill that formed the horizon. She seemed to pay attention but he knew it could mean little to her that so many generations of Grahams had looked to the same horizon. He caught himself waxing pompous and threw out all the Grahams from his mind and thought of what the skyline of her island would look like and possibly mean to her. He asked if there were any hills on her Copper Island, and she said that there were some but not like that one – and she pointed to the west.

The first barrier to tumble was his resentment that she was narrow and slightly juvenile in outlook. He was converted with much more mature tales from LA and more frank ones from Michigan. The nervousness that had caused her to come away with immature and obviously airbrushed school stories in the pub had vanished. She did tell stories of home from high schooldays until she suddenly fled. Stories from the deep snows of winter or the heat, humidity and mosquitoes of summer, but they were completely transformed and told as one looking back, although only a little, on the silliness of youth rather than presenting it unanalysed and not entirely as it had happened. She outlined her family to him without bitterness and the undefined hope that by some means unknown, things might get better with them – but she still missed any mention of the brother in jail. She told him too of aspects of urban LA that do not make the headlines. About shanty towns and drugs and outbreaks of diseases unheard of in modern times, while any decent housing was far out of reach to anybody not on hundreds of thousands and nearby restaurants where a bill for less than around $1,000 was not possible. She chattered on relentlessly, but he delighted in it all. As the afternoon wore on, she started to use some odd turns of phrase which James eventually asked her about.

"Like what?" she wondered.

"Like 'swampers' and what sounded like 'den' for 'then' and 'making wood' when we were chopping it for delivery – oh, and something that sounds like 'eh' after a sentence when you expect me to answer. There were others – but those I do remember."

She was delighted that she had said such things, delighted too that he had noticed them and told him that it was 'Yooper speak'. She said that it was from way back in the day and that she thought it came from Finnish and her granny had spoken like that. Although she said it was dying out, she still had to hand a good selection of them to invade her speech. She never used it in LA, where it would make her sound weird, but could only think that listening to him was making her revert to her roots.

"So 'cos you speak weird and old-fashioned, it's got me doing it too. It's definitely your fault, eh," she concluded, and laughed.

He analysed very strictly to himself over and over why he was entranced by this girl. She was inquisitive and interested but he reflected that the US education system must be especially bad to leave her knowing so little. She was spontaneous and funny and, most importantly, was by nature without guile. He knew instinctively that she was not working on his farm to impress him. He told himself that she was not classically good-looking but that was to little effect as he was already besotted by her face. He reflected that his ex-wife had managed to combine perfect looks with self-absorption and aloofness, which until then he had always wondered at himself for not seeing at the time, but now thought that blindness utterly inexplicable when he compared her with this. He went through all the basic mechanisms of sexual attraction. That we were programmed by evolution to select good-looking healthy girls who promised the potential to produce good-looking healthy children. He speculated that he was scenting her pheromones or something similar that he had read of. He wondered at her ability to select a mate as she seemed to be sticking with him, who was close to broke, with little income and a divorce behind him that had been inevitable to everybody's eyes but his own.

Then, when they were coming down from his hill pasture, his mind turned to the likelihood of meeting her at all. He went over how he had come to know her and saw that it was wildly unlikely. Roddy had demonstrated that the arrival in Glasgow had been truly a random one and completely unplanned and from what Judy had told him, their appearance at the Cross Keys was yet another totally fortuitous event. He thought of the chances of her ever having made her way to him, and decided they were as near zero as such a thing could be. He considered all the women he had known before and saw that with nearly every one of them, it was almost inevitable that he would encounter them such that at least an initial evaluation was possible. With his ex-wife, such an encounter had been certain, and what had been the result? He thought that perhaps some subtlety of mathematics in assessing probabilities was escaping him, but he thought not, and left off the speculation as one impossible to lead to anything meaningful.

Judy was once again just cruising in the present as any looking forward was too uncertain to contemplate. She had landed up on this farm with somebody she was very quickly coming to trust and care for. She had rejected him that once as part of her standard way of working. Indeed, this method usually involved many rejections until she felt it necessary to fall in with the spirit of the times and indulge in something physical. None of her encounters had turned out particularly successful. None of the men she had come across had ever proved other than merely acceptable, and that, temporarily. She was also led, as had James been, to wondering about the chances of meeting this man in a remote corner of a foreign country, although this was not quite so overwhelmingly unlikely in her mind as she still suspected some deliberate plan behind Greg Luce's movements.

It was well into the evening and bright but still cold when James decided to put off speculation of what the second night would bring. They would simply have to wait and see. He had decided to leave things to her, and Judy had also made up her mind not to encourage him – though she had innocently been doing nothing else all afternoon.

In the little hall, they discarded boots and coats and he had started to mention what he might make for dinner when their eyes met, and they exchanged looks of such intense endearment that it astonished both to see reflected. James bent over and gently smelled her hair then lightly kissed her forehead. Judy simply stroked his forearm. They did not, following the current mores, go off in an uncontrolled burn like two violently reactive elements, but the contract was sealed, and the timing was wisely left to be decided. The remains of the evening were spent eating and sprawling on the sofa while Judy watched her first UK TV. They got quickly bored and Judy went onto YouTube for videos of Keweenaw to show him.

They went late, but chastely, to bed.

Roddy rose very early to go to the airport. It was a renewed Roddy that got into his car in the cold dawn. He had completely shaved off his beard and taken a DIY trimmer to what remained of his hair. He had on an even newer and neater suit that he had discovered in the wardrobe. In this way, he planned, rightly as it would turn out, on keeping his identity unconnected to the unkempt Santa Claus figure that they might have already associated with Greg, Judy and James. There was no wife to see him off, as he had entered a strange marital arrangement since resigning early from the police and moving to the country. She was a decidedly a town person, and although she had initially followed him, she resented it. Then he had started his private detective work, and its dull and repetitive nature had been plain to her as had its poor rewards and lack of status in his wife's eyes. This brought another layer of resentment. Eventually, when her older sister in the city became widowed, she took to spending more time with her until she almost lived there.

Even the mundane bus-type flight to London was now a bit of an adventure in Roddy's increasingly quiet and under-occupied existence. In London, he went by tube and sought out the street he had from the number on Judy's phone. The neighbourhood was mostly Georgian terraced houses of the grander sort. It had seen good times and then bad but was now experiencing even better and more monied times than ever before. Roddy walked past the house quite quickly but had at once the impression, from the pristine decoration on the doors of the adjoining houses as well as the little bay trees in pots before them, almost blocking access, that this number gave access to more than one house. There was no name plate on any of these houses. He came back again on the other side of the street, trying not to be seen to loiter as it was a backwater and there were few pedestrians to hide himself among. The immaculate paintwork and perfectly maintained buildings, as well as the glimpses of expensive good taste that could be made out through the windows, meant that money had been spent. He thought that he would perhaps try to knock on the main door and come away with some bullshit if pushed but did not want to show himself like that. He took a wide detour and came up behind the building, where there was a mews lane. He dared not enter it as it was deserted and possibly under the surveillance of the house. There was, however, a coffee house with a perfect view up the lane. He went in and had to order coffee after coffee before he saw any traffic other than the council collecting bins. However, shortly after, a group of four girls who looked around twenty came out. They were almost caricatures of currently perceived perfection, absurdly good-looking and with improbably perfect figures. Traffic to the back door then increased and several small parties or individual girls, all of the same impossibly ideal aspect, came and went. Roddy left and went around the front again and made as many more transits as he thought advisable without being noticed, but there was still no movement there. He then noticed, just off the street, a small pub of the kind which manages to flourish in such neighbourhoods. It looked a normal pub on the outside, although as well manicured as the rest of the area, but it had converted itself into an expensive eating-more-than-drinking place on the inside. It had kept its old name of the 'Duke of Rothesay'. Roddy entered and sat at the bar, which was not really meant for sitting at. He got a wildly expensive double malt and weighed up the first of the lunchtime customers and the staff. At last, he selected a woman of early middle age who seemed to be in charge of the place and asked her across the bar very quietly if she could help him. She looked slightly suspiciously at him.

"And what is that you are wanting help with?" she asked in a South African accent – just slightly mockingly but with harsh nuances, as only that voice can combine.

Roddy directed her attention very carefully to the houses in the street just around the corner, taking great care that there should be no doubt which he was talking about. He then took out his old warrant card and flashed it at her while keeping most of it hidden by his hand.

"I just wondered if you knew what kind of place it was."

She paused, and shouted orders at some of the staff who were passing to look after the bar and that table 5 was ready to order and then came round to Roddy's side and led him to a secluded alcove where the table was still awaiting a customer.

"That place is some kind of expensive knocking shop, and some very famous faces pitch up there from time to time."

She paused and glanced around. "Now, as that place is a feature of this city, if your card was from here or even in date, probably you would know not to ask questions about it."

Roddy stuffed the card back in his pocket, paused and stared bewildered at her while she looked back at him, wide-eyed at his innocence.

"Can I get you a table for lunch?" she enquired, signalling a complete change of subject.

"No… no, thanks. I should really be off… it is time that… well, anyway…" And with a look that conveyed embarrassment, an apology for his innocence and deep gratitude for her help, he left the pub.

13

RODDY REPORTS BACK

Roddy also made his way back to Heathrow, and his mind concluded that Judy was being trafficked as a new girl for that place, but he as quickly rejected that as it would be near impossible to keep somebody in the middle of London against their will. He kept contrasting this possibility with the girls he had seen, who were obviously free to come and go from the place, and he could not square the two visions. On the plane coming back, and dozing intermittently, his half sleeping mind saw that himself and James, whoever had shot at them, the drinkers of the Cross Keys, Greg and the men who had taken him away, the policemen, the immigration people and the airline staff did not make sense without Judy to pull them all together as the key to the story. As an odd pseudo-parallel, he saw that all his boxes on the whiteboard were needing to be pulled together. There should be an extra key box at the top of the board whose function would be to unite and probably direct and animate all the other boxes and their linking arrows. When he landed, he texted James that he would be back soon and that he would require strong drink.

It was near midnight when his car reached James' place. It was met by Teribus, who advanced slowly towards this strange figure with a low growl, ready to make an aggressive dash for his legs when she caught his scent and retired. Roddy did not knock but went right in and entered the living room and dashed at once for the whiteboard in the corner.

"It's not complete – there is one key box missing," he announced without introduction or even looking their way. James and Judy were sprawled on the couch as a couple of long and intimate acquaintance. There was a bottle of malt in front of the fire which James had started already, and Judy took a bolstering gulp from a large glass of red wine in anticipation of imminent tidings. It was certainly Roddy's voice, and James looked over to him only slowly and then started and half rose, like his dog, to challenge this intruder. Judy took her cue from him and when Roddy eventually broke off from erasing part of his scheme on the whiteboard and eventually looked over to the fire, they were both staring at him over the back of the couch, looking incredulous and then trying to stifle a laugh. James rose and took a large glass of malt over to him.

"They only knew me as a sort of scruffy, woolly, old-man-of-the-mountains kind of figure, and I had to appear as unlike myself as possible in case they were paying attention."

"Who are *they*?" asked Judy.

"They are them here in the missing top box – they are directing everything. I'm not sure they are being obeyed by all the players in the game and I don't know what they are up to, but 'they' are behind this whole thing."

He convinced them that there needed to be some higher agency guiding and motivating his boxes. He dragged the stand closer to the fire and completed his redrawing of the whiteboard as they watched. He had a large box at the head of all the others labelled 'THEM'. He had also inserted another new box above Greg's column labelled 'LONDON HOUSE'. There were a few extra arrows to connect the diagram together in a subtly new way.

They pressed him for his reasons for the top box and he summed it up as a necessity. The diagram just did not make sense without it. Then they got around to what he had discovered on his trip, as he had confessed to discovering the necessity of the box while dozing on the plane.

"You could have saved yourself the fare and taken a snooze in this armchair here," commented James, with not a hint of levity.

"Aye, but that is where you are wrong, you cheeky young know-nothing bugger, because I found out something far more concrete besides," and he thrust at James with his felt-tip pen for emphasis but then looked doubtfully at Judy.

"Right – here it is – it would seem that the place that you phoned from the US that time, Judy, is some kind of very fancy… house of pleasure."

He was searching for some suitable circumlocution when he came up with this ridiculous term.

Judy's mind ignored the wording and leapt ahead of him.

"So, you are saying that that asshole Greg had me lined up for some kind of smart whorehouse. Jeez, this whole heap of crap just gets better and better!"

She paused and then blazed up again.

"Who does he think he is? Where does that nerdy little wuss get off trying something like that? If I saw him again—"

Roddy interrupted her.

"Well, Judy, the chances are that something much more drastic than you are considering has already happened to him, and I think I can say that it was not at all his intention to recruit you into that house – I am fairly sure that that was not what he was up to."

Judy fell silent and actually shed a discreet tear as she and James listened to Roddy's explanations.

He told them how he had seen the girls from the place coming and going freely from the back door. There seemed no question of coercion.

"But what if he was a courier delivering her to the place as... as... as some kind of punishment for Judy?" suggested James.

"Punishment for what? How could Judy have offended 'them'?" asked Roddy, stabbing his pen at the top box on the whiteboard.

"She had only known Greg a couple of weeks, what was her offence? And how would they have kept her there against her will in the middle of London among a lot of girls who are perfectly willing to function there... presumably held there by the money?" he added, in a final insight.

"And why would he have been desperate just to spend more time with me – because he was. I'm sure of that," added Judy, quietly and repentantly.

They sat silently for a moment and then Roddy started again to erase and add new comments to his diagram.

When that was finished, he quizzed Judy very closely about the time in the restaurant when she had demanded proof that the agency in London existed and had made the decisive call herself to a London number. She related again very carefully how he had first called somewhere that he had said was the US branch of the Gartfoil Agency.

"And did you hear anything – any names – who did he speak to?"

"The only thing I noticed was the name he asked for – it sounded odd – a Side-Martin or something."

Judy was quiet and thought a little after this and then realised that she had made a silly oversight at the time.

"If he was all fixed up with this agency he was sending me to, why did he have to get the number of their London office from the one in the US? He said they were in San Francisco. Why not just give me the London number and get me to call it!"

"Why not indeed – that had not occurred to me either," commented Roddy.

"And if this goddamn agency does not exist in London, why should it exist in California?"

Roddy nodded significantly at her to indicate further agreement. His first entry was "Greg L called here to get the number of the—" He stopped abruptly and cursed himself.

"What a numpty I'm turning into. There is no agency and no number…"

Judy then had a deep revelation and said slowly and clearly, "It wasn't to get an agency number… it was just to get any number… any number with a foreign code. I didn't know if it was London or Tahiti, but I knew it was foreign. And… and… and… and… I was wanting to get the number and call through to show that there was nothing wrong with the deal, but Greg went on and on a whole lot of crap for about ten minutes before he gave me the number!"

Then the pair of them broke into a great confused babble of talking over each other with both trying to say the same thing: that it was to give 'them' time to call the house in London and get somebody there to say that they were expecting Judy.

Roddy started with his new flip-chart page, cramming more in than before.

1. Greg called 'them' in SF to get a number to convince Judy that the Gartfoil Agency existed and that it knew who she was. The number was that of their establishment.
2. The business of 'them' is girls, etc., but Judy was not destined to be one.
3. He then rubbed out the second point and very astutely rewrote it as:
4. One of the businesses of 'them' is girls, etc. but Judy was not destined to be one.
5. Greg L worked for 'them'.

Although silent all this time, James then had his insight in turn.

"So, unless there is some totally mysterious third party involved in this, you have to assume that the shooter who tried to kill us was also a part of 'them' – and almost certainly it was the same men who took Greg away. And with your theory, Roddy, you have to explain what happened to change Greg from a loyal employee manipulating Judy – and doing whatever deception for whatever reason – to somebody they are trying to kill… and, on top of that, in a way that they must know risks attention being drawn to 'them'. And it is rather desperate times we are living through but not surely so bad that they just don't care. What changed?"

James looked to Roddy for an answer, but it was Judy who responded.

"He developed feelings for me," she said quietly and evenly, awed by the overwhelming and unsought powers that she had simply by being. But then, as a shiver passed over her, she made a visible effort to drag herself back from these thoughts.

"But where was he taking me? That's what we have to figure out. We weren't going to London to the agency that was never there, and we weren't going there to enrol me at their house of fun, according to Roddy. So where were we going… and why?"

They all sat quietly for a while and only the occasional crackling of a log was audible. James got up at Roddy's silent bidding and refilled him a large measure of malt. He gave himself a more moderate one and went with Judy's wine glass to the kitchen. He rushed back in the room only moments later with the empty wine glass still in one hand and stabbing the air in a wild gesture of triumph with the other.

"He was stealing you – that is what it was. He was supposed to escort Judy somewhere else for whatever purpose but decided to steal her and run away with her himself."

"That makes sense," said Judy hesitantly as she got used to the idea.

"It pans out when I think about how he was behaving on the planes. How he was such a good guy and all mushy at times with me and how he always wanted to never push things… the poor…"

Judy trailed off into silence and was again deeply troubled by the idea of Greg as the innocent simpleton.

"He was taking her to Iceland for some reason is what I think, but something major happened at the airport to divert him – can you not remember seeing anything?" James addressed himself to Judy.

"There was nothing. Nobody spoke to him and nobody even approached us. He just went into a major funk and then he made a hell of a fuss getting us through into the other side of the airport again – and there was the new flight to pay and all."

"Well, there was something scared him at the airport – but – London was just a place to call to fool Judy. It has nothing to do with this," said Roddy thoughtfully.

"Well, yes – they were supposed to be going somewhere else altogether," added James slightly impatiently.

"But this organisation – the 'they' you are talking about for your new box, Roddy – it somehow got word of it – it someway got to know where we were going – and… and… *and…* they had somebody at the airport already waiting for us and he saw them in the crowd waiting at arrivals. You could see right on through to the folks waiting for people coming off the planes!"

"Christ, you are good, hen," said Roddy admiringly.

"That must be it right enough," marvelled James.

"And as if that was not a quick enough response, they then had shooters on the ground – or here already – and tracking them down within hours of the pair of them landing after what was an escape from an escape. You have to admire their planning all right – we'll need to be careful," warned Roddy.

They took a break after that and Roddy mentioned that some supper would be welcome, and James got up to go to the kitchen, but Judy got up and pushed him back onto the couch, telling him, "You're not to be trusted with the responsibility, and besides, it is the only way I'm going to get some more wine around here."

Roddy was again stunned to see them behave like a pair who had known each other for months and was about to make some subtle comment to James about the seeming certain coupling that had happened while he was away, but checked himself just in time when he saw that any mention would be not nuanced but rather clumsy and intrusive.

Judy brought Roddy a superb sandwich, which he guzzled appreciatively with an even larger tumbler of malt by way of reward for the progress that evening and as an accompaniment to the joy he felt at not only being back in harness, but in a deeper and more thorough way than he ever had been in his career.

They went over and over the details and got things more or less right. Some bits they made errors on for the moment, and they could not decide where Judy should have been going, although they all had dark suspicions about why, though that they left unsaid.

Late on, Roddy took advantage of Judy's absence from

the room to suggest that he was in no state to drive even a little way to a cold and deserted house and hinted that he could maybe have James' spare room for the night. He was astonished to learn that Judy was in occupation, although he was made welcome to bed down on the couch. This time, he betrayed his surprise with a certain glance which James recognised, but he replied only with a look of his own and the raising of an eyebrow which asked teasingly how else Roddy had thought the land lay.

Judy came back to find James bringing blankets for Roddy. They said good night and went off separately as before. Roddy took off his suit and wrapped himself in the blankets and went off to sleep by the dying embers of the fire in a haze of self-worth and malt fumes.

14

SAID-MAARTENS' MISSION

Around the time that Roddy was leaving the pub in London to return north, Said-Maartens was taking a very early flight from San Francisco to LA. He knew that almost certainly he was being sent for over the complaint of the man from the burning sands. He was not concerned about any threat to himself as he had been instructed to bring at least an overnight bag and he had discovered that he had a first-class seat when he checked in. He had long since convinced himself that repeatedly selling his soul for The Foundation would render him safe, and was a long way yet from realising that the nature of The Foundation meant that it was not always possible for it to be rational about whom it turned on.

In Ms Saldanha's meeting room, he was briefed that The Foundation had previously decided to ignore Judy and abandon her to her fate in the UK until this intervention from the intended recipient. There was, of course, no mention of David, and this meshed in with the increasing awareness that Said-Maartens had been feeling that he had encountered a Foundation disappearance very close to him rather than as hearsay. Yet this reassured him as he was in a way a part of the team which had destroyed David. He was surely one of the inner circle now.

Ms Saldanha told him that it had been decided to reclaim Judy, but that it would be difficult for a stranger to fool her again into taking a flight anywhere. To kidnap and deliver her as originally planned would be far too disruptive as they suspected that she had become embedded with all sorts of new friends. They needed to find out about her circumstances in detail before deciding on what to do. Said-Maartens was given a folder with all they knew about James. He had the task of going at once to Scotland and, using any kind of cover he could think of, get himself close to them, to report back on what the situation was. Then they would decide on what was possible.

The meeting had taken barely an hour and he was dismissed with a new passport, credit cards and first-class reservations to Glasgow through London. He then made his way to the airport.

Said-Maartens landed at Heathrow early that morning. He noted the flat suburbia drift past as they came in to land. He did not react to it as home and did not think about it further. He had no need to delay his Glasgow flight and go up to town. He had no real wish to see London again. He had no friends to look up and surprise briefly and no pubs and no restaurants to pay nostalgic visits to. A small part of him might have liked to visit the establishment he had previously been in charge of, but it was only a shallow curiosity that drove this. The Foundation was obsessed with loyalty from its employees and absolute devotion from its members, which was why David was several metres underwater in his quarry, but it ranked all other abilities that any normal organisation would seek a considerable way below this. Said-Maartens was a just-adequate manager of known circumstances, a good soldier, but had little potential for improvisation or original thought. He had puzzled how he would find out what the situation was with Judy that afternoon in LA and at first on the plane but had got nowhere and had fallen asleep. On the short flight to Glasgow, he put himself to the problem with more urgency but could only come up with the idea that he would get as close as possible to them physically and then come up with some as yet unguessed-at way of getting to know what her situation was. As they approached the airport, Said-Maartens looked out on some bare hills with his customary detachment. They were still not fully greened by spring, but the sun was out and glanced off the surface of the many streams and lakes. Such was the geometric disposition of the plane that the water of David's quarry blinked particularly brightly for an instant as they flew through its reflection.

He discovered that the address he had been given was not too far from the airport but was in a small village with only the one pub-cum-hotel. Now, one of Said-Maartens' distinguishing traits was that he had absorbed a preference for luxury. He therefore rejected the Cross Keys and settled for a country house-type hotel that was about ten miles distant and which was difficult to get into even in late spring. At this hotel, he found the surroundings gratifying but no more, and critiqued one or two points to himself from the point of view of an ex-hotel manager. He took a shower then went downstairs and looked though the tourist brochures kept in a rack in the entrance hall and discovered one for the Cross Keys. He saw it did dinners, and a sort of plan formed itself in his head. He drove there in the early evening and parked outside – very close to where David's car had been fired on. He went in through the narrow front door and did not find the place at all quaint or old-fashioned. He saw only a total lack of ostentatious expense in the surroundings and disapproved. He found the tiny dining room at once, where two residents were the only occupants. He sat down at a table as there was nobody there to greet him. After a while, Shona appeared and, surprised to find him there, took his order. Said-Maartens had acquired a trace of a mid-Atlantic accent since his posting to the US, and it struck Shona that it was like that of the strange shy guy who had been in a few nights past with James and his assumed new live-in companion from America. Said-Maartens sat and ate and thought further about his position. He speculated that Judy might actually come into the place and his work would be half done.

While Said-Maartens was eating, Roddy came into the bar. He had left David and Judy after breakfast and gone by bus to the town where David's executioners had passed the afternoon. There he had installed himself in his usual pub. He had again tried the London address and Panomnes Productions, pretending to be various people and trying to get some more information. All his efforts had been very politely rebuffed. He tried to get some further privileged information from old police contacts, but he found his name was poison and he had run out of favours – a fact which should have had more significance for him than he gave it. In the end, slightly drunk and stopped in his sprint to ever greater professional glory, he took the long bus ride back and went straight to the Cross Keys bar to complete the job. There were only a few in and the comments about his smooth face were quickly over. He sat with his drink and brooded. Shona came in and out behind the bar and on one visit she whispered quietly to Roddy that somebody who spoke like the boy he was in with the other night was having dinner next door. This roused Roddy hardly at all but presently he got up and strolled to the front door and turned back to the bar and cast a look into the dining room in the passing. At that precise time, Said-Maartens looked up and caught his eye and saw only an old drunk. But Roddy knew this was his man. He knew at once intuitively that they had come looking for Judy with this emissary. In the short distance back to his bar stool, his mental processes raced, and he was in a strange and energised shock. He sat there and his thoughts veered all the way from telling himself that this was paranoia to restraining himself from going back through there and pulling this man up and telling him to fuck off and leave her alone. Shona could see there was something wrong with him but said nothing. A short time later, Said-Maartens decided to initiate his farcical investigations and wandered through to the bar. All eyes were on him except for Roddy's. The owner had by that time taken up position behind the bar and Said-Maartens ordered a drink and hurriedly engaged him in a hopelessly clumsy and ill-disguised inquisition. Roddy listened to the voice and shot darting glances at the bland and boring figure. After a few ludicrous questions about the area, Said-Maartens almost at once mentioned James' name and claimed him as an old friend and then went on to ask all sorts of questions about him which showed he knew nothing of him. The owner summed up what was going on almost as quickly as Roddy and had his terror renewed that the frightening manifestations of the modern world had again come to his establishment. He thought that it was now impossible to even keep his head down. He caught Roddy's eye and signalled his distress. Roddy as quickly shot back that he was away to warn James. He downed his drink and almost comically, casually and slowly said good night to some of the drinkers and went out through the side door. Once outside, he went quickly up the street to his car – drink, or no drink – and went off noisily towards James' place.

James and Judy had come back to the house late after another day on the farm and had just finished supper when Roddy's car was again heard, and he once more entered and came directly into the living room in a state of obvious confusion.

"Good evening, Mr McIvor – and how has your day progressed?" asked James, to all appearances, sincerely.

Roddy had distilled his thoughts and rehearsed his opening in the car.

"Something in their plan has changed and they have come back for Judy," he said with quiet certainty.

This started another loud overlapping confusion of an exchange. Who it was that had returned and how Roddy knew it and why was it for Judy were half articulated and then resolved into coherent questions.

Roddy held his hand up and recited what had happened in the pub. Then he reasoned forward on two points alone: that the two thugs had taken Greg but had showed no interest in Judy. Therefore, he declared this nonentity in the Cross Keys was from the 'them', and the 'they' had changed their minds and it was their attitude to Judy that had altered somehow. There was a long silence which James broke:

"We have just got to discuss everything this might imply for you Judy," and he looked at her seriously.

"Sure, I know, let's just go ahead. You know, for a minute, when Roddy came out with that theory I was scared, but it has passed now – I'm not scared of them because that is what these kinds of bastards rely on a lot of the time, isn't it?"

Roddy and James did not believe that those who had taken Greg away gave anything for the mental attitude of their victims but were glad of Judy's stance.

James took over the reasoning then.

"I'm sure it is not as serious as it was for Greg. If they wanted to get rid of you, it is not this stranger that they would have sent but the two thugs would have been back, and it is likely we would not have even seen them coming." He turned to Roddy. "And why is this guy parading himself around the Cross Keys telling everybody he knows me when he doesn't? He is hardly keeping undercover with his head down, is he? In fact, he is exposing himself with all this pretending."

"You could call him out any time," added Judy.

There was another silence and then James said that he wanted to see this man.

"But I should too – you guys are already sure he doesn't know you, but I might know him from the US."

There was an unarguable logic to this and so they all three set off in Roddy's car with his repeated pleas that they must be careful as the man must know what Judy looked like and most likely they had some kind of photo of James. Now, The Foundation had carelessly not obtained one, but it was a reasonable presumption. Roddy himself had been in plain sight before the man and he had shown no reaction. Roddy would have to go first. They parked outside and Roddy entered and went quietly to the bar door and looked discreetly round it and checked that Said-Maartens was still in the bar. He found him exactly in the same place but now with a few customers gathered around for the novelty and the possibility of more drink being bought. Roddy motioned to the owner standing behind the bar to ignore him and listened in just out of sight at the staff entrance to the bar. Said-Maartens was still going on about James but seemed to be checking on exactly what he was up to on his farm. Roddy was mystified but on the assumption that he would stay there, he went outside and signalled the two of them to quickly come inside. He then diverted them into the small room that had an old-fashioned hatch entry to the back of the left-hand end of the bar. He cautiously looked around the edge of it and saw that Said-Maartens was still fully engaged. He beckoned for the two of them to glance around the hatch and look at the strange and seemingly harmless visitor. They both did so and were then hurried out into the car. Roddy made off rapidly and was well down the street before he asked them the question, but neither of them had any idea who Said-Maartens was.

The rest of that evening was passed in totally unproductive speculation. They could not reconstruct the thinking of 'them'. Why the brutal and blatant excision of Greg should be followed by this apparent grey cipher who was declaring his interest openly. Before he left, Roddy again wondered what was so different in their interest in Greg as opposed to their new interest in Judy.

The next day, a restrained disquiet lay over the pair of them at breakfast as they planned the farm work for that day, as was now natural for Judy. Just before they went out, James' phone went, and he found himself addressed by the very phantom they had viewed the night before. In exactly the bland and detached tones they had overheard. He introduced himself by the name on his new passport, which he absurdly hesitated over, and declared the toweringly improbable idea that he had chanced past the Cross Keys last night and had learnt that James was into growing Siberian kale. James noted that they must pay more attention than he thought in the pub when he went on about his enthusiasms. The voice went on at great length with a tale that he was right into this incredibly heath-giving vegetable and was promoting it in the States and was even thinking of growing some himself. He went tediously on, repeating himself at times, about how he wanted to know more about a plant he evidently knew nothing about already. James listened with an impossible mixture of feelings; the tremendous danger this man might represent mixed with repressing an urge to laugh at his transparent amateurishness.

He knew he must go forward with this thought and put on the best imitation of delight for their supposed mutual interest. A time was arranged for meeting that afternoon. He called Judy back, as she was already on her way out into the yard when he put the phone down. He told her about the call and then sat in silence opposite her in the little hallway behind the front door. He remained like that for some time on the large frame that contained the shelves for their outdoor boots, and she settled herself in a big wooden chair of uncertain age.

"Right, we know that they would seem to be after you. Now, somebody in the pub may have told them you were here and then again maybe not. And if they are all the same 'them', they should know at least that you were here from those who took Greg away. But we don't want to make it easy for them, so your job for the day is to go up to the chalet and tidy it out for the summer tourists. Get changed again and away up you go – take something for lunch, there is nothing up there. You'll need to be right out the way. I'll call you when things are clear here." James sat a long while more right there by the door trying to think everything through. She reappeared and pecked him on the cheek. She knew that this was wise, and the thought was in her head that maybe the chalet was not far enough away. She strode away up the hill in the sunshine and was lost among the pines as a breeze softly sounded its way through their swaying tops.

James next called Roddy, told him what had happened and said he needed somebody else here to see this man again at length and be an independent assessor of what he might come out with. While he waited for him, he went through the house and removed every sign he could of Judy's presence and put them in a big old cupboard by the back door and locked it.

When Roddy arrived, he was told that he was the farm labourer for the day and was put into clean overalls and taken outside to have mud and shit sprayed up them. He was given an old baseball cap and told to wear it low. His car was parked behind the sheds, out of sight. When this man approached, he was to take himself into one of the sheds and if he arrived with any kind of company in tow, he was to get in the car and drive off by the chalet road and get Judy and then head away as quickly as possible for help. Roddy considered this and found it sensible and logical, and they sat down outside to wait. The sound of a car was heard through the trees and Roddy at once took himself off. But Said-Maartens arrived alone and crept out of his hire car slightly hesitatingly and came near to James with hand outstretched in a manner almost suggesting submission. James called Teribus to heel and stepped forward to shake his hand.

There then passed a few minutes in gauche preliminaries and even more awkward declarations from Said-Maartens of his enthusiasm for Siberian kale when a sudden rebellious inspiration came to James. He was mystified that whoever it was that was behind all these disruptions to his existence, and who seemed to be so menacing and given to violent solutions to their incomprehensible problems, should have sent this quiet-spoken junior clerk who seemed to have no hidden menace and who was also making a thorough fool of himself as he displayed no knowledge of the upmarket vegetable under discussion. Was this who they thought appropriate to search for Judy? He could not be in awe of such an incompetent nonentity, and he decided that he would have to be thoroughly humiliated – but in a way that he would not even realise, in case it stored up even more future problems for Judy.

A strange hour was then passed as James cheerily invited him to board his tractor which, as it was decades old and without a cab, involved him standing beside James and holding on as bits of mud were thrown up to foul his trousers and shoes. James took them lurching and bouncing much too fast along tracks between fields that led down and out of his own land to that of a neighbour who was farming more conventionally. There he stopped in a large puddle and motioned for Said-Maartens to step down and inspect a field of bright green shoots just newly invigorated in the belated spring. Once grounded, Said-Maartens stepped, feet-sodden, out of his puddle onto the muddy edge of a field of winter barley and went on extensively and as earnestly as he could manage about the apparent health and vigour of James' Siberian kale. James acted with his normal enthusiasm on kale but turned it up until it was overpowering. He was mocking this figure and saying to him that he was not who he was pretending to be. Said-Maartens had enough about him to sense correctly what James was about, but he could not even guess how. This left him feeling even more useless and awkward.

They went recklessly as before, back up to the farmyard, and dismounted. They were approaching the big shed when Roddy appeared pushing a wheelbarrow and going nowhere, with a pointless bale of hay perched unsteadily on it. He was playing his part and approached them and put down the wheelbarrow.

"This is a man from the US and who is wild about Siberian kale as well," enthused James. Said-Maartens, more mud-spattered than ever, just grinned and looked at Roddy but failed to recognise him from the pub, such were his lack of abilities for his new role as secret emissary. Roddy put a few completely irrelevant questions to him – 'just to get a feel for the bastard'. Then he and his load wobbled off and the two of them stood awkwardly with only small talk occasionally justifying their attendance. There was some duty still on Said-Maartens' mind. He looked towards the house, but James looked the other way. There was more silence and Said-Maartens knew there would be no invitation back to the house, and this registered with him as a way of hiding Judy. He then blurted out that he must be away but that he would like to use his toilet before he went.

"But this is a farmyard, man – you can go against anything you like."

This forced Said-Maartens to invent a phantom shit as his reason, which was doubly embarrassing for him to do as, besides being no actor, he was also a prude and inept at euphemisms.

James motioned towards the house and told him that it was at the back but made no move to follow. After an age, Said-Maartens came out again and mumbled something about having to go and briefly shook James' hand and was away.

Roddy re-emerged and delivered his view that 'them' must be short of manpower if the likes of that bastard was all they could find to chase Judy.

"Exactly what I was thinking myself," said James quietly.

"And he had a good look round the house for her as well!"

Roddy jerked his head back and looked incredulously at James.

"Ah, but you needn't worry – I put all her stuff out of sight. That was either the biggest dose of the runs he had, or he has looked through every corner of my house for her and found neither a hairbrush nor pair of knickers."

"I don't think that will put him off – though with him being such a useless wanker, it might just."

Later that afternoon, Roddy and James were endlessly and fruitlessly talking about who they had christened Mr Winter Barley. They knew he was not staying at the Cross Keys, and Roddy called the owner to see if he had mentioned where he was staying. Said-Maartens had apparently not bothered to hide his dislike for such a small place and had seemed keen to tell him he was at the Castle Hotel. Now this gave Roddy an idea. He called the Castle Hotel and asked for a certain under-manager for whom he had recently, in his private investigator time, buried a minor case of embezzlement because his opinion was that it would just ruin any chance the poor bugger had of making anything of himself in the world. He asked if their odd guest was still there and if he was around.

"Aye, he's still here, but he's no around that I've seen."

"Well, will you do me a great favour?"

"Whit?"

"Will you go away up to his room and take a look around and see if you can see anything at all on the boy?"

"Aw, fucking hell, man – what if he comes back?"

"Just keep an eye out for his car. It'll no take you long. You were bold enough that last time, just away you up, and it's nothing illegal this time!"

"Whit is it youse are lookin' for anyway?"

"Anything – any documents – passports – anything he might have left in the room."

"But he'll have aw his stuff wae him, will he no?"

"He might do, right enough, but I just want you to see if he has left anything behind – will you?"

"Christ, man – give us five minutes. I'll call you back."

And in five minutes almost exactly, Roddy was informed that there was nothing much there, only a passport left in a drawer, but that it wasn't in the name he had checked in under. It was for a Mr Said-Maartens. Roddy asked him to spell it. He also asked the details given on it.

"I knew you'd want aw the details, so I copied them down."

They now had a name and address and a date of birth. The address meant nothing to them, and they had to look it up, but he was born in London, which explained the accent.

"What kind of name is Said-Maartens?" asked James afterwards. "And why is he travelling under another name?"

"That doesn't need much imagination," suggested Roddy.

Then they sat in silence before James jumped up and shouted for Judy, who was restoring her belongings from the cupboard.

"We need to run this name past her!"

Judy came through and they asked her about the name. A look of recognition came over her face.

"Sure, I know it – and I've told you before when we were taking about Greg's moves to fix up a number for me to call."

They still looked puzzled.

"Your guy is Mr Side-Martin. The guy Greg called that day!"

"And does this address mean anything to you?"

"No, that's somewhere in the Valley near San Francisco, I think," was Judy's hesitant reply.

They resorted to Google Street View again, and the three of them sat wonderingly around an image of a very expensive house peeking discreetly out from a large garden onto a perfect palm-lined suburban cul-de-sac.

The rest of that day was passed in one of their long discussions on 'them'. They could discern a very sparse framework for the whole thing, though it certainly had huge holes all over it. They thought they could see its broad extent and reach; they knew its methods now would be anything from suspected sudden violence to wonderful incompetence according to their only guessed-at aims. They did not know its ambitions, but they could see dimly what they might be and more clearly what they were not. They had decided that they now wanted Judy back and that their attempts would go on. Roddy announced that strong drink might take up where the coffee had left off, and James decided to go yet again to the pub for dinner.

Roddy took them up in his car and the three of them installed themselves in a corner and continued their endless and fruitless speculations. They had their dinner and then let their obsession pass and moved to the bar and mixed. Later, Judy's phone rang, and she went out into the corridor to take it. She returned and her face had blanched and deflated, and she was close to tears.

"They've taken my apartment. I got nowhere – no home to go to," she said quietly but to no one in particular when she returned. Now, Roddy only had very approximate ideas about where or how she lived and though she had described it to James, he had not been paying complete attention.

"They can't just stop you renting like that – it's only been no time that you've been away," said James dismissively – and perhaps the new implicit contract between them allowed a touch of a paternal tone to creep in.

"Well, they goddamn have," she replied, vehement and loud now, and she turned on James. "I told you what that place meant to me. It was the only way I could afford to live in that city. I arranged the rental, and I placed the ad for the other girls to share with and I know it wasn't much and the place was never mine, but it was a kind of first move in my new life after leaving Michigan, and I thought I was kind of smart to have put it all together."

The tears started to seep out and Roddy took over.

"But what's happened?" he simply asked quietly.

"Well, what Rachel says is that there is some kind of new city ordinance that says that if the owner leaves any property vacant then anybody who wants can move right on in. Well, all the sheet-plastic tents from Skid Row have long since spread way beyond that neighbourhood and had just started to peek round the corner of our street. It turns out that there is some chief junkie asshole in charge of our section down there, and the minute he sees me leaving, he was into the apartment with his buddies, claiming the place. They threw out the girls and when they called the cops, he claims that I am the owner and that I've been gone for months – there is some time limit to this whole stupid law – but they don't care when they're told I've just gone. So… the cops don't listen and don't want to know and couldn't give jack-shit, so they roll over and take that jerk's side 'cos it's easier. They don't give a damn that I'm not the owner 'cos when they try to call him, it turns out he has bailed along with half the rest of California and had written off the whole block 'cos he saw that was what would happen and that he already knew it and figured the place was lost anyway and took himself off to Texas! So, I get declared the effective owner and we are all screwed."

There were a lot of consolatory noises, of no use whatever, made by Roddy and James, who insisted that they could not simply effectively re-assign the place.

"Sure, they can do that – they just goddamn did it, didn't they! And the best the cops could do, it looks like, was to get the girls access to get their stuff back. Of course, by then the place had been trashed and they are all lying around shooting up and shit and the girls are scared stupid, and it turns out there's none of their stuff left their worth having by then anyway."

There was silence from James and Roddy. Judy could not stop a few tears rolling…

"So, I got nowhere to go back to."

They left the pub and Roddy went off to his house while James, without discussion, walked Judy back through the forest. He said little and she went over in her head all that had happened in the immensity of time that had spilled into the few days since LA Airport. It was still just light. It was cool but with a scent of pine, broom and undergrowth. James discovered he did not know her well enough to tell her reactions, and did not interrogate. Judy felt increasingly serene and detached and assigned no importance to anything outside that present moment. She took James' hand but said nothing and did not look at him but just kept glancing around at the woods and the sky. She pondered the existence of a God whose duty it was to look after not particularly bright young girls from Michigan and lead them out of troubles, of as yet undiscovered depths, and pitch them up wrapped entirely in the moment with this company and in that forest.

Inside, she quietly said she was going to her room to think. The irony of calling it her room struck her, but she saw that it was as much hers as any other room on earth now. She looked round at the mismatched assortment of Victorian and modern furniture and imagined it to represent heirlooms of the Graham family, whereas a lot was from an auction sale that James had visited simply to furnish his farmhouse. James sat a long while going over the same simple thoughts: that he was taking a selfish pleasure in her misfortune as it made it more likely that she would stay, and he was certain that that was what he wanted, although it seemed now even more absurd and irrational.

That same evening, Said-Maartens, in his five-star accommodation, called in to Ms Saldanha to report progress. His lack of success was disguised as a work in progress, but his incompetence could not be hidden. Ms Saldanha, fearing for her own position and seeing herself being relieved of the responsibility, turned very nasty with Said-Maartens and returned him in seconds to the kind of fears he used to entertain about The Foundation before he convinced himself that he was a favoured person within it. He planned for the rest of the evening what he would do to restore his imagined position.

The next morning, Judy had fully re-established an internal serenity before breakfast. She had not decided much but had thought things over and had established what needed to be added to the things she admitted to herself were on hold for consideration. This was mostly the file concerning James, where was lodged as the main objections to him, that he was older and cleverer and foreign (sometimes to the point of opaqueness), and although she truly knew the answer, yet she would still not let it surface too clearly through her habitual caution over men and attachments in general. She had started off the previous night in her room feeling like a sudden charity case thrown back on his generosity, and then she decided that he had very little to be generous with and that this was the smallest farm she had ever seen and that by the state of his car and the tractor, there was not much money around. And he might be some kind of high-up lawyer of whatever kind they had in this country, but he wasn't working and didn't show any sign of ever wanting to. Plus, there was probably alimony of some kind, and she figured that her labour about the farm was as good as any fair rent and she felt better. As for being stranded on the far side of the world in a place she still did not fully know the location of, that she took with the equanimity she had found on the way home through the forest last night. That forest was very much like the ones on Lake Superior shore. And, in addition, she was the source of the mystery that was keeping them all interested and so she was also effectively providing for them – why, they were having such entertainment out of it, she should charge them to let them help her.

Breakfast proceeded with more, not less, of an atmosphere of domestic permanence. She appeared in a pair of denims that James had not seen before and a cotton top that seemed to be designed only to hang loose and delicately after stretching tightly over her breasts. James ached. She pecked him chastely on the forehead then went out to the henhouse for eggs. She made perfect eggs along with some bacon she found and brewed coffee far better than James ever managed, yet from the same old stained cafetière. The only tactical part of their conversation was to repeat that they were after Judy and that they almost certainly knew she was here but had not actually confirmed it. James suggested that they had not seen the last of Said-Maartens and then they went off outside into the dry and slightly milder weather to begin another exceptional day in her company for James. He endeavoured to suppress lust and advance enchantment. Judy continued to impress him with her intuitive understanding of new tasks that, in truth, had not long been mastered by James himself. Judy had taken her isolation of the previous evening to an advanced pitch and was perfectly cocooned in a wonderous present. James' prediction about Said-Maartens did not take long to be fulfilled. He had quit his luxury early that morning and called at the country town and equipped himself with an excessively expensive array of new clothes. A top-of-the-range anorak, waterproof trousers and walking boots, together with a rucksack and a steel flask bound in Italian leather should he get thirsty. He finished it off by buying a very heavy and expensive set of binoculars.

Said-Maartens drove his hire car until he thought he was approaching the village, turned off into the forest and parked in an unmetalled lay-by which he was certain was close to James' farm. He then set off and wandered about through forest and over moors for several hours and became totally lost. He was torn by the dead lower branches of larch as he tried to push through the gloom under tight plantations of towering trees, and torn even worse by spines when he fell among an area of gorse which he did not recognise for what it contained. It was only seeing James' farm in the distance that saved him. He made his way down and took again to the trees when he was near. He crouched down and had a clear view over the farm to the house. He made to free his binoculars from their case and did not get as far as attempting to focus when James and Judy came out of one of the sheds and stood before him less than fifty metres away. Teribus came with them and paused only for a moment before rushing up the slope into the forest, barking wildly. James looked after her and wondered that it might be rabbits that she was after but said quietly, half as a thought aloud and half to Judy, that she usually didn't bother making a fuss about them. Teribus went straight to Said-Maartens as he crouched in the undergrowth and decided that he did not need evaluating but was the enemy and made an initial snapping foray at his backside. Said-Maartens jumped clumsily to his feet and started a stumbling retreat, which he had hardly begun before he tripped badly on a fallen log and rolled uncontrollably down the slope to land in a shallow ditch almost at James' feet. Teribus followed and felt she had delivered the threat for examination and merely stood over him growling. They looked down at the ridiculously clad figure, who was still managing to clutch the binoculars.

"Why, Mr Alias, it's yourself. Now if you were wanting to know more about the kale, you should have just asked to come back today. Were you out for a walk at all?"

Said-Maartens, plastered with mud again, staggered to his feet and kept one eye on Teribus. Now, James had not thought that Judy had never caught sight of him before. But the significance of this intrusion took but seconds to add up in her head. She half turned to James.

"Is this Side-Martin – is this the son of a bitch who was trying to put me in the house of fun?" she asked very quietly.

"Said-Maartens," corrected James, to show him that they knew who he was and with the hope that he would think they knew much more about him. A look of dread began to deflate Said-Maartens' face when he heard his name.

Judy turned on him cowering in the ditch, and her voice changed to a strange screaming mixture of rage and exultation at being able to get to grips in person with some part of what had recently taken over her life.

"You are from them. You are the one who tried to send me abroad as a hooker. You probably got rid of Greg," and here she paused before resuming even louder, "but he was a son of a bitch too."

Said-Maartens climbed out of the ditch and started a retreat with the dread now manifested as outright horror as he decided they knew much more than they did.

Judy bent down and took up a handful of sizeable road-stones and aimed one at his head. It struck his shoulder with an audible thud.

"Get the hell back to LA and tell whoever dreamed up this whole fucking shit show to leave me alone."

Said-Maartens started to run away down the road, heading for the village. Teribus thought it her duty to pursue and kept up a snarling tearing at his trouser leg. Judy resumed her bombardment and bounced some more off the small of his back until, as he was getting out of range, she made a final effort and cracked him on the back of the head, causing him to stumble before resuming his flight.

James called Teribus back and gazed at Judy. He expected her to start sobbing but instead she let out a scream of frustration at the vanishing figure of Said-Maartens.

On the flight back, Said-Maartens started his report. He used as many invented details as he could think of and described himself as having skilfully and amiably intruded on their domestic life. He said that James and Judy were living together and that she would be impossible to separate from him as she was obviously already completely devoted to him and embedded in the community. He made no reference at all to the amateur incompetence that had allowed his identity to be discovered nor to the fact he thought James and Roddy had already worked out what was underway after Dave had gone native. He hoped that they never found out, and he would have it hanging over him as a threat as he resumed his life as part of The Foundation with the fear restored.

He sent it on return to San Francisco. The next day at the office, it seemed that his absence had never been noticed. He awaited the call from LA daily, but it never came, and neither did any acknowledgement of his report. Office life went on as before, but nobody mentioned David anymore.

Now, Ms Saldanha's first reaction to Said-Maartens' report and its indication that Judy would be impossible to wrest from her present position was to try to apologise to the customer in the burning sands and promise him the choice of a range of replacements for Judy. He, however, sensed that he was dealing with an organisation in some difficulties over the Judy delivery. He had no clue as to what might have happened to interrupt his delivery and embarrass The Foundation, but an instinct for maximum disruption told him to continue to insist on the original delivery being met. He rejected all the videos of fresh meat which they sent him but retained them for potential future value in his new pastime of causing confusion to whatever The Foundation was. Ms Saldanha therefore applied logic to the problem and saw that James and Judy had to be isolated before she could try any kidnap of Judy and elimination of James. The actual export would be difficult to complete but she thought it might be done if she was correctly drugged for the trip. She was sure there was a department she could contact for advice. She puzzled over how to induce their isolation and rejected outright terror tactics or threats which would have been less than productive. In the end, she had an inspiration, and the idea came to her that it had to be just those means – terror, threats and intimidation but in a perfectly open and indeed, in those times, commonplace form, which would be sure to drive them off the farm and into hiding. Now, everything in her department in The Foundation was but an ancillary arm of a larger body which promoted The Foundation's aims globally. She had to make enquiries about who to call but eventually was able to get the help of someone in an awareness promotion department. But such was internal security that she never even learnt where they were based. These people, however, were able to suggest just such a means of scaring James and Judy into self-imposed sanctuary. They of course needed to have all the details and it would take some days to arrange, but they thought it would serve the purpose and, moreover, cost The Foundation very little.

15

JUDY AND JAMES

After Said-Maartens had scuttled off out of range of Judy, they started another council of war on the spot, and not too long after that, Roddy's car came too rapidly down the same track that Said-Maartens had vanished up. He joined the conference and had first to be told what had happened. He asked Judy to go over her story of pitching stones at him a second time for pure enjoyment and then to go over the whole incident again to make sure he had missed nothing.

"Well, we are ahead of you, and we've gone over this already and all we can come up with is that he was actually making sure that Judy was here."

"It was like he just needed to see me for some reason. He wasn't coming on all threatening or anything – if I didn't know he was something to do with this whole thing, I wouldn't have got mad – he was just like a saddo duffus over there in the ditch."

Roddy was not convinced and asked where Teribus had found him. They both indicated the spot a little way up on the edge of the trees in undergrowth of bracken and broom. Roddy scrambled chaotically up there and shouted for confirmation that he was in the right spot. He searched around and then called Teribus, who did not respond until James echoed the order. She streaked up the bank and sniffed around for a few minutes but found nothing that Roddy's search had missed. He scrambled back down, and Roddy asked him what he was looking for.

"A dropped gun," he replied, looking gravely at Judy.

"No, Roddy – the men that Judy saw take Greg away were from whoever they are's SAS, but this specimen seemed to be more like one of their Boy Scouts. And… the only thing I can see this confirms is they did not know exactly where Judy was until now but—"

"Why do they have to know – and what is it they are planning next?" interrupted Roddy.

Their council of war went rambling on as the others before it, revolving around the same question again and again without making any progress. Roddy announced he was leaving to try to quiz Ian in the pub again about Said-Maartens' visit and then he was going to drive over to his expensive lodging and see if his contact was not around and get whatever he could out of him in turn.

"What are you looking for especially?" wondered James.

"I don't know – just whatever I can find. I'm not hopeful but refuse nothing but blows, eh!"

In the remains of that afternoon, James decided to start the sowing of the prized kale and he devolved a task to Judy that involved her taking the battered quad up to the hill pasture with a couple of bags of dietary supplement to spread about to help with the new lambs. No cooking afterwards, he said, and promised to go back to the Cross Keys that evening. She tied the bags on the back and dismissing sudden belated doubts from James at his own judgement, off she went up through the trees, almost sure of her route. James listened, and the high-pitched buzzing of the thing got slowly quieter and faded altogether as she climbed higher and rounded a ridge in the forest. She buzzed on through the trees in the sunshine, all alone and utterly happy, with Said-Maartens out of her head. The visit and what it signified she put forcibly from her mind. She would not continue their habitual lengthy discussions. If James could not figure it out who had been in some sort of National Guard, and Roddy could do not do better, who had been a cop, then what hope had she?

She took one wrong turning, but it amused rather than dismayed her and she turned back and found the true track for the hill gate. Once through and clear of the forest, she went slowly and bumpily along what was almost a footpath. There was fresh green growth everywhere and new wildflowers that were not here even those few days ago, it seemed to her. The sheep heard the buggy and started to stream towards it, such was their Pavlovian reaction to a free meal. She unlashed the bags and split them open and started to spread the feed pellets on a broader bit of the path where the grass was short. The cute-faced sheep jostled and mobbed her. She called for them to wait in line. When the bags were empty, she sat on a nearby boulder while the sheep searched out the last pellet. She looked around at ridge after ridge of forest and hill, with the great triangular mountain in the west. She was as contented as perhaps she had ever been but only recognised it and was not inclined to any further self-examination. Her thoughts turned to James down below on his, to her mind, impossibly small farm. She considered the planting of the kale and smiled to herself at the vision of him because the idea seemed unlikely to work to her. It was, however, altogether a sympathetic smile – the kale might be a winner for all she knew – and she could not but have a warm feeling at the vision of him resolutely toiling to make his idea work. At that moment, she was overcome with a longing to go back down to the farm just to see how he was doing. She at once checked herself and summoned the hard-bitten and cynical Judy of long experience to scrutinise this unexpected notion out of existence. She had fooled herself into such feelings just twice before – all the others had been merely lust and wine.

Yet her thoughts would return to James. She did remember him that first day as they approached through the village. Not just when he opened the door to her, but she had noticed him a few moments earlier as he strode alone up to the pub and had glanced at the car. The simple door incident had yet made an impression – but anybody around here, it seemed to her, would have made some kind of comment on squeezing through the door. Even Roddy would have made some puzzling comment that she would have had to assume was funny. Then again, she saw him striding up the hill and glancing in the car. Well, there were so few people on the sidewalk in this place. She reviewed her knowledge of where she was. It was a lot more complete than a few days ago but not at all perfect. Yet that did not seem to matter anymore. She was lost in a daydream of youthful freedom and decided that this place would do as well as any other for a home. Then she went further and settled on it as the place she could spend the rest of her days but then as rapidly swore at herself and called it a boring flyblown little Hicksville asshole of a place on the edge of the earth and tried to flood her mind with visions of the US. She decided that she would be longing to return after a month in this place.

She started up the quad again and set off downwards. The sheep surged hopefully after then fell back and dispersed over the hill. At the farm, she came across him and his ancient tractor coming back up from the kale field. She started zooming around it and passing it and letting it pass her again, only to overtake again. He laughed and called for her not to be such a silly bitch and she laughed back at him and did it again. When they got to the house, they both dismounted, and she ran towards him and gave him a hug. In obedience to the rules, he did not squeeze back but he again revelled in the scent of her hair and felt her breasts press against him.

He dismissed her offer of cook dinner and reminded her that he had promised her to go to the pub. She became a little distant and reticent and would not discuss it and just said that she would fix dinner. He offered to do it instead, but she insisted and planted herself in occupation of the kitchen. He gave in and retired. She knew what was to be found there by now and saw that it fell below any culinary invention that she could bring to bear to make it memorable. She found even concentrating difficult as she went about the now discouraging job. Her mind had suddenly recoiled from the fuzzy well-being that had seized it for most of the afternoon. Like with a hangover, all her mental processes were completely redirected. She became obsessed with how much older he was than her. She found it amazing that she had not actually found out. At least ten years, she thought, and then converted that to almost half her lifetime and panicked. About the failed marriage, she had had the essentials told to her already but now assumed that there must be much more to it than had been reported. She had admitted most of her past but had still concealed some of her naïve mistakes, and she thought that he would have as well – and as the level of his fancy, important and complicated life had been so far above her immature escapes then, she decided, so might the things he had missed out. He would have seen them as too much for her to handle. Too much to bother her empty little off-blonde head with. She would insist on meeting with this ex-wife.

She presented her dish, and they ate it in silence, both stunned at how bad it was. Judy ate to conceal her state of mind and James out of courtesy. He was puzzled by her silence – and their meal. Afterwards, he offered to wash up, but she insisted and whisked the dishes off to the kitchen, where they were washed and dried with much clattering and crashing. She emerged still distant, and James had set in his mind that she was reacting to the Said-Maartens visit and was belatedly worrying about what might follow. Taking advantage of the lengthening evening, he announced that he was away back out to keep going until the light faded. He expected her to come with him, but she said she would stay in and watch some television. This was not credible as James had the impression that she hardly watched in the US, and he knew that she found much of the UK output incomprehensible, and indeed admired her for that. He left and she settled on his huge sofa before the TV. She endlessly channel-hopped, never spending more than a few minutes on any one baffling presentation.

When it was almost dark, he returned and found her on the sofa. He did not bother to ask what she had seen as he knew she paid no attention to anything if the TV was on. He offered her a glass of wine, but she got up abruptly and said she was going to bed. She caught sight of how she was behaving and returned it a little to normality by observing the by then conventional peck of the cheek but still disappeared leaving a chill after her. James again thought she was worrying about Said-Maartens' visit and did not feel able to offer any comfort on the matter as he had no idea what would follow it himself.

Judy lay in bed in the over-sized pyjamas she had borrowed from him. Her mind continued its churnings, although she did not come up with any new aspects to be outraged about. Instead, she very slowly began to think of how they were probably all a load of crap. She had not completed this process when she fell asleep.

She awoke around four o' clock and found her mind made up without having to go through any further formal evaluations. She got up and, on reflection, took off the pyjamas and went quickly through the cold corridor, lit by the first grey of dawn, to his room. There she crept into his double bed beside him without waking him. She slowly thawed out and he was still not awake. She then nodded off contentedly. A couple of hours later, she came to and heard him still quietly making little puffing sounds. She nudged him gently and he wakened. He looked at her, perplexed, and she returned his gaze with a look that was resolute. He thought for a minute that she had become so scared at the prospects ahead of them that she had come to his bed rather as a little child would do. He reached out for her and found her naked and saw that he was utterly wrong. He rolled slowly towards her, accepting that she had at last decided this. The question as to why would wait until later, but then he thought that it did not really matter anyway.

He got up around mid-morning and made coffee and bacon rolls and they ate them in bed before resuming. At last, they went for a shower together in the draughty bathroom.

"At least this sharing will help with the lack of hot water round here," she said, giggling.

They did the minimum of necessary tasks on the farm then he took her off in his rusting car over a jumble of rough forested hills to a pier on a lake, where they took a trip on a little tourist steamboat that had survived the attempts of the Ministry of Tourism to eliminate the industry under regulations governing compliances with hundreds of politically directed restrictions.

It was a brilliant clear afternoon, and the complete lack of wind let the water mirror the mountains.

"I've lived around here all my life and I've never been on this thing."

Their ritual pecks at each other and the subtle passes of his face within the scent of her hair were now unrestrained, and they had to rein themselves in several times before the small number of tourists that were left for these trips. They drove back directly to the pub. Those present immediately took in the situation, and Roddy, who was there already, was confused and wondered if the impressions given really meant what he had thought they meant before. Roddy came over to them and told them he had found out nothing significantly new about Said-Maartens. Judy told him to forget Side-Martin and asked him to eat with them, relieving James of the worry she might have objected had he asked him. They had a very riotous meal with too much wine, led by Judy, with James close behind and Roddy dragged along. At one point, while Judy was at the toilet, James, without prompting and in a spirit of glorious and open celebration, told Roddy the news.

The two of them walked home through the forest again and when they got in, they moved rather slowly but certainly through the house, determinedly holding each other and making the removal of clothes awkward. They fell into bed for a protracted and slightly drunken session which seemed to go on for an age. Just before he fell asleep with her resting her head on his chest, James looked over this precious development. He had not given her pleasure; the act had, and, overly simplistically, both had to be present for it. The first few minutes of the previous morning had been a time of careful application of techniques learnt but after that he had felt no need of observed structure or planning. The audible pleasure she had experienced was not because of him or her

– it was because of them. With his ex-wife, the success of sex was just one more thing he was entirely responsible for, along with her new kitchen, the electric city runabout (and arranging a place to park it) and that ridiculously pretentious little house in the Borders – all inevitably lost in the divorce settlement.

They spent a perfect interlude of nearly a fortnight like this. Said-Maartens unthought of and the sun and simple unanalysed work by day and the shadows and unanalysed sex by night. Roddy came and went and tried to revive and update his flip charts every so often but with less and less success. His whiskers and hair were allowed to return, and grew back to their disordered former state. But it was only so long they had until Ms Saldanha, with the aid and input of the Awareness Promotion Department, would put together the means of driving them out.

16

SIEGE

One morning, as Judy and James lingered with each other when they should have been active on the farm hours before, there came the penetrating sound of a heavy vehicle entering the farmyard and a confusion of similar growls and whines just after, suggesting that more were following. James went to the front of the house, forgetting about his naked state, and looked out of the window. There was a large bus already in the yard and three or maybe four piled up behind it on the forest road. From all of them an assaulting army poured forth. There were strange figures in scarlet robes and white masks with terrifyingly impersonal minimal features drawn on them. Detached slaughter would come easily to these masks. There was a squad of enormous women in dungarees with faces which seemed permanently contorted in hate, and having the air of figures taking time off from crushing babies' skulls. There were huge young males, possibly students, with dead staring eyes, oddly uniform beards of all colours and wearing black sweaters with indecipherable oriental symbols on them. These were all the regiments apparent on first sight, but there were many other unkempt or outlandishly got-up aberrant creatures, having in common faces that had seemingly never laughed in their lives and a terrible unquestioning single-mindedness. They were all crowding around the luggage bays of the buses to retrieve placards and other more sinister weapons rapidly snatched up and instantly hidden inside various garments. There formed up in the van, a group of very deliberately scruffily dressed men and women of distinctly middle-class appearance. They were without uniform and were the plain-clothes organisers. They all wore expressions of glowing self-assurance and righteousness, irritating alone but rendered menacing by an expression that conveyed the belief that any measure of self-examination was unnecessary. They were advancing towards the house when one of the organisers in front spotted James, as nature intended, at his window.

"The patriarchy personified," screamed the leading woman, and all the others paused briefly to see where he was and then surged forward as one huge baying crowd. Several bricks were thrown through windows and James fled back through the house to find Judy.

The leading woman turned her back to the house and, pointing behind her, screamed again, "There was the patriarch fresh from oppressing his captive plaything!"

All the plain-clothes organisers turned in line towards the crowd to slow and contain them.

"We can't go as rapidly as we would like just yet, but we will achieve everything necessary before long."

The crowd checked itself and fell back a little, waving banners and bawling messages of hate at the house.

James rallied Judy and he and her dressed at once, with James ruling out any time for washing or preening. He did not know what was happening. His mind in the last few days had turned over all sorts of responses from 'them' – some terrifying, like the return of the shooters and those who had taken Greg away, and these visions had alternated in a confusing but reassuring way with that of the incompetent and harmless Said-Maartens. Judy complied and dressed in silence. She had heard the glass breaking and knew there had been a final shattering also of the idyllic goldfish bowl of existence that they had briefly made for themselves. He ushered her cautiously through to the front of the house.

"What's happening?" she asked him quietly.

"I don't fucking know – I truly do not." He answered her steadily, and by his very unusual use of a curse, she knew that it was serious, whether he knew what it was about or not.

They went cautiously into the living room to the increasing chants and screams from outside. They looked around curtains at either side of a small side window and saw rank after rank of them dammed up behind the overseers and all of them crying hate at them and waving banners with all manner of tailored messages.

'Climate Denier', 'Animal Cruelty Bastards', 'Gaia Oppressor', 'Carbon Betrayer', 'SJW against Elitist Scum', 'Old Law Dead-New Law Rules', 'Tree Killer – Merchant of Death', 'Child Exploiter' and *'Free Judy Ruono Now'*.

They reformed in the kitchen and sat and stared at each other. James had nothing to.

"Ah, this kind of shit happens every day in LA – when do you reckon they will go away again?"

James looked at Judy and wondered at how lightly she was taking this; he did not see that it was done only to try to reassure him.

"I know this is happening everywhere but why is it happening to us?" he said, deliberately not saying 'me' as he had seen the placard with her name on it – which Judy had not yet noticed.

"I never thought it was so intimidating until you see it up close."

He edged back towards the front of the house and took another quick look at them before coming back to the kitchen.

"Or is it an especially evil squad they have assembled to assault us?" he quietly asked Judy.

"What are they here for – and why now?"

But all too quickly, the answer had already formed in his head – this was the latest battle in the War of Judy. Once again, as with all the previous stages, he was sure what was the cause but baffled by why and how they were proceeding with the war.

They had a tense breakfast in silence as the chanting and hate-screaming kept on relentlessly.

"I need to call Roddy," he at last decided, thrusting aside his coffee cup. He tried the landline and found it was already cut off. A chill went through him when he saw what they were up against. He said nothing to Judy and called on his mobile. He recited everything he knew to Roddy, who had been caught off guard even more than James and had to have everything repeated to him until James cut him off by being obviously irritated and verging on fury with him.

"OK. OK, James," Roddy replied consolingly, "is there any way I can get down to the farm?"

James tried again with the volume of his voice held in.

"Roddy – you couldn't get near the place without a regiment of artillery," he said slowly, sounding each syllable.

James then went on and outlined his theory that this was a continuation of the war, not caring if Judy heard. She heard but it had already occurred to her as well, then suddenly Judy glanced out at them and saw something.

"My name is on their signs! What the hell is my name doing there?" and she started for the front door. James told Roddy he had to go and asked him to call the police.

"Yes, I know they'll be bloody useless… I have to go now."

Judy had already opened the front door and was causing a fresh crescendo of jeers. She spotted her name being waved aloft.

"What the fuck are you doing with my name – what are you going to free me from, you crazy bunch of hippy weirdos?" she screamed, fit to be heard over the braying mob. They paused a little as this did not fit in with what they had had sketched out for them. But such people rate facts nowhere at all, if they are going to get in the way of righteous persecution, so they almost at once started their chanting again.

Now, neither Judy nor James had thought of Teribus that morning. She had dashed around in the outer hall, seemingly terrified of the racket until now. With the door open, Teribus could see at last. She saw before the house the greatest manifestation of what it was her duty to repel – the very reason for her existence. Teribus dashed around both James and Judy and flew snarling into the mob. The mob separated, hesitated for a second or so and closed ranks again. There then began a terrible trampling, stomping and kicking. Atavistic squeals of delight took the place of the chants for a few moments. Then there was again silence and a particularly large dungaree clad lady hurled the bloody and misshapen corpse of Teribus to land just in front of Judy. She folded and emitted a strange, almost silent, cry of sorrow, and staggered back to take hold of the door pillar. James dragged her back and slammed the door. The crowd screamed with laughter for a minute then resumed their hate.

They retired again to the kitchen and Judy sat with her head in her hands sobbing quietly. She had now been the end of Teribus. James could not comfort her and fell into besieged silence as the screaming and bawling went on in shifts outside. He did not know if this was simply punishment for humiliating Said-Maartens but thought it was more than simply that but, as ever, was able to make nothing more of it since they just did not know the plot. His phone went, and it was Roddy begging to come down to the farm. James suggested that he could advance as far as the queue of buses but that was as far as they would let him go. He ended the call hopelessly.

Roddy decided to do just that, and some more if he could get away with it. He dressed down for the occasion in an old pair of overalls which he kept in the garage along with trainers with the toes out of them. He drove down James' farm road cautiously and came as promised to a traffic jam of half a dozen buses standing in the forest. He got out and was hit at once with the noise coming from just ahead, between him and the house. He walked forward past the bus drivers, who were in one of the buses playing cards and drinking beer. They paid him no heed as he passed. Roddy came to the back of the crowd and came upon one of the regiments having a break and nursing their voices. He had an inspiration and picked up one of the placards stacked nearby and gave the assembled troops a knowing look while nodding at the banner. Thus armed, he went in among the throng and edged forward near to the front. He started roaring as loudly as he could.

"Get the bastard oot here. String him up fae wan oh his trees."

Somebody touched his shoulder.

"Here, tone it doon, man – ye cannae go coming right oot wae that kind o' stuff in case somebody's recording us – just reign it in fur noo."

Roddy tried again and took his lead from some banners raised around him.

"CO2 Murderer… Gaia will be Revenged… Meat Eater – Blood on your hands."

He did this at an even louder volume than before, his voice rising above the mob, who were a little depleted as lunch breaks were being taken. He edged right to the front behind the sparse line of plain-clothes organisers.

Inside the house, his roars had been recognised as he hoped they would be. The pair of them went warily to the front window again and peeked around the curtains.

"Christ – it's Roddy out there shouting his head off," said

James with a quiet and incredulous laugh. Roddy spotted him peering out and took his chance. He swung the placard at the organiser in front of him and did as close to a sprint as he was able towards the house. He lunged at the door, and it was open. Gaining the porch, he went through the inside door, appeared before James and Judy and half collapsed with the effort against the wall.

"I would wonder at you leaving the door unlocked with that mob outside," he observed to James.

James looked admiringly at Roddy then said, "Well, that's the three of us trapped," by way of a thank-you.

They then began again one of their speculations but there was not a suggestion of why the mob should be outside. That it was contrived, orchestrated and probably paid for by whoever 'they' were was agreed. The mob had been wound up with some set of horror stories about James being every kind of fascist danger to society and oppressor of Judy, whose name they had been supplied with and whose story had been entirely fabricated. Later, they tried to have something to eat but discovered the electricity had been cut off.

"Treat it like another power cut," instructed James.

They consoled themselves that the water still worked.

Much later, the shouts died down and there was a loud knock at the door. James looked out carefully and saw two very young policemen. He opened the door suddenly and before they could speak, launched into a very incautious tirade about rights, obstruction and criminal damage. The younger – seeming of the two stopped him by yelling angrily at him.

"Right, that's fuckin' plenty of that, so it is! We've been ca 'ed roon here tae see what a' the fuss is aboot. As far as we can see, they people here are exercisin' their rights to demonstrate and object in a recognised and allowed manner. We can see nuffin' wrang wae't."

James held himself in and, very restrained, he outlined what he knew they had broken and how he was not allowed out of his house.

The other policeman then took up the story in what sounded a more reasonable way.

"I cannae see how ye can say that, sir – they're no keepin' you in yir hoose that we can see. An I'm shair they would move oot the way fur ye tae get on wae yir work as lang as they don't see onythin' wrang wae whit yer daen, that is. An' as fur criminal damage – ye'll just have to get a list o' whit it is ye are talking about – times an' that an' who it wis, names an' a' – an' get that tae us. Until we huv that, there's naethin' we can dae."

"But isn't it your job to—"

But the policemen had turned away and the crowd parted for them, and a spontaneous burst of applause had the pair blushing as they made their way back to their car.

James went back inside where Roddy and Judy had been listening. Judy asked, "I couldn't understand what they were saying – what were they wanting us to do?"

Roddy summed it all up. "I knew they would be no help, but I had not expected them to be so absolutely bloody useless."

The chanting recommenced, and they went back to the kitchen and sat around in silence. A little while later, there was another knocking at the front door. James went again and the other two took up their listening posts. A single male from the organisers was standing there. He was tall and skinny to the point of emaciation. He was around thirty, but he was going bald already and his skull looked as if it wanted to burst through its surrounding skin. He had the uniform and utterly permanent look of seriousness that characterised the officers of the besieging army, and an air of gravity that defied even imagining him to have ever smiled on any aspect of creation. He wore a long tweed coat over a denim suit as he was feeling the cold. Both were worn and faded. He farcically carried a clipboard and without any introduction, he raised it and read off it to James.

"I represent the Provisional Citizens Ecological Examination of Banachra Farm and the main findings of it are as follows.

"1) Wood Trade. We have determined that your entire stock of firewood is illegal and has been obtained from non-sustainable sources of a type not approved by the provisions of the latest firewood restrictions—"

James interrupted him and dashed inside and rummaged in his desk. He found his licence to extract firewood and the list of trees he was allowed to take and from where. This had all been issued just over a month since. He rushed back and presented it to the skeletal figure with the clipboard. The visitor did not even glance at it but tore it into many pieces and held them up for the breeze to disperse. A cheer went up from the crowd, which turned to menace as James lunged at the skeleton, but Roddy rapidly appeared behind him and drew him back.

The death's head was unperturbed and continued his reading.

"Something will have to be done about that," he said, not with menace but purely as a matter of fact.

He turned a page on his clipboard and continued:

"2) Sheep. We have had reports from the police that they appeared subject to extreme cruelty on their last visit, and we have had passed to us and order from the Animal Welfare Enforcement Committee to examine the situation provisionally on their behalf. We find it entirely upheld, and the entire stock of sheep have been removed and relocated to another more suitable farm. The reasons have been entered on Form 2408A here, but I am not permitted to let you have a copy. There may be some question of compensation but that is not in our hands. However, the fine for harbouring a non-approved breed will no doubt swallow any monies resulting."

"What approved breeds? There is no such list. Who decides there are approved and non-approved breeds?"

"There is indeed such a list, and it can be shown to you if you apply."

"Apply to whom?"

But the skin and bone ignored him and drawled irresistibly on.

"3) Your crop of kale has been found to be in defiance of new regulations concerning the limitation of diseases affecting brassicas and will be ploughed under."

James had had enough and lapsed into despairing silence.

"There are many other lesser infringements found but they will be communicated to you tomorrow."

With that, he turned and walked off with a strange, jerky and puppet-like gait.

The three of them reassembled quietly around the kitchen

table. James searched for some trivial politeness to rise above his ruin and asked what arrangement they could make for Roddy in the forthcoming night.

"Ah, but don't fret. I'll be able to go home – these bastards are going to observe office hours."

And at precisely five o' clock they all filed aboard their buses and were driven off. Judy rallied them and started putting together some food. She assured James that some way of getting back at them would surely be possible. James was not to be convinced and was in an apathetic state of incomprehension. He felt that he had crossed a huge gap from where he had existed previously, where the body politic was already distorted and certainly further threatened, to a place where it was forever and irrecoverably changed to a new reality without laws other than the will of some unidentifiable agency which manifested itself in this rabble.

Judy had not come close to serving her meal when the smell of smoke became apparent. James ran outside and called Roddy and Judy. His wood stockpile was burning, and such was the quality of his product that the flames were rapidly gaining ground. He rushed outside and thought of various bits of hosepipe and the whereabouts of standpipes around the farm. He cursed himself for never having rehearsed for such an incident in soldierly fashion. They eventually got two hoses connected to standpipes and found there was no water. They wandered desperately about the yard after James as the heat at their backs became assertive. James recalled, after a confused delay and uncharacteristic panic, where the farm stopcock was and decided the mob had turned it off. He approached the steel manhole cover which contained the valve six feet down and away from frost. Water was issuing from it, and it had partially lifted from its seating with the pressure. James kicked it fully aside and it was obvious what they had done. A large hook on the end of a chain had been lowered down and allowed to engage with the water supply pipe, and somebody had used his tractor to drag the chain until the pipe fractured and split. It sat there with the chain guiltily snaking away from it into the torrent from the manhole. James irrationally saw this momentarily as a betrayal by the tractor.

The flames went unchecked and started to spread to some nearby sheds.

"Call the fire department," yelled Judy.

James did just that and had to first tell them his name and where the fire was and then was required to say if there was any threat to life. He foolishly did not see how this thing was going and admitted that there wasn't.

"In that case, sir, we will have to prioritise your call and you have been put in the queue, but it may be some time before we can attend."

"I should never have told them where we were. Whoever it is has influence in all sorts of places!"

They arrived about three hours later and dampened down the embers that were the remains of most of his farm buildings. The house was untouched by a chance of the wind direction. The firemen seemed cowed, evasive and ashamed, and left shortly after they arrived, skulking off in embarrassment.

Roddy went home and promised to return early next day. James did not acknowledge him. He had been swamped by a vast numbing torpor. He barely responded to Judy either and would not even say whether he would eat or not. At one point later in the evening, he got up and went outside. Judy found him burying Teribus by the side of the stream near where the ducks had lived. Their dam and hence their pond had gone, and the ducks themselves had also disappeared. He then went in and went to bed. Judy followed and tried to lie behind him and gently comfort him, but she got no reply or response. James slept almost at once without the slightest agitation or concern. Judy dozed on and off all night and tried to watch over him, but he did not move. For all her attempts at monitoring him, she missed his awakening when, after a few hours' deep sleep and just after dawn, he got up and went outside. Judy stirred shortly after and reached out for him. She rose and dressed rapidly in the clothes of yesterday and went out into the bright and cool morning. Everything was birdsong and peace. The mob had not yet returned and there was no sign of James. She sat on the porch step to think and was just about to go back into the house on the assumption that he might only be in the kitchen when he appeared round the end of the house, struggling with a large plastic barrel. He laboured past her, saying nothing but giving her a strange look conveying renewal and determination. He took the barrel into the kitchen and came outside again.

"There are dozens of these old carboys that I got for… well, for some daft project that… that was daft. There is nothing has ever been in them. I'm rinsing them out and filling them at the broken main to have water."

He marched off and Judy followed. They made a sling from old rope and between them carried carboy after carboy into the kitchen. When they were getting tired and thinking about breakfast, Roddy turned up on foot.

"I thought to myself that when they come back, they will be looking for something else to destroy and I didn't want to chance the old wreck – it's not much but it is all I have," he stated quite directly by way of good morning. He at once decided this was a thoughtless and insensitive thing to say to a man who had just lost his farm, but James took no implied comparison from it and treated it simply as a sound, practical tactic.

"You did right without a doubt, Roddy,", he simply said.

There were only a few carboys left and the kitchen was full of them, so James led them inside for breakfast. When eggs and toast had been prepared and coffee brewed on a Primus, James stood at the end of the table and, when the other two sat and were about to begin, he held a hand up to stop them.

"To let you know what has happened to me, I'm going to make a formal speech here – but it's going to be very short."

Judy was anxious for him and had only detected an unexplained resolve in their hours of mainly silent water carrying.

"This whole affair is surely a sign for me."

He wandered over to the window and pointed vaguely at the still smoking remains of his sheds.

"I've been hiding myself away here and ignoring what has been going on in the world. I used to see the news and then started deliberately not seeing it. I have been *au-dessus de la mêlée* – effectively arrogant, if you like. It was nothing to do with me. I was here pursuing loftier goals – except I wasn't – Siberian bloody kale! And it has now solidly caught up with me anyway and swept me aside with its least little bit of effort. Effort ordered by some powerful new enemy out there – on behalf of whoever is belatedly chasing Judy, and why are they now…? I don't know. I have been destroyed by some agency I can only vaguely guess at. That is probably only one presence that I have chosen to ignore."

Judy was close to tears and felt an implied guilt. He caught her eye and with an odd gesture of his arms out by his side, and a look of ineffable compassion, he turned her around and caused the tears still to flow but for the very opposite of reasons.

He took a deep breath before going on carefully:

"But tiny minorities have usurped the truth to themselves and made it whatever they say it is from day to day, and there doesn't seem to be any challenge to them. The profession of the law has begun to be completely undermined and far removed in kind and distance from where it should be. I don't doubt that what happened to Judy is all part of the same story somehow – though we have no idea what it is. And while all this was developing, I was here hiding away from it and playing at being a farmer. At best, I was just avoiding bankruptcy. I was listening to those birds out there and breathing the good air while the towns burned. Well, they have forced me back and I'm going to do my best to take the buggers on – I have no conception about the manner of the struggle but anyway, I'll need to…"

"Well, I'm with you – I'm with you," said Roddy, bringing his fist down over-theatrically on the table.

Judy was startled then overwhelmed and absurdly felt herself present at some historical occasion.

Just then, the buses returned, and the mobs spilled out and the chanting began anew with a gloating and victorious overtone as they contemplated the ruin left by their fire. The three of them ignored them and ate the breakfast. Afterwards, James had an idea and told Judy to stay close behind him and film him with her phone.

"In case they want to flatten me."

He went out to confront the mob, who raised their baying to a new crescendo when they appeared. James to the fore, with Judy close behind with phone held high and Roddy flanking them with the air of a superannuated suicidal berserker should the role be needed.

"Racist – Fascist – Denier," went the chant repeatedly.

The bald skeleton from the day before jerked towards them from out of the crowd.

James was very close to him and asked in as calm but as loud a voice as possible what it was they wanted.

"The list was given to you yesterday," was the staccato reply.

"Well, your fire would seem to have dealt with most of the items on your list and made them irrelevant, so what is it you want now – why are you back?"

"Racist – Fascist – Denier," the skeleton screeched back, adding voice to the crowd.

"But what is it you want?" persisted James in a very loud but still measured way.

"Racist – Fascist – Denier, Racist – Fascist – Denier, Racist – Fascist – Denier," they chanted back, and kept screaming it over and over as the three of them went slowly back inside.

The siege went on all day as before, but they did not emerge from the house for any more attempted peace talks. In the afternoon, they decided to start keeping a record of what was going on. They started routine movies of the mob on James' and Judy's cameras and transferring them to James' laptop, which had a fully charged battery. When the mob ludicrously knocked off, precisely at five o' clock, Roddy belatedly noted the name of the company they had hired the buses from. They then went outside and filmed the destruction. They found the house had been thoroughly plastered with slogans which were strangely unimaginative and did not stretch beyond what they had been chanting all day long. Roddy went off and promised to return before the bankers-hours mob. As a first tiny part of the fight back, they gave him their phones and a tablet for recharging. James was now thoroughly committed to this uncertain new life, and it seemed worth living in a way that none of his previous existences had been.

*

The next morning, Roddy turned up with working phones and a bag of more supplies from the village shop. James glanced into the bag; well, they would just have to live on pies, eggs and sliced bread, it seemed. The mob returned and they tuned them out again. They had another futile attempt at analysis.

"But if they are only doing somebody else's job for them for a reason they cannot know, why are they so enthusiastic in their hatefulness?" asked James quietly.

"Just because these people hate everybody – it's what drives them. We got plenty of them back home – plenty! I don't think they are even very fond of the guy throwing rocks next to them – or even themselves, most likely!"

"Judy has it exact," said Roddy, "and we should be grateful it is like that because it stops them getting organised. The only communal spirit they have is the near bloodlust they muster when they really get stuck in."

"Ah, but they have enough organisation given to them from above, though," added James quietly.

It was Judy that then stepped in to get some focus brought to bear.

"Look, guys, we are going off on one long discussion again about what's happening. They haven't got us very far in the past. Well – they have – but not nothing like as far as they should have done – sorry!"

James and Roddy said nothing but made contrite gestures.

"What it comes down to is that when they decided to get Greg, they sent in the bad guys and took him right on out of here and then… and then, most likely…

"But now that they seem to want me – first, they send in that Side-Martin geek to prowl around the forest like a weekend hunter that was flushed out by Teribus. Then, after an age, this mob turns up to pen us in and burn James' place, but it don't look like they're ever going to do us any harm or kidnap me or anything."

James made a slow nodding gesture with his finger pointed at Judy but lowered towards her feet.

"That is the sum of what we need to untangle. Because with Greg they were doing something to us, but now they want us to do something for them."

This was welcomed as progress and the speculation went on.

But it was well into the afternoon before Judy had an

insight which seemed telepathic in its origin and might have come directly from the mind of Ms Saldanha.

"They want me back in the States for some reason – or they want to send me wherever it was I was going before Greg interfered. But they've discovered that they can't do it from here. Everybody knows me already – you guys and… and… and a whole bar full of folks. If they snatch me, the chances are that they're going to have to get rid of you and Roddy… or else you're going to make a hell of a noise. And if they take me and have to get rid of two bodies as well, then the whole pub is going to be shouting. The cops here can't cover that up, even these days. So – they want us to run away and hide. To get away from all these crazies. They want James and me to hide away from everybody – leave no forwarding address in case somebody squeals on us to this right-on mob of rioters. They expect that we will even tell what we are up to – say to the village not to expect to see us for some time. But then *they* will find us – you can be sure of that as they have everybody in their pockets. And when they do, it will be easy to take me and make James follow Greg. And nobody will miss us for months – and you can be sure that the cops will find a routine answer and say we must have disappeared someplace and not make some big deep case out of it."

Roddy and James were silenced. They looked at each other significantly and thought. They got up and Roddy leant against the sink while James perched himself on a stool in a corner of the room. They looked across at each other several times before James broke the quiet.

"It must be that simple – it fits all the facts that we know. That mob out there does not know why they are here. They've been told a load of lies, had the keys put in the holes in their backs and their springs wound up and pointed in this direction for the latest fascist oppressors to destroy. And who did the winding – or the paying – because you may be sure they are not giving of their time freely – but that is for later. On past form, none of them would have been needed – they could just have given Judy the same treatment as Greg and all at the one time. But here they are. And the farm has been destroyed but not the house – they could have burned us out but like you said, Judy, it might be a step too far. One or other of us might have gone up with the house – trying to save… to save all the invaluable Graham heirlooms!" He motioned round at the old pieces of forgotten furniture and chuckled sadly to himself.

"I think you are spot on, Judy. This way, you would be daft not to run off somewhere to get away from these bastards… and what gets me about them is that they are so bloody stupid. I don't suppose one of them could tell you—"

"That's OK, Roddy," interrupted Judy, who saw the intelligence of the mob outside as irrelevant, "but what are we going to do now?"

"We are going to get out of here and hide in full view of as many people as possible. We could take up residence in the pub – I'll think of something," concluded James. Roddy made a long and half-hushed call to the pub – he told them all that had happened.

*

The rest of the day passed in an atmosphere of steady determination and grim humour. When the time came for the mob to leave for the day, however, there was an evil surprise. Another set of buses turned up and a fresh mob piled out and became the night shift while the day shift left for their lairs. Roddy was trapped and called the pub to report what had happened. Shortly after that, Judy contributed to the gloom.

"I just got a text from Rachel – she thinks the landlord of our apartment was right to abandon it and get right on out of the state – it looks like the whole block was taken out last night in fires from the rioting."

The night shift brought airhorns to guarantee that sleep would be impossible in the house. At one point later in the night, they thought they had managed to fall asleep despite them, and a few broke in and sounded off outside the bedroom door. When confronted, they again screamed their meaningless formulas of hate and sauntered away out the main door, leaving it open. James decided to post himself by the door to let the others sleep. He was not there long before he started to receive a series of visitors, all of whom ignored him completely after making it clear that violence would be swift if he did anything to object. They all wandered around the kitchen and took what they fancied, only to hurl it away as soon as they were out the door again. Some decided additionally to relieve themselves on the kitchen floor. He tried to mop the mess up but saw it as useless when an enormous and seemingly female eco-warrior came in and was minded to join this latest form of demonstration. She hitched up her skirts, produced a penis and repeated the performance, but all over James' 'head of the table' chair. James could not but stare.

"Look at the evil bastard enjoying himself," she called to the crowd in mid-flow.

"Have you never seen a woman's prick before, you cis scum, eh? D'ye want me to keep it out for a while 'til ye have a wank to yourself?"

When they had lost interest and drifted away, James gathered up what was left of the food and hauled a carboy of water through the bedroom. He went next door, woke Roddy and ushered him into his bedroom. The three of them would need to try to defend this one room and secure passage to the bathroom.

"James, that is no way to live," and he got on his phone to the pub again. After he finished, he announced that they must just hang on until that afternoon but would explain no more. He announced this with a look of expectant triumph mixed with an air of anticipated disappointment.

17

THE RELIEF

Around about two o' clock in the afternoon, when James was considering what food remained, there arose a racket from outside that penetrated the bedroom above the continual chanting. Roddy led the way cautiously through the kitchen, which had already started to stink. They looked out the window and took in a scene of chaos. It was some minutes before they could see what was happening. The mob still had three buses waiting on them and blocking James' approach road. These were visible from the house but beyond that the view was partially blocked by trees, but they could see something large and yellow edging backwards and forwards. This was a huge yellow digger with bucket attachment which had engaged the back of the first bus and was manoeuvring it close to the edge where the ground fell away from the road. The three drivers had emerged from their card game, had been told to fuck off and that they should be ashamed of themselves and were escaping past more tractors and another gathering army who were following on. They all had shinty camanachds, baseball bats or simple lengths of 2 by 2 and made a great show of menacing the drivers, but no blows were struck. The digger manoeuvred round the side of the first bus and nudged it sideways, where it rolled off the road onto its side. The next bus was in a more favourable position and was soon cast aside in the same manner. The mob saw what was happening and surged forward, but the new army was clinging to the digger and surging around the side of it and merrily cracking heads, such that the mob fell back. They knew of nothing but inspiring fear and bullying and simultaneously sheltering behind their assumed righteousness, and were not used to opposition. The digger took a run at the third bus and simply pushed it before it into the farmyard. This all then became visible from the house and James and Roddy shouted out as they recognised the improvised assault vehicle and who was driving it and most of those who were hanging on or surging forward from behind. The tractors spread out when they gained the space of the farmyard and scattered the mob in all directions. The fat ladies in dungarees got no distance before collapsing in panting heaps on the ground where the mob left them, and the newcomers went past in pursuit. The main body of the retreating rabble then made an effort at regrouping and formed up a wall next to the still smouldering pile of firewood, and screamed rhythmically back at them one last time, "Fascists – Fascists – Fascists…"

Out to the head of the pursuers who had paused before the wall came Ian from the pub.

"Right, let's give them the answer."

This was evidently well rehearsed because they started at once and even louder than the mob with, "No, we're not – no, we're not…" then a brief pause followed by, "We don't give a fuck about you – we never gave a fuck about you," repeatedly, in exactly the manner of their enemy.

This triggered a group of mixed anarchists, anti-fascists and eco-warriors who charged them with previously unseen knives prominent before them. The line faltered briefly but agile wood was wielded, and arms were broken, and heads were cracked, and no steel was allowed to get through. The eco-warriors turned in retreat to witness the main alliance of the resentful already in full flight in every direction. They followed them into the woods, abandoning a handful of wounded. The three prisoners of Banachra left their viewing gallery and went forth into the confusion. Judy led through sheer reckless haste with James behind, half-heartedly trying to hold her back, and Roddy panting on behind in triumph. They passed the tractors with shouts of recognition to their dismounting drivers, arms raised in combined gestures of thanks and victory. They passed the fat dungaree-ed ones struggling up from the ground, and Judy kicked one of them back down with a swift foot to her immense behind.

"That's for Teribus."

"And for pissing all over my kitchen," added James over his shoulder as he passed by.

"Fascist – Bigot – Racist," was the response, but delivered in quiet but desperate, wheezy and almost reflective voices, which seemed to be more a curse on their present helplessness than a persistence of hatred.

They arrived at the front line just in time to see the charge of steel repulsed. All three of them noted a half-dozen or so non-combatants deliberately deployed and recording it all on their phones. James was impressed by their organisation and astounded by Mr Ian Nicol of the pub, apparently in charge and still giving orders. He could not keep this thought from showing on his face. Mr Nicol noted it and smiled briefly but was soon giving out orders for the mopping-up. He assigned various parties to scour the woods and others to return to the village to keep the mob away from it. They gathered the abandoned wounded, mostly with seemingly broken arms in a circle, and Roddy announced that he would call for help for them, already half anticipating the response. He called emergency and again was asked not about the wounds, much less the number of injured bodies, but only about where they were. There was a long pause before the voice replied, clearly ashamed, that it would be some time before any help could be got to that farm. The conscience-stricken ambulance controller had no idea about the siege and thought he was denying help to the farm's owner, who had been cancelled for reasons whose origins and nature he knew not to pry into.

"Because you have chosen the wrong place to get hurt in, it would seem that there will be a prolonged wait before they will come and get you to hospital. Entirely your own fault. I hope it's no too painful in the meantime. Hell mend you!"

"Just let them take it," he announced to any of the relieving army in earshot.

Ian of the pub completed the dispatch of the pursuing groups.

"I don't care where they go as long as they get the hell out of here with a long walk back to their holes – and James, you better go after these ones that went away up the hill in case they destroy your holiday house. Take a few of the lads with you."

Roddy stayed with the main force and called after James to be in the Cross Keys for explanations later that afternoon. James felt a wonderful conspiracy acting around him that Roddy apparently knew something of and which, incredibly, old 'do-nothing-and-keep-the-head-down' Ian Nicol was in charge of. Three of the boys from the forestry that he knew came with them as they strode up the hill. Judy knew them too and they were, as she had said before, 'Just like the guys propping up the bar at the Copper Country Tavern'.

The followers caught up with a group of the dispersed about to torch the holiday house. They fled at once.

"Fascists – Oppressors – Racists – Deniers," they shouted back at them, with decreasing volume and frequency but never changing the content.

"They have little conversation, these lads," observed James.

"They just yell the same old crap over and over," responded Judy.

*

It was early evening before they arrived at the Cross Keys to find the whole army of siege-lifters assembled there. The bar was full, and the remains had spilled out into the small square that fronted the community centre. The atmosphere was not simply one of celebration but also of intense relief. There had been a return to normality and the joy of not having to pretend anymore. The crowd parted when James' small party arrived and clapped them into the building. James paused and roared above the din, "It is not you that should be applauding us. It's us that should be thanking you!"

"That's right – what the hell – a big thank-you. It was you guys that came charging down the hill," contributed Judy.

Judy and the rest of them peeled off into the crowd, but James went on inside after a last shout to the assembled. "We are late because we had to be sure we had our contingent well and truly wandered before we came home."

He had to find Ian of the pub and Roddy and find out how it had happened. He was intensely curious to know what had turned Ian from the one who took no part in controversy to the apparent leader of the resurgence. He pushed through crowds to the bar, all of whom feted him like those outside and to all of whom he protested. Before he could find Ian and Roddy, they found him. They already had Judy with them, and they all went into the small private family living room behind the bar. There in the quiet, with the crowd just audible outside, Ian started to explain before James could ask.

"The reason I led the charge to relieve the fort this afternoon was because I'm in what you might term the committee."

"The committee?" repeated James.

"Well, it's not a committee or anything like that – nothing as organised, it's just a bunch of us who have said we will take a lead if anything sparks off in our patch. It's cellular in that we only know a few others to communicate with, but we are not organised in any way. We can't be, because you must assume you are being listened into and so we can't send much to each other, anything beyond the briefest information. We haven't got codes or any of that kind of thing. And that is why I'm always a good government man in the bar and make them all behave when the talk turns seditious! But the idea is that we will be guaranteed secrecy by not actually saying very much to each other until something happens. Like your farm, James."

"Well, what is left that I can say… I can only thank you, and now I'm worried that I have been the cause of you having to come out in the open and all that it could—"

"Don't worry about that – the principle has always been that if we have to declare ourselves then the vast crowd of ordinary folk who are also on our side – and effectively more or less on the committee too for all we can do to organise or plan – well, they will come to the fore and then *they* will not be targeting me but hundreds of spontaneous rebels as well. And that, I am glad and thankful to say, is what has happened here!"

James looked at Roddy, who narrowed his eyes and shot a slight confessional smile back at him.

"Ian told me some time ago – because I was in the old-style police – was that the reason?" he asked Ian. "But, anyway, he told me a while back, and that is the way I knew that a rescue party was on the way."

Judy listened and was silent. She was once again touched by all the forces that had come to her aid.

They were interrupted by Shona, who told them that the whole crowd were waiting on them through – in what she called, observing the convention of the house – the function hall. This was just a large barn of a place that had been added to the side of the inn, just by the car park where they had been fired on. Indeed, its timber frame probably concealed bullets. James made his way past the kitchen and went in. Again, he was welcomed as the hero and, yet again, he protested it was the other way around. He went to the front, and they all perched themselves on the edge of the stage. There arose a general expectancy that James should address the crowd rather than Ian or Roddy or any of themselves telling him whence had come his salvation. Roddy nodded to him, and Ian motioned him to stand up. Mystified, James got to his feet.

"I have to say for the third or fourth time in the last five minutes that it is me and Judy – that's the American lassie for those not in the know – who should be thanking you… and us that should be asking you how it was done."

A tremendous confusion of replies came in response, the essence of which was that they felt they had let James down in the past and not treated him seriously. Ian stood up to speak for all of them.

"We've all kept our heads down in the past – and me more than most." He looked round at various faces. "I've tried to keep you quiet in the bar when I thought you – or quite a few others, you know who you are – were on about the government or the polis or when they might think about letting us have another election. But no good it has done me – or any of you. The situation just keeps getting worse – and ignoring it… ignoring it… I have come to admit to myself, is the last thing that is ever going to put it right!"

A cheer went up and all sorts of shouts about the impositions everybody was labouring under. Ian held his hands up for quiet.

"Well, this worm – and I admit to seeming just a bit of a worm in the past but there were reasons for that – has turned. And in the last few days. Roddy here told us what had happened to you. Well, we just all got together, and the rest just snowballed. I didn't lead it – everybody did when they heard what was going on at Banachra."

Roddy gave James a look that said, *I was almost sure they'd come today.*

McDonald, a small-time contractor who had supplied the JCB which had led the assault, stood up.

"And why at Banachra – what the hell is it about your crazy kale or knitted sheep that they object to so much? If they can come down on you like that, they can get any of us. I mean, my diggers run on diesel and they could decide that my diesel was destroying the planet while Lawson's diesel was good for it and come down and close me down just the same. They can tell you anything, these bastards." He was referring to the owners of the buses from the nearby town that the mob had used for transport.

James and Roddy went into a huddle and decided that Judy should be brought into things. They would attempt to show complete trust in this miraculously arisen army. James went out to get her and ushered her in front of the stage. She was reluctant to come forward, but this was overcome by the two glasses of wine that she had downed on an empty stomach, the effects of which were discernible only to James' eye.

More shouts of welcome and encouragement went up. Roddy now held his hand up for patience and to pull her in, he addressed the room.

"They seem to be everywhere and have the police, that mob and even worse maybe, at their command, even in this corner, so who is to say they don't already have a sympathetic ear in this room."

"Is it OK with yourself then?" Roddy quietly asked aside to Judy.

She did not reply to Roddy but turned towards the crowd and yelled, "Roddy here is asking me if I am happy to trust you all with what has happened to me…"

She looked around and would have accepted a microphone had any been offered, but instead broke the informality and climbed on the stage, the better to address them and be heard. More shouts of encouragement went up in answer.

"Like I said, am I happy for you all to know what has happened to me, 'cos there might be spies in the room?"

They laughed at this, and Roddy looked hurt.

"Hey, I'm not saying that Roddy is wrong but it's just that I don't give a flying… a damn anymore if there is."

Another sympathetic roar greeted this, and Judy was not only the angry pursuer of a cause but a performer driven by her audience, which is an effective combination.

"I don't know a half of what or why I ended up here – and James and Roddy have helped me a lot to try to find out – we'll explain it all to you – but I was kind of traded or sold or some damn thing, but it all went wrong and here I am."

Noises of righteous outrage arose.

"But… but… the one thing I'm sure of and I'd bet the farm on, is that it is the same folks behind all of it. Sure, they won't all call themselves the same name and I'm mixed up with some particularly bad ones, but when worst comes to worst, they are all the same. When the guys after me called in help, they called in the same mob that is coming out with the same crap that is interfering with all your lives. Oppressors, deniers, fascists – who am I oppressing and what am I denying… and what the heck is a fascist anyway? The same outfit that burned out James' farm is kind of really the same one that took my apartment away from me and got it burned out in the end."

There were more sympathetic noises here as they assumed it was Judy's flat, and she did not see the need to explain that it was only sentimentally hers.

"Anyway – we'll fill in all the story in a minute but the main thing to answer Roddy and you all is that no, I don't care if there are any spies out there – are there? Put your hands up now if there are any anti-fascists noting this all down."

The crowd were delighted by this.

"Nope? None of you are spies then. OK, then I'll just say how I see this. I reckon you are just like me in this. Even with James and Roddy working to help me, we still don't hardly know a damn thing about what is happening to us. 'They' have all the high cards in this game, and I figure it is just the same with you guys. You can't satisfy them. If you do what they want, they just come up with some other way to get you. Some demand that sounds half reasonable that they sucker you in with but which you never heard of before."

The hall erupted in an outraged roar of agreement.

"So, the way I see it is that the more we can let them see that we have figured out how they work, the better – the more scared they will be 'cos in the end they got nothing... they got nothing – they've got to be told we know that now. So, if there is somebody back there taking notes then just get it all down right and don't go making any mistakes now!"

The crowd was hers, and amid the ongoing cheers, she signed that she had said enough and sat and slid down off the edge of the stage.

James waited some time for calm again. He stood there, not appealing for space but content to let them howl their approval. His face was straining to remain expressionless, and he fought back tears. The room subsided enough to let him talk.

"She has it spot on! This is what we are all up against and we should—"

But further roars went up and when they in turn subsided, Judy, James and Roddy just went directly into the whole history of how they came to be besieged. The grey-haired widow who ran the village community shop stood up. She saw her time had come as a student of organised crime.

"They've postponed elections, hemmed us in with a' their apparently endless series of virus threats, more or less done away with the polis or at least staffed it with a lot of corrupt eejits o' their own, and given us their thought control laws – nobody can say a word about anything for fear of being clyped on. But this shooting carry-on – this is something new. Could they send them after us as well if we fight back?"

They knew what they had been through but wanted to

know about their neighbours, about whom, at most, all they had learnt were a few cautious whispers in the pub. They had to feel free and get all their stories out in the open before they could think about going forward. A great earnest exchange started, and all quite formal, and voluntarily controlled with few interruptions. The stories came freely out at last and the fears that had held them back still had foundation, but the battle of Banachra Farm had dissipated them, for it had shown that something could be done, and they were not minded to consider the consequences as a result. Stories of jobs lost and lives ruined over the slightest resistance to the thought police or objections to their extortions filled the rest of the evening.

18

REPERCUSSIONS

When they at last poured forth from the Cross Keys in the early hours, James had to resist them trying to carry him shoulder-high. His transition from victim to be helped, to leader to be consulted was complete. Roddy had asked them to stay with him that night as the farm was without power and water. As they walked uncertainly the short distance to Roddy's house, James resolved to get the power and water back on the next day, but it would, in fact, be many months before he would. Roddy's house was kept excessively clean and neat by his own hand and there was a feminine aspect to the decoration, which surprised Judy. Yet another power cut wisely sealed the decision to get some sleep.

*

The next morning, they had just finished breakfast when Ian came to Roddy's door.

"They don't know where you are – but you'd better come up to the pub right away – there is so much coming in for you, well, for all of us!" he announced, with an odd mixture of joy and anxiety.

"Come in – and what are you on about?" asked Roddy, ushering him forward.

"I can't – and you can't – you have to come up to the pub. Everybody all over the place is needing you. They all want to know how we did it. And the police... the police... you have no worries about them. They will have too much other bother on their hands to come looking for us. They will have to persecute hundreds of us – the whole village – and now thousands more."

In the pub, they were led to the function hall and found it transformed from the night before. Tables had been set up and were manned by people taking calls endlessly on their mobiles and noting them down then pinning the news in bits of paper on a huge board like Roddy's investigation log. Shouts went from table to table, asking about, and being informed of, progress so far. A large screen in a corner played a very professional movie of events at the farm. Roddy had given them all his material from his phone last night, and there had been huge amounts more taken at the lifting of the siege. Overnight, Mike, an ageing hippy self-under-employed web designer and supporter of the bar, had professionally joined them all together and edited them until it all looked seamless.

"Mike has it posted on all sorts of sites and it went viral as soon as it was up. The world is looking in at your farm, James –

millions of hits already – it's just what folk have been yearning for. Somebody abused as they are and yet fighting back. We can't handle the calls of congratulations and demands about how we did it and can we come to their aid as well!"

The three of them just stood and stared at the pictures from the fight. They saw themselves facing the baying mob, the aftermath of the fire and the relief column arriving. At last, James looked up and around the room.

"But how did you organise all this, Ian?" he asked, waving a hand over the busy volunteers.

"I didn't – it organised itself – I told you about Mike… well everybody else was more or less the same. They just saw what was needed and did it.

"But it is you that is the victim and you that is the hero," he added in a quieter voice, and addressing James directly.

"I'm no hero – and if there is to be talk like that then it is herself here that should be the heroine."

They stayed and even helped take calls. There was mayhem across the country, with marches and demonstrations spontaneously breaking out. Few were now scared.

Towards noon, James slipped away from the confusion of figures with phones. Roddy was deep in conversation with a distant part of the country and interrogating the caller about the details of exactly what was going on. It seemed that the police in a corner of England were in the process of violently reforming themselves, with pitched battles between the new postcode recruits, led by the corrupt and politicised wing, fighting the remaining traditional wing, who had not been forced out already. The callers that Judy took recognised her accent and instantly identified her as 'the American girl at the heart of all this', so rapidly had the identities and roles of everybody involved in this rapidly seeding struggle spread and started to turn them into legends.

James exited the hotel with nobody seeing. He took his car down to the farm. He wandered among the burnt ruins of his sheds and outbuildings, thinking. He ended up as follows: that his first duty was to Judy. He had to know what had happened to her and free her from the persistent threat of whatever it was that hung over her. To help Judy would mean the US. In the house, he got two suitcases out and filled one with as many of Judy's sparse belongings as he could find. He sought out her passport. He did the same for himself with the other suitcase and put them both in the car. He went round the house and dragged the fouled rugs out into the yard. He went round the remains of his sheds and found tools and nails and enough surviving boards. He went round the whole house and crudely boarded it up.

At the pub, things were still frantic. News had spread to England and Europe long ago, and since the early afternoon it was bounding like a net-borne wildfire across the States. Judy was in an innocent frenzy and kept breaking down into tears as she was passed call after call in her own accent. The pub was now mobbed, and the bar was full, and a wild party was in progress. James' reappearance was greeted with great joyful roars of approval. He only acknowledged them to show reluctant recognition but not any sign that he thought them deserved. He sought out Ian in the hall and told him of his decision before even Judy or Roddy.

"But we need you here, James," was Ian's apparently sincere objection.

James waved at the surrounding crowd, still loud and ecstatic.

"Aye, you really need me, eh? Go on yourself, Ian!"

He dragged Judy and Roddy and herded them outside past repeated delays getting through the detaining crowd. He asked them to go back to Roddy's house.

"But there are rumours that the wee pretendy Parliament is panicking, and not a word of any of this in the MSM!" was Roddy's plea.

"And I have so many to speak with in the US now," was Judy's.

"Well, I have something to tell you and I think it needs quiet to do it – and to think about it as well. After that, you can decide what you want to do. It will be up to you."

19

SETTING OUT

Back in the formal domestication of Roddy's front room, he told them briefly that his fight was first to stand with Judy and get her free of whatever was still threatening her, and that as he saw it, that meant going to the US. There was some money that he had fenced off for the next stage of the 'project' which had now so completely vanished. He then asked them if they were with him; this absurdly to Judy and needlessly to Roddy.

"Well, you can't hardly go there without me," Judy announced with a choked-off snort of surprise and derision. "And who'll keep you right with everything like driving on the right side of the road and stuff..."

"Hey, I've been before," was James' comeback in a ridiculous New York accent.

"But, sweetie, you won't know where to go and where to avoid," was Judy's very serious reply.

"But you can't leave me," said Roddy, verging on pathos. "They don't need me here – there are huge mobs of volunteers coming forward to the cause, but searching these buggers out would be real work.

"And I can pay my way," he put in as an afterthought. Judy gave him and his whiskers a hug. James went out to the car and returned with the two suitcases.

For the next few days, they worked in the plainest sight possible. They went to the pub every day as a token appearance. Powers cuts went on as normal but did little to hinder them but after a couple of days, the village went into a deliberate permanent black-out, but by then there were a thousand more centres at the task. They planned everything, meanwhile, from Roddy's house. They worked on the basis that 'they' were so well embedded in government that they probably had access to flight records and were by now alert to Judy escaping back to the US. They gambled on Canada and booked flights from Glasgow to Vancouver on a cheap tourist airline. Judy objected to the suitcases as farcical, and they borrowed three backpacks instead. The night before they left, Ian came to the door and handed James a slip of paper with a name and address in Sacramento.

"I know the general direction you will be taking, and this is a guy you can look up for help. It's not the only one by far and it's probably not the nearest, but it's the only name I have been allowed… but I've no doubt he'll be able to give you plenty more once you get there."

He would not come in and wished them luck and was off back to the pub.

*

With word to nobody, they left next morning early for the airport. They just managed to get out of the country in time before Edinburgh panicked at the growing chaos and illegally shut down the country in response. This was for no real practical reason to advance their fight back and arose only from their conviction that more control and suppression was always the answer. They arrived in Vancouver without coming to the notice of 'them'. They took a train to Seattle and cleared immigration at the station before boarding, with no notice taken of two tourist visa waivers and a US passport. There was a record somewhere of their entry, but The Foundation never thought to look for it. In Seattle, it was raining, and they spent the night in a cheap chain hotel.

Very early the next morning, Roddy hired a car like an awkward tourist. It was still cold and raining and there were miles of burned-out sections of the city, with pavement-camping down-and-outs.

"This place is worse than LA," was Judy's opinion. The clerk at the car hire desk agreed and advised on the safest way out of town, and traced it on a free city map. Roddy looked doubtfully at it.

"They've got opposition in the last couple of days, you know," he announced in a deliberately matter-of-fact voice. He paused and looked them over before continuing in a near whisper, "And not before time, I say." He then gathered their documents and indicated where their car was before, as a last comment, he said to them that it was not just demonstrations and riots, it was now battles they had to deal with on the streets.

"Just the regular civil war like everyplace else these days."

They journeyed all day south towards California. There was relentless political graffiti by the road, with a simple repeated taunt of "Four Years?" It was well into the evening when they pulled off into a small town. It had stopped raining at last but was still cold. They found Main Street and pulled over while Judy got out and asked for someplace to stay. They were directed to an unlikely but comfortable bed and breakfast only a few blocks away and wandered forth to follow directions they had for somewhere to eat. It served Italian food and was still open.

"Well, we have arrived – sort of," James said by way of starting the discussion of where they would point themselves next. All they had to go on and all they had therefore discussed was Sacramento and Panomnes in LA. That was where their only clues lay.

"Well, we just have to keep on south," said Judy.

"If that is the sum of your insight…" said Roddy, and the food arrived to stop further bickering.

They were tired and hungry and ate with only a few words to each other. They did not notice a table across the aisle, paying great attention to them. Two black men in their thirties were eating there, and one of them looked over at James and Judy repeatedly. The other man had to ask him, "What's so special about those guys over there?" quietly, as the tables were quite close.

"Well, I think that… no, gimme a minute or you'll think I'm crazy."

He took out a tablet and got among the rapidly growing number of websites that were up and publishing all manner of stuff about the fightback. He navigated to Mike's site. On there had been posted not only the movie assembled from the phone footage but also various photos of James and Judy and even one of Roddy, who was captioned as aiding the struggle. Ian had taken the decision to put them out there as he decided that he wasn't releasing anything that any of their enemies did not know. The man at the opposite table looked at them and then the photos and back at them. He did not say anything to his companion but just handed him the tablet and nodded at James' table. The other man did the same double-take routine and conceded the point with an almost reverent nod.

"Those are the guys who started this whole ball rolling," he announced quietly to himself rather than his friend. "But here…?"

"I have to go over there and talk with them." The other man thinks more and has the wit to see that if they are in this unlikely corner then they are maybe wanting to stay unrecognised.

"Unrecognised – shit, man. The whole world is looking at them. They'll never go unrecognised again. I'm going over there." His companion gives in and rises to follow him.

They introduce themselves in an instant as Ross and Ricky Taylor, which is not quite heard as they follow it with an overwhelming cascade of congratulations verging on adulation, repeated mentions of their names and avowed support for the new cause. They are effectively silenced and reduced to a few incoherent half-questions in response. They realise that if they could be found out by these two in this corner, then they have no chance anywhere.

Without appealing for permission, the men got the waitress to help them pull their two tables together and set about an endless stream of questions about how the battle of James' farm came about and the whole history of Judy in these events. The two brothers went spilling onwards, uninterrupted. In the old American fashion, they presented a hugely over-frank potted history of themselves with complete honesty in a way that by then had mostly become a form of public suicide. All three of them saw this and thought that these must be reckless or driven men. But they had more in common with them than seemed possible.

The brothers had run a small radio station in San Francisco which was renowned for its outspokenness. They championed all sort of unapproved causes and as the political climate steadily worsened, they had got in more and more trouble. They had endured writs and several court cases and won them all using facts and logic. When the authorities had subverted the law to circumvent these underhand methods, they had drawn in their horns on legal advice, but this did not save them, and their station was closed on grounds of subverting community welfare, which by then needed only a few notable voices to declare that the community was offended, and it was considered to be so. They had disappeared for a few years but had recently bought a small local station under the name of a partner and had remained unnoticed but were now just surviving on a bland mix of music, religion and safe syndicated propaganda bulletins. But there was growing legislation against radio, newspapers and websites and they knew their days were getting short. Religion was severely restricted, and advertising seen as suspect. There would shortly be very little permitted content and even less revenue. They would not need to ban them; they would simply bleed to death, and only public radio would be allowed.

"Would you guys be willing to come on our station and be interviewed about your story? It would mean a huge amount to us and if we are going down, at least we would go down rebelling."

The three of them looked at each other in confusion and the brothers took the opportunity to continue without a reply.

"It's not as if nobody knows who you are – the whole world knows now. The whole goddamn world – or anybody who avoids the MSM and gets their news from the web – which must be nearly the whole world!"

All three of them were taken from their state of exhaustion and confusion to one in which they could no longer even think coherently.

The brothers went to start up again and it was Judy who brought things to a conclusion.

"Right – OK – we have to stop things there. It's too much to think about, guys. You have to see that. Can we see you again tomorrow?"

And so it was agreed, and cards were submitted with the address of the station on a minor hill road as it exited town.

"Don't worry – we will find you," was James' parting shot. They walked the short way back to the B&B, entered and went up to their rooms. Roddy seemed about to say something just before he went in his room, but Judy held up a hand.

"Sleep on it," was her patient command.

*

The next morning at breakfast, James started it off.

"Well, after that fine night of jetlag, what have you decided... Roddy?"

"I say we do it. Those men were right, our anonymity has gone. Without false passports, 'they' probably know we are in California already. Why not try to get as many people on our side as possible?"

"And, Judy, what say you?"

But before she could open her mouth, he added, "Because, Roddy, we haven't discussed it already – not at all."

"I'm with Roddy. And I am always thinking how little real information I have been able to give us... and I think that it is – that it is too crappy a lead – and somehow, now that we are actually more or less here, I feel it worse. But this way – who knows how many may give themselves up to help us."

"Agreed all round," shouted James, and turned heads in the breakfast room. He went on in a quieter way with conspiratorial enthusiasm.

"Imagine the reaction of 'them' when they hear that we are here. The buggers think we are hiding in Scotland and are no doubt trying to find us there. They will be reading into our position all sorts of strengths that we don't have yet."

*

The radio station was only a slightly larger version of all the other timber houses on the edge of town. It had a large notice outside defining it as 'THE HOME OF THE BLUES IN NORTHERN CALIFORNIA'.

They went in to find a reception desk, that was unmanned, and were starting to wonder where to go to find somebody when the brothers exploded out of a side office. This was the big gamble that would either make them or have them fleeing underground. The place was small, and passing a tiny studio manned by a youth wearing peeling earphones and supervising a shabby consul, they entered a second deserted studio.

Ricky was going to do the interview and they had allotted about twenty minutes to it but if it took longer, then they were to speak as much as they wanted.

"I used to do most of our live material back in the day when that was what some radio stations did," he said by way of a wistful explanation.

They told him that Judy would do most of it and they would only add things occasionally, if at all, after the introduction. He agreed and cautioned Judy.

"I'll be a little prying at times but just come right on back at me if you want to – I won't mind."

They were all composed and ready and the recording was started.

"Here we are with a US first and indeed a world-first interview with the folks behind the incident that has the whole world talking. It went viral a few days ago and has started all sorts of trouble in Europe and the US. As you folks know, this is not the kind of thing we normally do here but I think the times have changed. But this is exactly the kind of thing we used to do back in the day out of San Francisco. So, let's have another shot at it and see if we still can!"

He introduced Judy as a very brave young lady who was at the centre of the events in Scotland. Judy just kept herself sharp and receptive. The only point she raised her voice a little to refute suggestions that she may have been a bit naïve to have fallen for the offers of foreign stardom.

Judy was not nervous or tense, simply purposeful. She had an intense, concentrated look. She was now fighting back big-style and had all these new friends to help her, and she was doing it here in the US. She went over everything. She interviewed well, and Ricky was happy with her, and they began to spark off one another in an almost rehearsed manner with no talking over. All the names were mentioned: Greg Luce, the Gartfoil Agency, Panomnes Productions and, most important of all, Said-Maartens. They stuck to their agreed script, and she did not mention their speculations. She several times summed up the purpose of what had happened to her by saying it was a mystery – but that they did know she wasn't going to London to an agency that did not exist. When asked about the fate of Greg Luce, she went through what she had seen when he was beaten to the ground and taken away in the car. The mention of the names was to cause major disruption in The Foundation, and the mention that Dave had been harmed and, as they all instinctively knew, killed, was greatly troubling among the staff. She concluded that they were back here to find out what had happened to her and to try to make sure they didn't sucker any more girls into their scheme. At no point was there mention of who they thought that 'they' were, but it didn't matter too much to the audience as they knew anyway – the nameless presence that seemed to be behind all that went on.

When it was wound up, they sat in silence for a few

minutes. The brothers had come down from their euphoria and were giving way to anxiety. Ricky broke the silence.

"That will be going out in about an hour after the syndicated *news* bulletin in the local slot. The *lost and found* bit. And again, twice in the evening and as often as it takes after that."

"Or until they close us down," added his brother.

"Can I ask a sensitive question?" said James.

"Go ahead, my friend," said Ross, "but I suspect I know what it will be."

"Will you not get a little better handling from the authorities – with all their endless talk of everything being racist and the need to stamp it out… and such like…?" James asked, his voice slowly dying away in embarrassment.

"Will it make a difference us being black?" Ross asked back sardonically. "Not now it won't, but it got them to cut us some slack back when they closed down our last station. We used to do lots of hard-hitting stuff on race questions, but trouble was, we did lots of even harder-hitting stuff on all the bullshit and hypocrisy that was growin' up then. They even made us an offer to keep the station open if we only did our reports on race questions – and only in their way."

"Were you not temped to give in in those early days? Anyway, I was a completely silent member of the useless majority then," said James.

"Now that, my friend, is just white privilege speaking."

James sensed he was in dangerous territory and opened his mouth to make amends but did not get that far.

"Listen, racism is what it is, and I could just about take what was left of the old style – the kind Martin Luther King fought an age ago. But now these sons of bitches have invented a whole new meaning for it. They need us to divide up the country and they despise us worse than the worst rednecks ever did. They really do. They see us as a useful tool – that's all. They patronise us and pat us on our silly little curly heads. They arrange to pull down statues in case we are offended but really to make their followers feel all right. They change curriculums in case we are too dumb to follow them, and they reinvent the past – the bits we didn't appear in. It's all like some humungous humouring of a child – don't trouble yourselves, you poor little *chillun*, we will make it all better for you because we just know you want to split up the country. I used to be American but now I'm one of my 'people' getting patronised to hell and having my soul soothed at every turn while they encourage me to hold every grudge they can think of and invent new ones all the time to keep us bitter over every damn thing. And all this while it is their tactics that really make me mad as hell… and it is all right there in the story of how that station became our present pathetic excuse of a place. That's the real modern whitey racism."

They sat around while the brothers went into the other studio and arranged for the recording to go out in the local spot after the next news. They returned and suggested they take them out for lunch as it was now after noon. All agreed, but James insisted it was on him.

*

They went back to the station and were barely out of the car when they were met by the youth Chad running out to intercept them.

"You guys have to get in here – I can't do this on my own. The phones have gone crazy since that thing went out!"

Inside, all three lines were ringing constantly and the brothers' mobiles had joined in. They sat around the front desk and started a long session of trying to answer them all; the brothers and Chad, together with an elderly lady receptionist who had appeared since they left. Soon Judy had to join in, but they did not get all the calls.

The calls were all wild congratulations and sympathy for Judy expressed in all sorts of ways, some highly political, others in an innocent and naïve fashion. About the same time, the sound of car horns was increasingly heard from outside as passing traffic expressed their approval and later started giving up their afternoon to drive around the block, hooting as they went. In the end, a crowd appeared on the lawn outside and called for the brothers and Judy. There was no discussion and they hoisted them shoulder-high and carried them to the back of a waiting pick-up. They were driven slowly in triumph several blocks to a Roadhouse on the edge of town. Roddy and James tagged themselves along, explaining to random people in the crowd who they were. A wild evening followed and the whole town seemed to call in at one point or another. At the end of the evening, nobody in the place seemed capable of taking in that they were staying at the B&B, and Ross insisted on taking them home.

They got to a pleasant wooden suburban house and met Ross' wife, who had heard all that had happened and was as apprehensive at their prospects as the four of them were drunkenly euphoric.

*

In the morning, they woke up in a strange house and went sheepishly through when called to breakfast. They found Ross' wife welcoming and committed to them now, and resolute in facing the future with the courage that they themselves now felt to be failing them.

His two little children, a girl of five and a boy of three, sat at the other side of the table, overawed by these strangers who had appeared from nowhere. Eventually, the little girl broke the ice. She looked long and hard at Roddy and his whiskers and asked, "Are you Santa Claus, sir?"

Just before they left, Ross stepped forward and slipped a piece of paper into James' hand.

"Try this guy – I know where he came from, and he should be able to help you some."

It bore the same name and address in Sacramento as he had been given by Ian on Roddy's doorstep.

20

THE QUEST PROGRESSES

As they passed further south, the radio began to speak of the police being summoned to quell riots in various cities, refusing, and in several cases joining in.

"That is really a game changer," remarked Judy quietly.

They came to Sacramento and followed the sat nav into a very affluent territory of large houses, large lawns and many trees. Most houses were deserted and boarded up. They passed a lake and at last turned into a small suburban road with room for only a handful of these discreetly ostentatious dwellings. They pulled into the driveway of the right number and hesitated. The door opened and a thin and nervous-looking man of around forty emerged and could not restrain a glance around him before he advanced to the car. They came slowly out of the car to greet him. He was wearing jeans and a cheap tee-shirt with the logo of a hardware chain on it. They entered a large room that could have doubled as the lounge of a small hotel. It seemed to relax him somewhat to be there and he at last introduced himself as John Snyder, shook hands all round and told them to sit down. He told them Ian had said they were coming but that he was worried as they seemed late. He quickly asked what they would have to drink, more to give himself one than to put them at ease, but Judy sensed a threat that she could not name. She glanced anxiously at James as the man returned with the drinks and he gestured to her cautiously, asking what was wrong, but she could not answer.

The drinks were set out on some very expensive little tables without coasters and already watermarked in rings. The man was just lowering himself into a leather armchair when the connection was made in Judy's brain as when the leader of a lightning bolt, making its way slowly through the air, suddenly opens a route to earth and triggers the flash.

"Jesus goddamn," she yelled, jumping back to her feet. She was pointing wildly at him with her right hand and making appealing gestures to James with her left.

"He's one of the sons of bitches who made my video at Panomnes – I remember him – he was the guy on the camera and stuff. It was him, I swear."

The Snyder man spilled his drink on the carpet and held up his hands in a gesture of reconciliation. He deliberately stayed seated.

James and Roddy, however, rose to their feet after Judy.

"Is this right?" James asked him. "Are you one of them?"

Before he could answer, he added more reflectively and half to himself.

"Christ, have we fallen among them after all?"

James stood over him slightly farcically to prevent him rising out of the chair, when he was making no attempt to do so. He just sat back and continued to make placating gestures with his hands held out in a gesture of helplessness.

"Whoa, whoa, whoa – let's all calm down here."

"I'll cool it when you can tell me why one of the guys who started the ball rolling with my whole kidnapping thing is sitting here in the house that Ian in the bar and the Taylor brothers told us to come to – are you even for real? What have you done with the guy that they were really wanting us to see?"

"Do I look like somebody with back-up just hanging around ready for you?"

James stepped back a little and started to speak, but Judy held up her hand to him while staring hard at the still-seated and acquiescent Snyder.

"Well then, Mr Cameraman, you tell us how you came from telling me I was doing great when you were making that nail-bar commercial to one of the good guys all of a sudden."

Snyder sat himself a little more upright in his armchair and reached over for the fallen glass.

"We'll even get you another drink to help you along – Roddy, go get him another beer in that kitchen."

Snyder took the beer and drained most of it in one go. He sat hunched forward with his elbows on his knees and then looked up at them sitting audience-like opposite him.

"Well – when Ian told me who was coming, I recognised you from the video of the farm and knew you were the girl that had been one of the last I worked on."

"What do you mean, 'worked on'?" asked Judy, now apprehensive rather than aggressive.

"Wait and have patience – I'll get through everything – or everything I know.

"We were a quite successful small production company and I had been in it around ten years. It was mostly corporate videos, commercial stuff and all kinds of promotional material. Then, cutting a long story short and without all the detail of who shafted who else, we were suddenly bought out. It was all very irregular, and I guess they made an offer that couldn't be refused but none of it came my way. Anyway, I stayed on under the new management and at first all seemed to go well. They poured in huge amounts of money – money none of us could figure could possibly be justified. They built us a whole new set of studios – the ones you visited, Judy. I can call you Judy?"

Judy nodded a reluctant agreement.

"We moved from our old place, which was much smaller, and then they changed the name to Panomnes. Pretty soon, though, it all started to get a bit weird in the new place. They gradually phased out all the commercial work over about a year, no more – said that was against all the thinking of the new company. All our work changed, and we started making government… well… just plain government propaganda about climate change, minority rights, the oppression of any number of groups – you know the kind of thing. Anyway, we did the whole nine yards – and for all manner of governments and increasingly for the UN. That stuff was a non-stop repeat message about how nothing would ever be changed until we all came together under one organisation. About that time…

well, pretty much from the time they moved in, they started bringing in new hirings. Some of them were needed – foreign language speakers and such – but a lot were just... just... well, spacemen. Kinda zombies if you like. They all got jobs that had not existed before, with meaningless titles, and they did not do much all day as far as any of us could see. Nobody got close to them – hell, they wouldn't hardly even speak to us most of the time – but these guys, they were in the know, while it was more and more made clear to the rest of us that we weren't. I tried to find out about these new owners, but I got nowhere. You weren't allowed to know much more than who was giving you orders. All the rest was gossip from other departments but pretty soon you learned not to ask too much. I looked on the net as well for hours, but I got nowhere. It was a registered charity – they were damn rich for a charity – who was under a shadowy foreign trust fund that you couldn't discover the names of. Soon people began to leave – mostly because they were pissed-off but some when it was made plain to them that they were not trusted somehow – it was never explained exactly how they didn't fit in – but just that they didn't. More new zombies would always appear to fill the gaps. In the end, it was mostly zombies with about ten percent – no more – of us left from the original set-up. I guess we were kept because they needed us. They showed us just a little bit of acceptance – we were given to understand, and even that very indirectly, that we would not be among any further force-outs, but it was always the zombies and the original guys – them and us."

He paused and thought of a lot of other details that he should put in here but stopped himself as he knew nobody would want to know.

"Any road up, not too long before your video, Judy – I got called to some Ms Saldanha's office – and that was one level up from what I had previously known, that was how it worked – anyway, I got called in there and they announced that they were making a return to commercial work. Long story short, we started making pretty much the same kind of stuff we used to make. It was all ads for local TV and the like. But – after a while, I got suspicious. A lot of the productions didn't seem to have any customers – yours was different as I recall, there really was that nail bar – but a lot of them did not have any customer input. I started to investigate the companies they were meant to be made for and found that there was no record of them. I couldn't figure it, why were they spending so much effort on making stuff for phantom companies? Then, not long after your video was made, some character came by the studio asking some stuff about you, Judy. He just wanted to know what we had learned about you while we were working together. Mostly just kinda trivial personal stuff was all. I got brave that afternoon and asked him why he needed to know that. Now I assumed that he was one of the zombies, but he didn't altogether act like he was. He seemed a little nervous – or more anxious, if you like – anyway, not the usual zombie performance. A zombie wouldn't have answered me, and he didn't much either, but he did say that he would be looking after your case and wanted to know a bit about you before meeting you. I asked were they thinking of using you again for some other ad and he paused before he answered – I can still see him today 'cos he suddenly spoke in a different tone – like he was suddenly some tough guy and bragging a bit, but frightening as well –

anyway, he says, 'No, we're using her previous work as a sting to draw her into something much more important.' Then he changed back into a company man – back to his zombie self – and he was out of there quick as you like."

"What was his name?" asked Judy in an even and restrained voice.

"Now that I do recall – it was David Johns."

All three of them had been hanging on the answer but were knocked back and dejected by this.

"After that, I decided it was time to get out. I just disappeared out that place 'cos by then it was an outfit you were scared to reject. I sent the wife and kids off to stay with a friend in Alaska in case. I came here as a favour from the family. It belongs to a sister of my brother-in-law, and since the collapse of California property values she can't get it off her hands. The only reason you are here is 'cos I've known the Taylor brothers for ever and I called them asking if they had any leads for work I may be able to do. They figured who I was on the run from and recruited me into the network. They have probably told you that nobody knows too many others – Ian in Scotland was one of the few I was assigned – but I'm sure they figure me as a prize since I used to be sort of on the inside. I hear lots of rumours about what they are up to and where the money comes from – drugs, for instance – and who would have figured that one. It gets more like the mob with every extra lead I pick up – but the mob only want to make money. These guys want to control the world, it looks like to me."

All this time, Judy looked rather distracted until she jumped up and pulled her phone out of her pocket and began wildly swiping away at it. She produced a photo that Greg had prompted her to take of them on the plane. She swung it round to be in John's face.

"Is this your David Johns?"

John peered at it and then took the phone from Judy and looked closely.

"Yea, that's the guy!"

Judy took the phone back and then turned it slowly so that the other two could see the image of Greg and her in the plane.

In the light of this step forward, they began a long, frantic discussion about what they knew so far. The three of them pressed John for more information about Panomnes, but he insisted he had told them all he knew.

James then sat silently for a moment before he started to sum up their progress after this latest information.

"So, Judy gets an offer of work and does the ad for the nail bar, and they use it—"

But Judy interrupted him.

"So, I get suckered into doing that dumb ad and after that they decide—"

But James cut in.

"You did a perfectly genuine ad for the nail bar. We have nothing to suggest that the nail bar was anything but genuine, although many of the other girls – that we knew nothing of 'til tonight – really were tricked with false work."

He shot an enquiring glance at John, who confirmed this with a resigned shrug, hands held out again slightly and head bent a little.

James made a calming gesture towards Judy.

"'They' then build on this work already done and send in this Greg Luce or David Johns – the man with two names – to present himself as an agent looking to recruit girls for more work abroad. He says he has seen her nail bar ad through Panomnes but says he is nevertheless independent of them and is simply an agent with contacts. Now Judy checks out all his claims as thoroughly as possible and decides—"

"Not nearly thoroughly enough, though – I was pulled in by that guy."

"So, at any rate, you get promised work in London with the Gartfoil Agency, which as far as it exists turns out to be a sort of brothel, which provided them only with somewhere to call to suggest that there really was a destination in London. But then you fly with your 'agent' to Reykjavik where you were—"

"Greg was not meant to be there at all," interrupted Roddy with sudden insight.

"I bet Judy was really supposed to fly to her intended destination unaccompanied."

"That's right, Roddy – he made all sorts of excuses to me about why an agent should have to go with me – he must have thought it would seem strange to me."

"I think you may be right," said James slowly and quietly. Then he gathered himself and went on.

"Some time before they left, this Greg/David started to get romantic ideas about Judy and decided to steal her from 'them'. Why he chose Iceland – maybe just somewhere remote that he thought 'they' wouldn't find them – who knows. But for some reason, something went wrong there, and he took the first available plane, which is how they got to Glasgow.

He then decided they would go on a small holiday, and they ended up with us and the rest is known."

"Pretty much," agreed Judy.

"One thing on reflection, though," answered James, "we have come all this way and actually met somebody from the inside, somebody who has fled 'them', and we are still not that much further forward at all."

"The two names were probably just to isolate David from Panomnes should anybody think to trace him," put in John as an afterthought.

Soon after, John showed them to their rooms.

"This place could do with a good pull-through with a wire brush," was Roddy's housewifely comment when John was out of earshot.

*

Roddy was up first next morning. John Snyder was already deep in a distracted conversation on his phone while the house phone rang unanswered and another cell phone warbled in the kitchen. He asked whoever it was he was speaking with to hold a minute and put his hand over the phone.

"You need to get the other two through here – we'll need as many hands as we can get."

Roddy went through and roused them.

"Quick as you like, you two – dressing gowns or jeans and sweaters – no time for ablutions or make-up, just get your asses through here," he added in his best American accent.

"You're not funny, Roddy," Judy called after him, sitting

up and holding the sheet around her as he disappeared back to the kitchen.

He paused and shouted back gleefully at them, "No, really – you have to get through here now – it's just like Ian's function hall."

When they got through, John was ignoring all the phones to have time to brief them.

"Two things seem to have happened overnight. First, the cell structure we had set up, like the amateur professionals we were, has broken down. Nobody gives a shit anymore. Because there is so much happening – I'll get to that – everybody has just come right on out and wants to talk to everybody else and get some real fight-back begun. And the second thing… the second thing – and I ain't got no time for details, but just trust me, there is shit breaking out everywhere. All round the world – in England last night and all kinds of bits of Europe. And it has already started on the East Coast. Marches, demos, strikes – all kinds of good shit. People have been shot, I hear – I just don't have any details – it's chaos."

He paused but they said nothing and just stared back at him, hanging on for more in a stunned and joyful trance.

"Your farm siege video seems to have somehow sparked off stuff that has been building up for years now. That and the Taylor brothers – they have unofficially sort of syndicated your interview on all kinds of other sympathetic channels. They've suddenly figured that they can't cancel everybody. Everybody can't lose their jobs – and if they whack the ones in the spotlight then everybody is going to realise about them."

The phones continued an even warble and a monotonous ringing.

"Isn't any of this on the news yet?" asked Judy.

"I don't know. I just have not had time to get anything together," John said hopelessly, and waved at the TV and the laptop in the corner.

"As far as I can tell, the MSM won't touch any of it – big surprise there – it's just those radio stations. I do know that there are all sorts of blogs suddenly popping up all over the place, but they are being pulled down as fast as the shadow side of big tech can get to them."

He dashed round the kitchen and assembled a box of cereal, a huge container of long-life milk and a big jug of coffee on the table and put down a pile of scrap paper to jot notes on.

"Breakfast while you answer," he joked, and even as they made a move to start, their own cell phones started into life.

There then began some intense hours. There were again, as in the hall at the Cross Keys, story after story of lost jobs and persecution. Of slight transgression against the new morality being punished by lives destroyed. Of resistance to police corruption being crushed and again the rumour of much worse – disappearances or camps.

They eventually broke off answering the phones when the rate of incoming calls eased a little. They still warbled on, however, but they ignored them and sat around collapsed in relief and just drawing their breath. It was early afternoon.

"Well, I'm needing some coffee and something a little more substantial than Coco Pops," announced Judy.

"Hey, I like Coco Pops," protested John, in the voice of an offended child but laughing at himself.

"I'm going to fix some sandwiches anyway."

She rose to go through to the kitchen.

"No – let me," offered Roddy.

"Hell no."

"Well, I'll go," said James.

"No – you won't hardly know what anything is in there!"

John started channel-hopping on the TV, looking for a phenomenon that he had been told about that morning. When Judy came back with a big plate of sandwiches and a jug of coffee, he had just discovered that things were even as it had been reported.

"Look at this," he instructed.

He put on several of the MSM channels on TV and there was nothing about anything that was going on except a few mentions, well down the running order, of disturbances by anti-social elements, but nothing about what had happened.

"And now look at this stuff that is eventually breaking through…"

He put up website after website that had somehow come online and not been shut down. They were versions of the tales that had been told at the meeting in the pub hall just a short while before, or like some of the disjointed calls that they had taken that morning. Many were much worse.

"It's 'them', and everybody sees it – it's all the same 'them', but who the hell are they?"

"Jesus – no one is scared anymore," whispered John. "Suddenly nobody gives a shit."

*

Later in the afternoon, Roddy had to get some air and

went out into the garden for a look around. Beyond a bank of tropical-looking trees to his eyes, he found a small lake. There were several other very large houses dotted around the opposite shore. Roddy thought that this must have been an expensive piece of property. He was almost at the water's edge when a small scruffy boat came quickly along the shore and slowed to call out to him.

"Say – are you that retired policeman that is here with Judy Ruono, the girl who was kidnapped?"

"Yes – that's me," he replied, his head a turmoil of panic as to who this might be.

The boat at once turned for a landing stage and an athletic-looking specimen in his late twenties leapt from it, tied it up and strode towards Roddy, hand outstretched. Closer up, he was less impressive and was wearing a stained tracksuit.

"It is a privilege to meet you, sir – Phil Berglund – and you're Roddy if I have picked it all up correctly – I stay over on the other side there."

He shook Roddy's hand eagerly and firmly and explained that he had only just realised that John Snyder and he were in the same secret chain when the names of all the different cells had started to leak that afternoon.

"Who knew," he asked brightly, "and just across the lake too."

He then asked tentatively if he could meet Judy.

They re-entered by the French windows, and everybody looked enquiringly at the new face. Roddy explained to all, and Phil engaged John with tales of secrets from the network coming out into the open. He revealed that he, like John, was separated from his family, who were in hiding while he was living on the charity of a rich sympathiser in what was originally the gardener's house. His story was remarkably like John's. He had been forced from his post as a web designer when the company he was with was taken over. He had questioned a lot of the stuff they were told to do and was not sacked, just told to leave. His wife and family were threatened and then, when he persisted on a claim of unfair dismissal, he was beaten senseless in the car park in full view. The passers-by passed by and sensed who they were dealing with and did not call the police.

When the introductions were done, a summary session began.

"Well, I suppose we have not contributed much to this fight and none of us were any part of this hidden network that you men were in… and Ian at the pub," James added thoughtfully.

"We weren't in any network, but Judy has been tricked, abducted and transported halfway around the world and you two came close to having your heads blown off," commented Roddy, who had become doubtful that this secret society had achieved very much.

"No, I don't suppose we have done too much to slow the bastards up," said John quietly, with an enquiring look to Phil.

"No – not too much, I guess."

James then asked them, "I don't know what you two men are going to do now that things seem to be changing so quickly – are you bound by any prearranged scheme of things from this secret network?"

The two of them looked at each other blankly in a way that said there was no answer to that question. They had never got as far as being as organised as that.

"Well, I suggest that you both put yourself forward as much as possible. Get yourselves into politics – there are going to be a lot of vacuums to be filled after the next few days."

"And if any opportunity for revenge presents itself..." growled Roddy.

"Well, firstly, it's going to be 'North to Alaska' for me," declared John happily. "And then I will see."

"Yes, reunion first and then whatever I can do right after."

They all sat in contented silence for a moment or so after that.

James then brought things back to their quest.

"Where we are is still not much further forward – we need to find out what happened to Judy and to be sure that she is out of danger" James stated simply.

"John has given us the first real help we have ever had, but it hasn't got us much further along the road."

"I can trace what guys I can from the old set-up. They might know more than me – but they're probably going to be complicit in what went on and are going to resent me for getting out when I did. They're not likely to want to talk," offered John.

They fell to discussing this suggestion but had not got far when the front doorbell rang.

John answered it and they all flowed after him and lurked in the hallway, just out of sight to hear who it was. When he opened the door, he was greeted by a sort of reception committee. There were around a dozen figures, men and women, young and old, and they had evidently appointed a representative. An attractive middle-aged lady stepped forward.

"We are sorry to intrude but we just had to come – we heard that Judy Ruono is staying here and we want to talk with her if that is possible. It would be awesome."

Behind her were more folk on the lawn, and cars cruised past slowly with their drivers waving and honking their horns.

The rest of them edged forward into view behind John.

"Oh my God – there she is – it's Judy, folks!"

John had gone instantly from a fear of encountering a representative of 'them' to one of a stampeding mini-mob trampling him as it surged through the hallway. But the crowd decided to let a few of their number into the house to negotiate some form of more general meeting. There was a sort of formalised adoration of Judy, which turned her welcome into embarrassment.

"Come on, you people – I didn't do anything – I had it all done to me!"

They protested, as carefully as possible, that they could not go through the whole story for just these people, which was the wrong thing to say and caused matters to be taken out of their hands. At once, one of the men suggested a much bigger meeting the next day. More advice flew and quickly coalesced around a much bigger reception with temporary bleachers on the lawn and a platform of sorts for Judy and the others. And a sound system – they decided they would need a sound system. Names were suggested and appeals were shouted to the growing crowd outside. Soon, sources at local schools were found for all the bleachers, and somebody knew a guy who did the sound for sports meets and county fairs and that kind of thing.

"I'll haul it all – you just tell me where you want the truck tomorrow morning," shouted an unseen figure from a car.

After what seemed like only minutes, they were all gone with the promise to return early the next morning. They returned inside and sat around in silence for a few minutes before it occurred to John to wonder out loud how all these people had come to know where they were.

"I could have texted a few friends in the neighbourhood this afternoon," Phil confessed sheepishly.

"Well, that is the last of our security shot," said John resignedly. James and Roddy nodded slowly.

"Hell, it was more or less gone anyway – and besides, we're too famous to shoot," countered Judy.

Early next morning, in the still-low Californian sunshine, they were all awakened at once by the noise from the lawn. Squads of men were carrying prefabricated wooden stands from a huge truck parked outside the house. There was shouting and hammering as the bleachers appeared in a large semi-circle around a similarly constructed stand at the other edge of the lawn. A short while later a van appeared, and a couple started deploying loudspeakers and cables around the place. They were having breakfast when the good-looking middle-aged lady came in through the French windows without formality.

"Morning, you guys – have you seen what is happening in Washington?"

She gestured at the TV. And continued with a different topic completely.

"We'll be ready for you any time around twelve if that is OK for you, Judy?"

Judy assumed an almost professional competence.

"Sure, twelve is fine by me."

They put on the TV and found that what was described as a provisional committee was now in charge of the US government pending an immediate election. Arguments were going on about how to accommodate this within the constitution, but delays caused by going to law had been completely rejected. The police had partially refused to control things and had even taken part in proceedings by arresting various members of the government who were not already in hiding.

The morning passed quickly, and they went out into the growing crowd and James even helped to fix up the stands. Judy was mobbed and had to retreat inside again until her time came. Next, there miraculously appeared a TV truck from a network that had been banned for years. They mingled with hand-held cameras. Towards twelve, the crowd had outgrown the accommodation on the bleachers several times over. They sat on the grass in front of them and assembled on a bank of grass between the bleachers and the flowering shrubs. Still, there were some who could only get into the corners with no sight of the stand and hoped only to hear what they said.

Judy, James and Roddy appeared together on the stage at precisely twelve and insisted on John and Phil being there too. The next hour was mostly Judy, who did a repetition of what she had done for her broadcast. The atmosphere was festive, so her talk was met with wild whoops of approval. A chaotic question and answer session followed with the good-looking and middle-aged lady trying, but not entirely managing, to convene the event. Almost as soon as they were done, the network – who had previously been banned – succeeded in getting them on air in the Bay area at least. Many in the audience who had been recording on their phones also got coverage onto all manner of websites.

21

THE FOUNDATION CATCHES UP

In the days just gone by, the initial silence towards Said-Maartens, the patience of Ms Saldanha and the ignorance at the higher layers of The Foundation of what was going on in the world were all greatly changed. Ms Saldanha had repeated reports of the siege of Banachra and was becoming very impatient with the lack of progress towards her goal. The besieging army did not seem to be achieving Ms Saldanha's aim of getting her targets to run and hide. A worrying idea lurked on the edge of her consciousness that the tactic might prove counterproductive, but she kept it there as she could not come up with any other way of dealing with things. How to deal with Judy and James if they did succeed in isolating them was another matter. She still had only vague plans in mind for these tasks.

While Ms Saldanha was anxiously waiting, Said-Maartens' concerns slowly subsided again as the days passed and he continued to be ignored from above. He continued with the supervision of the couriers and a new batch of girls – until the day of the raising of the siege. Such was The Foundation's disdain for the world, whose flawed existence it was in the business of correcting, that its lower levels, and even the middle-to-upper layers, were not expected to pay any attention to what was going on around them. Thus, with all the mainstream media having been drawn into The Foundation's orbit, the only news of the raising of the siege at Banachra and all its thousands of consequences stretching to the Taylor brothers and beyond did not reach Said-Maartens or Ms Saldanha – not even through her contacts with the besieging mob, as they kept silent while they tried to find the right words to convey utter failure. So, days passed in complete isolation from the events outside but some of the lesser staff at Said-Maartens' office had seen the material on the net and were making connections and becoming scared.

Those at the very top of the organisation saw from the beginning what was happening, though. They rapidly assumed the fury of the pious, who had been thwarted in their struggle to impose their will. They decided on vital corrective action but held their hand initially. But a few days after the trio became established in Sacramento, another blow fell which had The Foundation launch a more desperate attempt at covering its tracks. The man in the burning sands had to suddenly abandon his tactics of high-level mischief making for its own sake and start to adapt them to saving his own skin. The portion of the burning sands which this man inhabited had been under an increasingly radical Islamist regime for a while, but the man had been able to adapt. It was dictatorial but corrupt and he had been able to protect his many business dealings by the paying of suitable bribes. About his moral life he had no worries, since it was an American he intended for sex servitude. However, with remarkable speed, a grassroots faction of the ruling party had risen from local politics and taken over the top. It was carried forward on claims of religious purity but was really driven because it coveted the money streams being absorbed by the ruling faction. The attention of this new faction fell on the man in the burning sands. There was some material in his file that referred to communications with the US regarding a female. He was arrested and taken to the usual basement, and it was made clear to him that he was about to disappear in violent circumstances. The man in the burning sands, however, was quick-thinking and managed to convince the new faction that some organisation in the US was trying to bribe him to work against them by offering him a girl. He suggested that the new faction could make great use of this in the international scene to discredit America. He let his name be used and made available emails to show that somebody in the US had offered this service, but suitably altered to delete his acceptance of it. This, he thought, would ensure his survival if he threw in the proceeds from a few of his business interests and as an afterthought exposed The Foundation-run establishment in the capital. The purity police called on it and arrested everybody and added its existence to the list of devastating indictments it was making about what it presumed was the US Government. The local management was tried and swiftly hung, and the almost exclusively Russian girls were sent home as they were seeking favours in Moscow at the time. Loudly proclaimed protests about US attempts at moral corruption were therefore added to The Foundation's troubles. Moreover, the man in the burning sands had been able to give them the names of Ms Saldanha and Greg Luce. When all this broke at the same time as the broadcast, it sealed Ms Saldanha's fate.

The bubble burst and the corrective action became much more drastic. They rapidly turned their guns to point downward through the organisation. The live flesh exporting had to stop at once and they would follow with the establishments. Now the top had initially approved all this, but as in all despotic structures, the blame fell lower in the line of command. Said-Maartens would have to go and Ms Saldanha possibly as well but her they would have to debrief first. They put out a job card for the local department of violence with Said-Maartens' name on it. Fortunately for him, the bureaucratic inefficiency of all such organisations interfered to give him a vital interlude. His description and details were not fully passed into the hands of the liquidators, and they did not recognise the name, so while they enquired back upstairs, he was ignored for a day. That morning, he came into the office and discovered the door locked and the locks apparently changed. The place was deserted.

This left the temporarily overlooked Said-Maartens alone in the car park and going around peering in windows at an office cleared of all furniture and any signs that anyone had ever worked in there. A suspension of reasoning affected his brain, and it could only decide, at a very simple level, that there was no point hanging about in the car park. He set off home again, which was the last place he should have gone, but the men with the guns were still awaiting confirmation and besides, they had a little way to travel to this first place they would check for him. By the time he got home, Said-Maartens knew that his world had collapsed but he was lacking the details. He sat numbed and unmoving before his screen in his home office. His wife entered and asked him why he was not at work but did not wait for a reply. She then asked him if he had seen this and clicked on a pre-selected entry on social media that she had ready for him. He still said nothing, and she lightly told him that she was off out to one of her committee meetings. He turned to the screen to see the broadcast. At the mention of his name, his bowels were overwhelmed, and he soiled himself. His mind returned just enough for him to know that he had no time to shower and that he must not use the car. He cleaned himself up imperfectly and stuffed a few clothes in an overnight bag together with an emergency bundle of dollars he had hidden in the recesses of his walk-in wardrobe. This he crammed into his pocket. Even the time to do this panicked him further and he staggered off outside. He went as far as the main route that skirted his privileged estate and stood in line with the Mexican help at a bus stop. He went on board and sat with the Mexicans and the usual sprinkling of crazies. He blended in perfectly with the crazies and smelled worse than any of them. He got off the bus at the California Ave. station and took the train to San Francisco.

Ms Saldanha was not so fortunate. She lived alone, and with no warning, they came for her. She was subdued, gagged and frogmarched out in plain sight and bundled into a car as

Dave had been. They took her to a private airfield and put her into a small jet. They flew a very long way for hours on end, during which she was given neither water nor food. At the other end, there was another car journey, this time in the boot. She was unloaded at a huge and isolated building in the country, entirely clad in glass which anonymously reflected the outside world. There she was taken a full three floors down in the earth and thrown into a cell in a prison installed in the depths of the basement. The door closed behind her and she was left in perfect darkness and silence to grope about for her bed and a foul-smelling toilet.

On the train to San Francisco, Said-Maartens sat in a corner by a window and quickly cleared a space with the smell coming off him. His bag was on his knee and the notes were crammed into a pocket. He half stood and pulled it awkwardly out and hid it at once behind his bag. He was still well beyond rational planning and thought only that a good first step would be to count the money. He did this discreetly behind his bag, though nobody was paying him any attention. The money was from his old nervous days in California before he let his continued existence lull him into thinking it would always be so. There was around ten thousand. This was not enough for… but then he could not name what it might not be enough for as he had no idea what he would do. He replaced the money by stuffing it into the same pocket, folding and tearing a few notes in the process. He then sat and gazed out at the cheap motels, the loading bays of strip malls, the truck rental lots and the patches of scrub which even the most affluent suburbs retained to line the railroad.

In town, he put his bag over his shoulder and wandered north into the city. For the first time, his mind focused on why the dollars were thought necessary and he realised that his bank account would have been frozen by The Foundation and that he dare not try to use it as it would give his location away. He had, however, a private account and he sat on a bench in Union Square and contemplated how safe it would be to attempt to access it to get more money. Enough to support some as yet unimagined scheme. He was by then strangely not aware of his own smell. He wandered the streets in areas he had never been before; in fact, he hardly knew the city. Everywhere he ventured away from the most affluent areas he found the junkies and mind-addled in charge. The tent cities had spread everywhere, and old needles, trash and human shit decorated streets that tourists used to inhabit. At last, reality dawned on him and he became confused and scared. He turned again towards the centre. Passing an ATM – which looked dirty and abandoned – his befuddled brain made a ludicrous connection between the abandoned aspect of this money machine and the time it would take for anybody to detect the attempted use of his card. He stood conspicuously before the machine in a street with an excess of men staggering around roaring curses at passers-by or at thin air, and pulled out his wallet to extract the card. It is then he had the good fortune to be mugged. A wreck of a man who looked about forty but was not yet twenty, unshaved and dirty, appeared from nowhere, shaking for lack of Honey, which was the name of the current instant high on the street. He was new to such desperate methods and his brain was much more deranged than Said-Maartens' and he snatched the card, grabbed Said-Maartens' hair and wrenched his head back. He pressed a knife to his throat and pushed it until the skin just gave way.

"Give me the fucking number," was his obviously unthought-out demand.

It was far too much for Said-Maartens and his bowels once more let him down.

"9703," he whispered in a disarmingly honest voice and this, together with the little stream of liquid shit trickling out over Said-Maartens' shoe, was taken as a guarantee for the number given and the thief was gone. This had happened for all in the street to see but nobody paid any attention, and nor did they when Said-Maartens slowly collapsed in despair into his own emissions with his back resting on the filthy and unusable ATM machine. The mugger was from the other side of the Bay and at once took the BART to Oakland. It was there that he attempted to use the card and found it was retained by the machine and was useless. They had even managed, with their almost limitless connections and favours due, to cancel Said-Maartens' account. So, it was on the east side of the Bay that they set their hunt for Said-Maartens and that allowed him to escape them.

Meanwhile, back at the ATM in San Francisco, he sat long and utterly apathetic in his own mess, approaching a feeling of resignation. At last, he got up and rambled slowly at random. He noted that his bag had gone but could not recall if it had been taken or if he had maybe left it somewhere. His bundle was still in his pocket, but he did not think to check it. He was feeling neither hunger nor thirst but was simply exhausted and, in the end, he subsided down in the doorway of a long-boarded-up hardware shop and dozed off. He was perfectly safe, as he presented such a wrecked and desperate appearance that there seemed no point in mugging him again, and he slept the whole night.

*

At dawn, he got up slowly and, completely unremarked upon, he pissed against a building, as seemed to be the local habit. He might have emptied his bowels as well but that had been taken care of. He floated slowly around, aimlessly observing the natives and their tents made from scrap. He came to think that he may use his remaining bundle, which nobody seemed to have suspected was there, to buy some of whatever these people were on. It started to appear to him that he belonged here and that there was nowhere else on earth that would have him anymore. It was still early in the morning, and he was wandering without purpose when a priest, who scoured the area trying to help at least some of the inhabitants, spotted him. This priest used to patrol the neighbourhood alone as he was recognised and left unmolested. These days had long passed, however, and by then he had to move around with back-up in the form of three or four young volunteers. The priest spotted Said-Maartens right away as he presented an enigma. To a practised eye, he did not look as if he was using; indeed, he even guessed that he had never touched the stuff, yet at the same time he was in a worse state than almost all around him and it was plain that the stains on his trousers were not mud. In an instant triage assessment, he thought that Said-Maartens might be salvageable. They called him over and suggested he come to their shelter and get cleaned up and possibly stay a couple of nights. They expected resistance but Said-Maartens offered none. They took him round the back to where a church hall had been converted to a vagrant shelter. The first thing they proposed was a shower, and Said-Maartens did not object. They showed him to a cubicle in a small washroom. He undressed and they took away his clothes while he stood under the hot water. He felt very thankful, even after his only brief absence from normal life, to be returned to the cleansing properties of hot water. He was also relieved to find himself guided once again in however small a measure. They took his clothes and discovered his wallet and bundle, which they put to one side before throwing the clothes away. They looked out clothes from their store of donated gifts and selected some which would fit him. When he was clean, and the stench was gone, he quietly dressed himself in the offered garments and was taken by the priest into a small office and presented with his belongings. Patiently, it was explained to him that his bundle marked him out as possibly not needing as much help as many others out there but that he was welcome to stay for something to eat. If he wanted to talk further to him, the priest would be back later that afternoon. He was then shown to a refectory where volunteers were giving out basic meals under a statue of Our Lady. He went as peacefully as ever and managed to remember to thank the priest and promised him he would try to speak to him later but knew that he could never even begin to tell him what had happened to bring him there.

He ate what he was given as he moved along the line with his tray. He sat there among a mixture of men and women, young and old, who all looked at once desperate, thankful, but also resigned to the idea that they would soon be back out there again looking to score. A TV was mounted high up in the wall and one of the volunteers was channel-hopping with the remote. A view of the house by the lake and the crowd assembled for Judy's talk came up. They left it there and Said-Maartens watched, astonished, as it unfolded. There they were: Judy, James and Roddy on the stand along with a whole group of others that he did not recognise. He did not completely take in what they were saying but it did register that it was very much like the broadcast he had heard the previous day. It was like watching people from another life who had suddenly appeared in his present nightmare. And they were doubly removed as they had been a geographically distant part of his previously settled and safe professional existence who he had never expected to turn up in California and appear to him in the completely unexpected pit he had descended into. He watched, numbed, for a while and then a feeling of paranoia took over his thoughts. He could only believe that they had come there specially to hunt him down, and it all added to the hopelessness of his position. He decided that he was being hunted from both sides. When this came over him, it almost caused his bowels to react anew. He sat for almost an hour in a state of numb, unthinking panic. His brain had switched off again. Suddenly, however, an epiphany spread through him, and he realised that he must seek redemption. This was followed by a simple joy at how this changed everything. He must go to Judy and seek her forgiveness. There were others that he had wronged before that – since he had so naively left the hotel for The Foundation's establishments, but he would catch up with them all in time. The first and most supremely wronged was Judy. He knew the house was somewhere in suburban Sacramento and he must go there at once.

He wandered to the city centre and asked how to get to Sacramento. He did so with such an air of hope and expectation that a lady answered him and directed him to take a taxi over the bridge to Emeryville and catch a train. This he did. Unfortunately, Emeryville was on the other side of the Bay where they were concentrating their search for him, and he got spotted at the station. The in-house department of violence was watching the station and the bus terminus and as many other places as they could cover and got lucky when he turned up to take the train to Sacramento. His bundle easily covered the fare. Said-Maartens should have been shipped with Ms Saldanha. They had lost a vital day and as a result he had gone to ground. That they found him again was more good fortune than they deserved. The girl watching the station had searched desperately for a way to stop him from entering the train until others could arrive. She approached him and, with an almost hidden sexual projection, in a practised and normally effective way, she told a tale of luggage trapped in the escalator and asked for help. Said-Maartens came out of his sheep-like trusting attitude from the mission and was at once afraid. He bolted for the train, which was just about to leave. She was just announcing her failure to the boss when it pulled out. The boss, who was high up in the department of death and fancied occasionally that he might be very high up in a global sense though in the tradition of The Foundation – he had no real idea – was in town to supervise this one vital job. The news that Said-Maartens was on a train for

Sacramento made the connection in his head with the recent broadcast of Judy's rally, and he instinctively knew he was off to spill everything he knew to the revolution.

He at once set off with two of his operatives and headed to Sacramento. That they had to take Said-Maartens was perfectly understood. However, if he had to be hit in an open shoot-out then that would have to be what was about to happen. They arrived and parked anywhere and rushed into the station. The train had just got in and the crowd were pushing towards the exit. They mingled, desperately looking for a face they had only seen in photographs. The photograph had been full faced and confident, but Said-Maartens had been much changed by the last few days and now looked haunted and drawn. He walked close to the two lesser operatives as he moved towards the taxis. Then the boss thought he recognised him but was not certain. He followed on behind him and it was only when the boss felt the dread that he might get away from them again that he took desperate action even as Said-Maartens was just about to get into a cab. He called out Said-Maartens' name. Said-Maartens just turned his head a little in response before a fresh wave of panic overwhelmed him and he rapidly got into the cab and, in a strange hoarse and desperate voice that was almost a whisper, told the driver to get on the road and he would tell him where they were going.

The boss shouted desperately for his two helpers and kept his eye on the cab as long as he could. They sprinted back to the car and with the boss driving, set off in pursuit. There was now no possibility of seizing him – all three of them saw that.

In the cab, Said-Maartens asked the driver if he knew where the rally he had seen on TV had been.

"Sure," he answered, "I was there myself to see it all!"

Off they set and so did the department of death. The taxi was out of sight and, at first, the boss went on instinct and the general direction the taxi had headed in. The troops got the address up on the map and he desperately tried to second-guess the taxi's route. It was obvious now that they could not take him, and as they had only handguns, they would not have the possibility of seeking positions with their more normal and appropriate death-at-a-discreet-distance-type hardware.

The taxi pulled into the little street in sylvan suburbia and stopped at the entrance to the drive, which was about thirty yards long. The house sat quietly at the other end with no sign of life. The trio, with John Snyder and Phil Berglund, were sitting out the back enjoying the evening. They had had a busy day helping clear the bleachers away.

"This is the place," said the taxi driver.

"Are you sure?" asked Said-Maartens. Now they were no longer travelling but had arrived, he was facing the previously unconsidered manner of his reception. He remembered Judy's aim with the stone that had almost split his skull.

The taxi driver nodded to the number on the mailbox.

Said-Maartens unfolded his bundle and paid the man and was just getting out when the pursuers cruised slowly past and unleased rapid fire from two automatic handguns at the car. Said-Maartens knew at once what had caught up with him. There was an instant, when he saw the top of the taxi driver's head being jerked violently to the side and turned to a red spray, before he started to run to the house. Some residual shots came from the car as it overshot the end of the drive. One of them grazed his upper arm as, about halfway up the drive, he came to a raised flowerbed which had served as a traffic island in the area before the house. It invited cars to circulate in an ordered manner when dropping people at the door. He did not dive and roll in any semblance of athletic control into its shelter but collapsed chaotically with limbs flailing in panic and maintaining forward momentum through a frenzied kind of swimming motion across the gravel. He came to a halt, and nobody appeared at the house. From the road, he heard the noise of the car apparently driving away. He knew this was not finished but his bowels held this time and a strange kind of calm started to form in him as he confronted what he had feared for so long, strangely finding it less dreadful than his imaginings. The car went forward only to the next house and turned, tyres squealing, before returning. They had seen where Said-Maartens had gone and all three of them got out and started up the drive.

Now back on the decking behind the house, all of them recognised the sound of gunfire but only John and Phil reacted instantly. Phil got up and shouted to John that he had his with him and to get the rest inside. He then went cautiously round the side of the house to see the three of them advancing towards the flowerbed, guns in hand. He raised his gun and loosed off the whole magazine at them. They had not even noticed him appearing around the side of the house and were coolly advancing towards an anticipated execution. The shots all missed but one, which caught the boss in the shoulder. They dived for the cover of the flowering shrubs by the side of the drive, all in silence, even the boss, who was not given to anything as unprofessional as cursing. Phil then ducked back behind the house and went through to the front. John had just opened a drawer and drew out his own gun. There were two in there and he offered the other urgently – James took it and the two of them were just taking position by the window when the attackers, now coming under no fire, came out again to dash forward. A fresh volley of shots came from the two guns in the house and a third was added when Phil reloaded. They dived again for the shrubbery. A stalemate then ensued. The range was too great for much accuracy. There were occasional lulls and in one of them all three of them spotted Said-Maartens in a heap in plain view behind his little wall. James recognised him at once but said nothing and had to make signs to the other two to hold their fire as they were ready to take shots at him. Judy had been instructed to stand well back inside the room and shouted for them to call the cops.

"We can't, Judy – it's too early in all this thing – we can't be sure what sort would turn up," was Phil's response. John nodded a grim agreement and James saw they were right.

Roddy had offered to patrol the other rooms on the ground floor to see if they tried to outflank them but was told to be careful. Occasional shots still rang out, but outflanking was exactly the tactic they had decided on. The boss designated one of his troops to go around the side and try to get in the house. It was a desperate mission, but they saw that they would all soon be in Said-Maartens' position as hunted men if they did not get to him first.

Roddy was in the kitchen when he heard a noise from a small pantry area by the back door. He went in to see a figure squeezing himself through a small window. He had one arm and leg in the room and was in the process of getting the rest of him to follow. His gun was foremost in the hand that had entered, but his head was squashed down in an effort to get through the gap, and he could only partially see the room by squinting upwards. Roddy, almost without thinking, saw that once inside, this gun would change the whole situation and that they would very likely all die. He looked about and grabbed a strange metallic tubular device that they later discovered was an over-elaborate bottle opener. He pointed it towards him.

"Let it go," he said, in a voice that was not to be disobeyed.

The man still could not see clearly and only caught an oblique sight of a shiny metallic object. His position and, oddly, the foreign accent and the indefatigable pitch of it finally of it drew all the fight from him and he let the gun fall to the floor. He would throw himself on their mercy as it was a better prospect than what was facing him outside if they did not get their target. An army can only be driven forward by the threat of brutality if they fail, when they are certain that the enemy will be as brutal if they do fail. Roddy was wondering whether to dash forward for the gun or to call for help when Judy came in the room. She came rushing forward shouting, "Son of a bitch."

She picked up a large ceramic jar marked 'Flour' and hurled it at the still-trapped figure. It smashed on his head and flour went everywhere. He was knocked unconscious, his body relaxed, and he was at last able to slump forward into the room, raising even more flour into the air as he fell. Roddy looked at her, astounded.

"I thought I kind of had that one covered – but all help welcome," he commented quietly.

Roddy searched the drawers of the room and found a huge roll of duct tape. He left her tying him up, hands and feet, so he could not move when and if he ever came around. He took up the gun and went back to join the other three. They asked what had happened.

"However many there were outside, there is one less now – and we have another gun."

He took position, tried to recall some firearms training from decades before, and started to take aim uncertainly at whatever presented itself from the shrubbery.

Out there, it became apparent that they were on their own and that the third man was not coming back. They now counted four guns firing back. The boss was losing blood and starting to get weak. They began to rehearse in their heads the various plans they all had for this kind of occasion. The cabins in the woods well away from civilisation or the false identities they thought they had prepared. Just then, a shot from the house hit home. It got the remaining soldier in the abdomen. He was not as restrained as the boss and fell back into cover and cursed loudly.

"Motherfucking cocksuckers!"

It did not turn him to revengeful fury, however, but just put retreat firmly in his mind. Without asking the boss, he started back towards the car. The boss had no option but to creep after him. When they came close to the car, they had to be out in the open and all four thought of taking more shots, but none did. With the boss driving, the two of them sped off. Both were losing blood and getting weaker. They got on the freeway and pushed the car as fast as it would go, not thinking straight and not in fact thinking much at all, but merely as an acknowledgment that they were now fleeing their previous lives. They did not see the truck in front changing lanes and went into its rear corner at a relative speed of more than 60 mph. They leapt off sideways with the car now beginning to tumble rapidly as its ordered forward momentum was converted to chaotic rotational energy. They did not hit anything further in the inside lane but rotated right over it and the crash barrier and went down into a small ravine in a ball of flames. The car went spinning on up the opposite slope some way before rolling down to the bottom again and setting the scrub on fire.

22

THE FOUNDATION VANISHES AND WHAT THEY DID NEXT

After the car screamed away, an absolute peace fell on the house with the last of the evening light. The same single bird kept up a strange call in a minor key, which nevertheless sounded hopeful. The four of them put their heads up above the sill of the holed and, in places, completely smashed window. There were no police sirens approaching and John simply said that as most of the houses around here were boarded up, there was probably nobody to have heard the shots. The four of them looked out at Said-Maartens still lying there and now, in a state of almost serenity, he was gazing back unfocused and without seeming to see any of them. They noticed for the first time that he was bleeding. James and Roddy had both to signal once again to the other two to keep quiet and ignore him for a moment longer. Judy had meanwhile re-entered the room when the shooting stopped and, unnoticed, had collapsed into a huge armchair and started to sob. As the silence reasserted itself, they heard her and turned to face her. James went forward but before he could get to the chair, she stood up before him and explaining, before explanation was sought of her, she lamented, "It was all because of me. You could have been killed and all because of me – because of the shit I've brought down on you..."

James hugged her.

"They didn't come for any of us at all – and I want you to keep calm because I'm thinking that there is a lot we have to learn in the next wee while."

The tone of his voice alone stopped the sobbing and she just asked him quietly what he meant.

James signalled for Roddy to go outside and bring him in.

"And take that gun with you and menace the bugger as much as you like. But don't for any favour shoot him," he added.

Roddy returned with another figure, but Judy couldn't make him out at first. John was curious to see who he had brought as well and switched on the lights. At once, Judy saw who he had found and leapt up again, to be restrained by James, who was in place for just this move.

"It's Side-Martin – it's that son of a bitch Side-Martin again. Was he one of the bastards shooting at us? How d'you find him out there, Roddy?"

James had to hold her back more firmly and was going to answer her when John stepped forward.

"If I'm guessing right, he was the one they were trying to get at all along and… we didn't find him. He found us and brought those goons in on his trail."

Said-Maartens said nothing but motioned to a chair and Roddy let him sit. He was weak and at peace at last. This shone through the exhausted state he was in and the effects of the hole in his arm, and managed to make even Judy hold back and wonder at him.

"I'm here to tell you all I know. And I'm sorry about who followed me here – I suppose I'm not very good at any of this."

He then lapsed into silence and started to doze off for little spells.

"I know a doctor who we can trust – I'll call him," said Phil.

Said-Maartens was given water but refused anything to eat. John stood over him, feeling slightly superfluous with his symbolic gun in his belt. Said-Maartens sipped the water and came to a little and sat drowsily looking around him. He seemed to be in no pain, and he had the same disarming expression of subdued relief on his face.

"Don't I remember you from Panomnes?" he asked John.

He was relieved now to be able to treat their tenuous relationship as if it were something from the normal world about which one could exchange small talk, though small talk was not his usual habit.

Meanwhile, in the kitchen, Phil took the first lead in the analysis of events.

"The way I figure it is that this character… what did you call him?"

"Said-Maartens," answered James.

"Yea, Said-Maartens," repeated Phil with some effort.

"This character has somehow pissed them off big style. Now in my experience that has either been because they have let 'them' down badly or have had the balls to go against 'them'. But this guy doesn't look like he has anywhere near that amount of guts – he seems like kind of a wuss to me."

"He is a wuss," commented Judy in a resigned voice. She was recalling her change of heart after throwing stones at him at the farm.

"OK then, I think it has been decided that he just let them down in some way."

James then thought of a question.

"But what about all this shootout carry-on? They don't do it this way back home. An odd person has been disappeared in the last few years – Greg was disappeared – and with us they tried to snipe us out of existence from a couple of hundred yards away. But nothing like this."

"No, likewise over here," said Phil reflectively.

"They don't like anything to be seen – yea, you're right, this is kinda new."

Roddy had a sudden insight.

"These soldiers had lost control," he announced. "They would have liked to have done it like Greg outside the pub – I bet their standing orders would have been to do all their work like that. So that people disappear, and nobody can link it to 'them'. That was how they were meant to be acting but they one way or another lost control of their target – this Said-Maartens."

James started to speak but Roddy broke across him

because, having articulated his first revelation, another had come to him.

"It was to stop him getting to us. That was why they were so desperate. Judy mentioned his name on her broadcast, and they knew he could be linked back to 'them'. They didn't know we knew who he was until that broadcast. He's involved in Judy's story – you can be certain of that – that's why he was sent to look us over at the farm."

James' thoughts had been catapulted forward by Roddy's idea.

"It's because of what he could tell us," he stated.

"It's because he can tell us what the whole bloody thing was about. They couldn't even let him in the door here."

"So, they really weren't trying to wipe us out again at all," Judy almost whispered.

"No, I think you really are too famous for that now – and probably have been since after the whole shooting thing and the disappearing of the guy who brought Judy to you," added Phil, who was not without insight.

Changing the subject, he went on. "So, what do you want to do with this Sai…" he stumbled over the name.

"I just call him Side-Martin, it's easier," suggested Judy.

"Sure – Side-Martin – sounds better too. Anyway, what are you wanting to do with him? We should get as much incriminating stuff out of him as we can, and it is probably going to go a long way to explaining what happened to Judy."

Just at that moment there was a crashing sound from the little pantry next door. Roddy looked to Judy in alarm; James and Phil just looked mystified.

Roddy got up and headed for the door to the pantry and Judy followed him.

"Don't worry, Roddy, he's not going anywhere fast. I've got enough duct tape round him to keep him down."

And, when Roddy got into the pantry, things were as Judy had promised. The gunman had his ankles and wrists tightly would round with the tape. Furthermore, a strong band of tape looped back and forward many times between the two bindings, drawing his arms behind his back and his feet up almost to his behind. As a finishing touch, he was gagged by a large strip of tape across his mouth and wound right round the back of his head. He had the beginnings of a large bruise on his forehead and a small gash which dribbled blood but did not look drastic. He had regained consciousness and was groaning and struggling and had tried to turn onto his front as preparation for trying to kneel but had upset a small table in the process. He had fallen back resignedly.

"You managed to clear up most of the flour, I see," was Roddy's only comment by way of understatement.

"Sure – I'm a neat worker," answered Judy in a mock indignant voice.

Broadly, *What the fuck* summed up the others' reactions.

They had it explained to them. Meanwhile, the gunman had shuffled to a half sitting position with his back against the wall.

"So, this is one of the soldiers – I've never seen one before this," quietly explained Phil in an intrigued voice.

"I have," said Judy.

The gunman glared back at them in a semblance of defiance but there was something missing from his expression.

He was only in his twenties and had a hard, cold face and a shaved head, with surprisingly small blue eyes. He had an air that denied any possibility of reform, but only of stunned acceptance for a while with the pretence of cooperation with humanity before, in time, another means might present itself for taking revenge on society for whatever were its faults in his eyes.

"One of the fanatics – but not specifically for 'them'," was how James accurately summed him up.

They left him there and went back into the huge main room and told John what had happened at the other side of the house.

James wanted to discuss what they were going to do with Said-Maartens but instinctively thought that it would be better if Said-Maartens knew nothing of whatever they decided.

"There is a kind of den down below here in the basement," said John, with a nod towards the floor.

"It has a couch and a toilet and everything."

So, they led Said-Maartens, totally docile, to a little door off the hallway and down the stairs into the den. He looked supremely content again. Judy followed them down with some food and bottles of soda. He did not even comment as they promised to get to him in the morning, and retreated up the stairs and locked the door.

They had only just started to think about what to do with their captured soldier when a car came up the drive and stopped right outside where Said-Maartens had been cowering.

"Don't worry, it's old Doc. Rospendowski," said Phil.

A slim figure around sixty came in through the French windows. He had an expression of great innocence, preserved over the years against all the odds. He looked around and recognised Phil but just frowned slightly at the others. He waited to be introduced and the situation explained. He was then ushered towards the door to the basement but hesitated.

"Before I go any further, you should know that you have a taxi shot full of holes at the bottom of your drive and a taxi driver with half his head blown away – nothing to be done for him."

They all looked out through the smashed windows and saw the rear of a taxi cab just protruding into their field of view around the shrubs.

They went down into the basement with the doctor and asked Said-Maartens about the cab. He confirmed that it was how he had got there, and that the driver had had a bullet to the head but didn't seem overly troubled by having witnessed the occurrence. The doctor cleaned up his wound and bound it and gave him a shot. Through all this, Said-Maartens never flinched. The doctor was going to advise them further about the arm, but they urged him up the stairs and quickly followed him. They relocked the door and were ultra-cautious, needlessly manoeuvring a large sideboard across it.

"All I was going to say is that it isn't serious but that you should have him checked out in a couple of days or if it gets any worse."

"Can you arrange a shot to put somebody under for about half an hour?" was Phil's irrelevant reply.

"Sure, I've something here – if I only give half of it, it should—"

James interrupted all this.

"What are you thinking about?" he asked for the rest of them.

"Well, I think I know what to do with our soldier – we send him back to the scene of his crime and blow the whistle as loud as we can," explained Phil.

The rest still looked mystified, but it suddenly dawned on Judy.

"You mean, put him back in the taxi and call the cops?"

"Not just the cops but every news outlet we can think of that will run it. I know some that have turned already and there is more of them every hour. There are the Taylor brothers for a start, and they must know dozens more."

"And all the blogs we can think of," added James.

"That way, even if the cops are the new style, they won't be able to sit on it and we can embarrass them into doing something."

"And we get a major scandal of 'them' actually shooting somebody out there in the public eye for the first time," announced John.

So, they arranged to get the doctor to put the struggling soldier out for just long enough to carry him to the car. First, they cleaned up his gun, the one Roddy had used, and with all his prints removed, Judy, meticulously wearing rubber gloves, dotted the limp soldier's fingers all over it. They then carried him, between four of them, down the drive. Getting near the car, the doctor warned them that it was a gruesome sight and James insisted that Judy hold back. John stayed with her, but Phil was able and between him and James and the doctor, they got the unconscious soldier into the passenger seat. They dropped his gun on his lap. As a last inspiration, Phil noted that the deserted suburban road was inclined slightly downwards along the line the car was pointing. To make the whole incident look more mysterious to the police and to take attention away from the house with its shot-up windows, he took the handbrake off and pushed it with his shoulder. The soldier was just starting to groan again as it rolled gently down the straight road for quite some way before crashing into a tree in front of one of the few houses in the neighbourhood that was not boarded up. It encountered the tree at a moderate velocity – enough to cut up and bruise the soldier further and make enough noise in the silence of early evening. They waited a little until the light in that distant house went up and, after a moment, screams were heard. They then knew that they did not even have to alert anybody themselves.

They would have awoken late the next morning but were disturbed by the sound of hammering from the front of the house. John came through into the kitchen yawning and unthinkingly scratching his behind. He looked into the big room and a smile of recall lit up his face. With a look of profound gratitude, he nodded to himself and raised his arm in thanks to the joiners who were busy replacing the windows and patching up the front of the house where bullets had struck. The foreman waved back his acknowledgement, but nobody even paused as they worked. The rest of them came through into the kitchen almost simultaneously.

"I just figured last night that even if the car was found further down the street, we don't want any sign of what happened to remain. I called some guys I know that we can trust, and they are working their balls off for us out there," he explained, even before he said good morning.

"Thank God for the few that were onside."

Roddy saw the point of this first.

"That's good work, John – good work. You can never be sure what that shaven-headed little bugger will say to get himself out of his mess."

They were past with breakfast when they remembered Said-Maartens in the basement. They put together some fresh coffee for him, shifted the sideboard and cautiously unlocked the door. There was no need for any hesitation as Said-Maartens was sitting quietly below them on the end of his improvised bed, watching television. He looked up as they came down the stairs and switched off the television and stood to greet them and accept the coffee with thanks. It was all done formally and totally impersonally. Small talk was not a feature of Said-Maartens, and it was not seen as appropriate to the occasion by the others. Roddy did his bad-cop performance to make it clear what they wanted.

"You're down here 'til you tell us all you know about Judy's history. There is nobody out there from your employers that wants anything to do with you anymore, except the execution squad that we rescued you from yesterday."

Said-Maartens looked round at them, a genuine picture of innocence. He considered, after what he saw as his recent multiple trials and tests, that he was a new version of himself, and that confession to Judy was the essence of his new incarnation. He could not understand that others could not see it. He was dismayed by Roddy's approach.

"I'll tell you everything I know – everything," he declared directly to Judy in a tone both familiar and contrite.

He started into his tale right from the time he joined the establishment in London. He was not any time into his confessions when Roddy made the first connection.

"Was this place just round the corner from a pub called the Duke of Rothsay?"

Said-Maartens said that that was exactly where it was but did not ask or even try to guess how Roddy knew. He no longer thought of himself as a part of that world and had no interest in it anymore and no concern with how anybody else thought of it either. He would tell all that he could recall but it was not for him to enter their processes of deduction. This early disclosure that Said-Maartens was connected to the agency to which Greg had ostensibly been conveying Judy gave a new solidity to their speculations.

He outlined why the establishment existed but emphasised that this was initially only his speculation. Nobody had ever contradicted his assumption of influence over important people but neither had they specifically confirmed it. It had been the inevitable assumption that dawned on everybody and became the thing that everybody then knew but never talked about.

"That's pretty much how they would work things," put in John.

Said-Maartens then went on in a matter-of-fact way to describe his promotion to administering the whole chain of global establishments, all of which had the same function of political leverage. He then went on in an only slightly less pedestrian manner to describe the expansion from houses to supplying girls to specific targets around the world in an extension of the need to influence the important people who may have resisted The Foundation's plan for the future of the globe. That this revelation would have a profound effect on his audience Said-Maartens should have been able to anticipate, even though he had already mostly forgotten his own first reaction to the news, but he still had no intensions of entering their thought processes. They stopped him and he very politely indicated that he would wait, sitting there with an expression of patient good humour. This beam of light descended and illuminated that which had been the great puzzle until then.

"It was none of my idea. I was merely given it to organise," added Said-Maartens.

"So, I was being sent as a sex slave to somebody that you needed to have something on," said Judy directly to Said-Maartens, her voice a mixture of relief at finally knowing the truth but revulsion at what she had been told.

Said-Maartens did not reply but a look of confirmation came with a slight raising of his eyebrows and widening of his eyes.

"And Greg tried to steal me away from you and you had him wiped out because of it."

"That was Ms Saldanha's doing," replied Said-Maartens.

"The mysterious Ms Saldanha again," commented James.

"She was just someone I reported upwards to. She was at Panomnes."

They looked to John.

"I only saw her that once, but nobody knew anybody they did not have an absolute need to know. It will have been the same with this sorry asshole here."

Said-Maartens was again dismayed at this language and that they were not recognising the new man he had become.

"And why did you come to spy on us at all? What was that about?" asked James with anticipatory curiosity.

"That was at Ms Saldanha's instructions."

"To see if it would be safe to wipe us out too?"

"Yes – I believe she wanted to drive you into hiding."

There was a silence. Judy sat back in her chair and stared into the distance, and Said-Maartens resumed his air of detached contentment and relief.

Roddy broke the silence.

"Well, we got most of it fairly right – we got all the twists correct. It was only the big question that we couldn't work out – and no bloody wonder. There should be no ill to any of us for not being able to make the leap of imagination to that particularly hellish fact."

Said-Maartens took no interest in Roddy's summation; he did not care how they had handled what had happened to Judy. He was starting to think of the future now.

Judy got up and went quietly upstairs to think. They watched her go, slightly anxiously, before turning to Said-Maartens again.

Roddy continued to probe.

"So where was Judy being sent – who was it to, and how did you select him? Was he demanding a girl by return in the post or was all this Saldanha's idea?"

This was the cue for Said-Maartens' scant documentary

evidence that he had put in his bundle before he left his house in a panic. He brought the bundle out of his pocket and laid the notes on a small table but separated a small sheaf of papers from them. These he looked through and then handed Roddy one with the name and address of the man in the burning sands. He said it had come from David. James leant over and examined it.

"Thank heavens for that poor bastard Greg/David, eh?"

"I have no idea how they were selected, but I believe they were approached rather than coming forward themselves."

"As I said – that was how they worked – obsessive secrecy always. Tell us again then all that you know," said John.

With complete candour, Said-Maartens went through every detail of his days since he was introduced to the girl export business. The only detail he missed was his craven behaviour in the last few days and the degradation he had been rescued from. Before he was done, James whispered to Roddy, half joking, "You get every last detail you need out of this specimen– I'm a bit worried that Judy is up there looking for one of the guns!"

In the big room, the repair gang were packing up and had almost all their gear back on their truck. Judy was sitting quietly, looking calmly out at them but not acknowledging that she saw them or indeed anything.

"He's not even a wuss, is he? He's way less than even a wuss – he's just a nothing. I think he sees he's done wrong – but not so much in his eyes. And that about sums it up – it wasn't really him – Side-Martin – was it? It was this whole huge goddamn outfit he was working for… and what was I being shipped for?"

"To give them something to hold over their target – something they could use to get more power."

"That's great. I just had to know, like. That's OK then – as long as I understand!" Judy erupted sarcastically.

"I would hate for it to be a mystery after all."

"Roddy's getting the last of the details now. Said-Maartens is being completely cooperative."

"Well, good for old Side-Martin. I'm sure it is making him feel a lot better about the whole damn thing," she spat out in the same bitter tone.

But then she relaxed back in the chair and continued much more softly.

"Just doing what he was told, huh? I guess it was a case of just doing what he was told, and good old Greg? Yes – he was as well. Until the poor schmuck had to go and rescue me and got disappeared for his trouble. Jeez!"

She lost control briefly and a look of distress came over her face and she shed a brief tear for at least a part of Greg. Then she fell silent but was quickly re-animated.

"So, Side-Martin was fixing to trade me into some kind of sex slavery – can you believe that low-life nothing – why, he couldn't even hit on me in a bar," she announced indignantly and somewhat illogically, but understandably.

"I was afraid you might be up here for a gun," said James quietly.

"Where would be the point in that? He's just a bit player and halfway crazy the way he is speaking down there. He's trying to make out it's all nothing to do with him… and I guess he is right in a way."

Down in the den, Said-Maartens had truly exhausted his

narrative. As a last gesture, he had given Roddy a list of all the girls who had been shipped. This last point was flourished as if it was the crowning piece of evidence in his defence. He handed the list over, again emphasising in an oblique but nonetheless plain manner how good it was of him to have gone to these lengths to help them.

Said-Maartens attempted a very humble enquiry as to what else they needed from him and when he might be allowed to go.

"You're going nowhere at all," was Roddy's brief response before they went back up. Said-Maartens again despaired that they were not seeing his new self.

Back in the big room, Judy looked up as they came in. Roddy waved the paper at her.

"It wasn't just you."

"What do you mean?" asked Judy, completely turned from her previous thoughts.

"Well, there were seemingly some before and after you and maybe more even than appears on this list – he has just given it to us."

Judy paused and went up and down the list and then read out the names. They meant nothing to anyone except Judy.

"I kinda know these girls."

They all looked at her doubtfully, hoping to check an excess of sentimentality.

She caught the mood and went on.

"No, I don't mean I really know them – it's just that I can see them all hopeful and falling for the same crap that I did. I can see them all happy and excited and getting on a plane…"

She fell silent for a while, and nobody said anything.

"But nobody rescued them – they didn't have a Greg – and where the hell are they now? Jesus, what are they having to..."

She quietly began to weep gently, and James sat down by her and hugged her.

Some minutes passed like that in silence when suddenly Judy freed herself of James and bounded to her feet.

"We have to find out who these girls were and where they have been sent and go after them."

This initiated a spell of anything but silence. They tried to convince her that they would never be able to do that. They could just about find out who these girls were, but the way The Foundation was set up was as secrets hiding secrets for layer after layer. John and Phil began a long discussion about how the country was going to emerge after this revolution just begun. All the men agreed that it had to be publicised and put in the hands of the authorities, but they ended up with simply vague hopes for the possibilities of any rescue. Judy was not satisfied and sat quietly as the discussion dribbled to a subdued close, and it seemed like the next thing was a suggestion of lunch, when she saw a way.

23

THE RUONO GIRLS

"We can't do it – but they must have family, friends who are wondering where the hell they have gone… because… because – you can be damn sure that they were all fooled into keeping their trips hidden by being suckered into one of their scams. Nobody will know anything – they will just have disappeared – they're all missing persons. Somebody must have called the cops about them."

The rest of them started to slowly alter course in line with this new approach.

"And who is going to follow up better than the families? We just have to contact the families and set them loose on the case."

This was seen and became agreed, and they fell to work at once to find those who would fight for this mere list of names.

Contacts were tried with the authorities and the police; people who were sympathetic but frightened previously were now much more forthcoming. They started another great phone session that went on for the rest of the day. They grazed briefly in the kitchen and Judy remembered to feed Said-Maartens. Judy then found a giant presentation flip pad and tore pages from it and pinned them to the wall for each name as they were identified, and the details accumulated. Well into the evening, when it all started to dry up and they thought they had got as much as they could, they paused and reviewed it all. They had a description and family to one extent or another for all of them. Incredibly, and because The Foundation did its selection so well, they had four sets of contacts for names who were apparently never registered as missing persons. They had the names to call but already saw these girls as lost completely. Although it was late, Judy insisted on calling them all right then as they were chiefly in California. When they called, they found most of them were already thinking about contacting Judy as they had made the connection with Judy's story appearing viral on the web. Some had not thought it out yet but were still impossibly over-optimistic. They just wanted to get some new help in their search for a missing daughter. They were all given the address.

"Well, at least we've done something here," proclaimed Judy softly before they turned in. But even as they dispersed, James called them back into the big room.

"What are we going to do with him down below? We have to think about it. We could turn him in, but all these other families are going to want to do that – or a lot of them might want to beat him up or worse – we just can't anticipate."

Judy resolved the thing for them before anybody could put any ideas forward.

"He has told us all he knows – we aren't going to be able to break this foundation down and neither are these poor folks that are coming tomorrow. And I don't see police or the FBI or whoever it's going to be from now on doing much better with or without him to help them. We'll give the folks the list and just keep him down there and then later just… just let him go. If there is still a hitman out there looking for him, well, just… anyway, it's no business of ours to keep the sad son of a bitch protected."

Judy had spoken and it was her call ultimately.

Around late morning, cars started to arrive. The folk were invited in and soon enough another car would turn up. They had driven from all over the state, some of them overnight. By afternoon, they had a house full of anxious people. They tried to give them what information they could but urged them to wait 'til they were all there. In the afternoon, they gave up waiting and delivered a long lecture. They covered what had happened to Judy over again, that they had discovered the list (fortunately nobody asked from where) and how they had then contacted all of them. They told of the location of Said-Maartens' office, Panomnes Productions, and every piece of information they had on The Foundation – all except Said-Maartens' name. He meanwhile sat and waited contentedly in the basement with no knowledge of what was going on above his head.

Swollen by late arrivals, the noise of the discussion was impressive as they compared notes on what little they knew and exchanged photographs of the missing. Many of them broke down and cried and then tried to comfort each other. They formed into little discussion groups to decide on action. They detailed people to go to the office in Cupertino and break in, if necessary, to see what evidence there might be still in there. They similarly had people from the LA area promising to blockade and invade the Panomnes studios. They started to get together lists of news outlets they would lobby and politicians they would demand join the fight. They already knew that this would be bound up with the revolution roaring on ahead around them. An obviously supremely dedicated and angry black woman, who managed to deliver a damningly logical condemnation of it all while letting tears fall for her lost daughter, was spontaneously elevated to chairman coordinating them all.

Phil commented quietly and grimly to Judy, but out of the women's hearing, that it was good to see that The Foundation upheld its policy of equality of outcome in all its activities.

After only a couple of hours, they all dispersed to their cars with an air of urgent business to be begun. A few stayed behind for a little and helped tidy the place up. They exchanged details with Judy and promised to keep her up to date with anything they found out. Then they departed in turn. The whole swarm of them dispersed to magnify the Judy effect a thousand fold as they got the disappearances – which collectively they had already named the Ruono Girls – and all that lay behind them made know across the world.

Now, after passing on the information, they were left a

little flat and tired and for the first time Judy felt sidelined a bit. The fight was no longer completely with her but with her new army, who were off and raging across the country. They sent out for supper and made inroads into John's relations' wine cellar. As they parted for bed, Roddy remembered Said-Maartens.

"Let him stew," said Judy, "he's got plenty of water."

*

Next day, without any discussion, they all felt it was the conclusion of the battle. John and Phil, above all other considerations of what they were going to add to the hoped-for new order of things, had to restore their family lives. Over breakfast, it was apparent that there was to be no lunch together. The morning was all packing and closing the house.

"And where are we going?" James asked Judy.

"I know it doesn't make any sense, but I want to go back to LA. To Panomnes and the old apartment and... It's just what I'd like to do. We can talk about other stuff on the road."

James agreed and went to tell Roddy. Roddy didn't care and just wondered what the rest of California might look like.

It was well into the morning before a kind of telepathy ran quickly through all five of them and, with expressions of amazement at how they could have forgotten again, they remembered Said-Maartens. They unlocked his basement and called him up. He emerged into the hall to be told that they were going to release him. He was given no reasons and it was clear nobody wanted to talk with him anymore. He had the clothes he stood up in and had nothing to fetch from the basement. There was at first a suggestion that they could not send him forth like this.

"No – just let him go wander the streets like he is," said Judy.

She relented a little when Said-Maartens asked for the loan of one of their phones to call his wife. It had not occurred to her that a creature like this could have any such connections to another member of humanity. He got 'number unavailable' responses from his wife's phone and the house phone. He did not puzzle over this and, as he only then had started to think of her, he thought to himself that some drastic change in her circumstances was inevitable. He saw no connection between this sinister alteration of her circumstances and his having brought her unknowing to being a wife of The Foundation and taking her to California. He then asked to be taken back to the train station.

As the trio were going to leave first, because as they had such a long way to go and the other two were still planning their trips, they were pressed into taking him there. Judy was not happy but relented. After restrained farewells to John and Phil in front of Said-Maartens, they went off, promising to keep in touch, which they did for years afterwards. They drove in silence downtown with Judy at the wheel. Said-Maartens was deposited in front of the train station. There was not a word said in farewell and they went off in search of the freeway to San Francisco.

Said-Maartens retraced his steps and ended up in the late afternoon at California Ave. Station. He walked to his house. Finding it locked and being without keys, he knocked. After a long interval, the door was unlocked and the maid appeared.

She was in the process of clearing out Said-Maartens' stuff but had lately been unable to get any response to her request for further orders on the matter as The Foundation phones had gone dead as part of their general rout into hiding. She only knew that it was dangerous to even be seen now with Said-Maartens and started up a terrible tirade against him in Spanish, and ran screaming back into the house for her husband. Said-Maartens took fright and fled. He started the mental process of looking on his wife as some past presence while not dwelling at all on how she should have come to be so. In fact, if they had managed to get their hands on Said-Maartens, she might have been gently let go by The Foundation with mutual expressions of mystification at why he had disappeared. But as they had blundered and let him escape, he might have come back to her telling all and that could not be allowed. So, she had been shipped on the same plane as Ms Saldanha and been dealt with almost as soon as she got to the other end. She had, however, spent the whole journey in a perplexed and confused state and was not at all apprehensive until the very last moment, and even then, she was too surprised to graduate to terror.

The world was becoming liberal and free again and Said-Maartens got hotel jobs and eventually gravitated back to London, where he became once again a manager at his former place of employment. After a while, he took up with another receptionist and was moved to investigate the time that a wife had to be officially missing before he could marry again.

24

CODA

Judy and James and Roddy went spinning off southwards through California. They stopped on the way to LA and treated themselves to an upmarket hotel in the woods not too far south of Said-Maartens' old office. All the way there, they avoided connecting to the net and just listened to the news coming through their car radio and on the TV in their hotel rooms. There was already news of the Ruono Girl crusade and a whole range of similar cries of protest that had boiled over now that the lid had come off the pot. These were the beginnings of a burgeoning number of similar attacks on a myriad of inequities inflicted by The Foundation but significantly, hardly any on the range of confected oppressions which The Foundation had always used to keep people divided.

Sitting that evening on a balcony in a redwood forest, and bolstered by some Napa wine, Judy permitted herself a little self-congratulatory reflection.

"Well – we made a difference – we sparked a riot!"

The other two sat back and inwardly allowed themselves a similar self-admiring reflection.

When they got to Panomnes Studios, there was no sign of life. The main gate was closed against them and there were no cars in the parking lot and not a movement behind any of the windows. A bored security guard of late-middle years and an expression of habitual weariness wandered out to them to turn them away and, while they were making a measured appeal to be let in, he recognised Judy and the usual scene ensued. It was wearying for her by then, but she played up to it this time to negotiate entry.

"Well, seein' as how you're the chick changin' the worl' right now, why the hell don't I just let you go in," he announced.

"Don't go stealing anything now," he warned with mock seriousness, "but I don't reckon you could get very much in there 'cos all them arrogant motherfuckers already loaded everything worth a damn into trucks and took off over the horizon – it seemed to me like their asses was on fire."

They wandered through deserted studios, with most of the stuff gone and wires left hanging out of the walls. Judy located the studio where the nail-bar ad had been filmed. It brought a new level of verity to the episode for James. They wandered into the large office where outside, the water had been left running through the formal garden to disappear into the sand as normal. They searched almost at random for any paperwork in filing cabinets, but they had no idea where to look. There was very little and there appeared never to have been anything as traditional. All soft records would have gone, they presumed, but if there was anything remaining on the various machines still there, it would take an age to find, and many of them appeared to have been damaged deliberately.

Judy drove them downtown to her street. Her whole building had been gutted by fire in the riots and there was nothing to visit. All was boarded up with warnings about the risk of the remains of the building collapsing. The tent city had also been cleared, either by the fire or the recent changes at City Hall. Judy suddenly felt what she should have anticipated: the immense gap that had opened behind her and suddenly banished her past life and made it frighteningly distant. It had the opposite effect on James and knitted Judy's story together as an only now visible whole.

Roddy ignored the slightly unsatisfactory ending of his greatest case with the pursued villains mostly evaporating beyond any conceivable reality. He thought of that as an unimportant imperfection to his part in a revolution of which he was possibly a little too self-congratulatory. The next day, he detached himself as courteously as possible by claiming to have played gooseberry too long and flew home. His wife had already formed even grander notions of his role and was inspired to a renewed professional respect for him. She moved back to his house in the village. After a short while, though, as his part in the reconciliation, he sold up, gave up his place in the Cross Keys and moved back to town. He kept in contact with James in case, as he said, something further came up and he could do with a hand again.

James and Judy, floating on a flurry of fees from chat show appearances and the like, went across the US in some style for a while and became even more famous until they became finally disillusioned with the frequently insincere circus that it all was. The politics of the entire West seemed to have changed. There were new people who weren't quite as new as they pretended and there were new freedoms and prosperity which were similarly not quite the revolution they suggested, though things were so much better that almost nobody noticed. Underneath, the same old, almost unheard *ostinato* was repeating over and over and very gradually gaining volume. The people very gradually and unconsciously were induced to ignore that the dangers threatened by those who have a plan and seek to be right and therefore obeyed, is vastly greater than any posed by all the rest of the greedy galloping circus of humanity.

They went, after much nagging by James and reluctance from Judy, to Copper Island to let James see the remaining bit of her life. Her mother had ditched her alcoholic, failed liquor store guy when he took the plunge to financial ruin and physical degeneration without being able to recognise that either of them was upon him. She had started a modest new existence and had sobered up. She talked of moving away somewhere, and the reunion of mother and daughter still had the undercurrent of perceived desertion about it. She even hinted about a new start abroad, but James did not notice, and Judy did not take her up on it. James was taken one night to the Copper Country Tavern to meet the remaining friends Judy had in the place. James felt old and foreign, but the night went well enough. The company did not annoy him, and he more than once wondered at the civility still shown by so many of the young of this place in an environment of alienation, cynicism and distrust. He was again bewildered for yet another reason at how he and Judy could have come about but did not doubt that they had.

They both saw that their time in the US was coming to an end. There had been many conversations between them recently about where to go next and what to do. Nothing definite had emerged and it was Judy who outlined a possibility. She wanted to go back to the farm and the village and even Ian's pub. She was aware enough to worry that she was possibly trying to recreate her deliverance. She knew the farm was finished and that such a horizon was going to be far too limited for either of them now. But she wanted it as a base, and not only physically. He had talked of continuing the fight – trying to become a campaigning journalist or something in politics – he had nothing clear in his mind yet. Meanwhile, he thought he could get work of a kind through old contacts. Judy promised to do anything available or start some new enterprise out of the farm. The unrealistic sheep and kale were forgotten. They had enough money now to restore the place and maintain it until they got their intentions resolved. Therefore, as the days started to shorten, they found themselves taking a plane home. The option through Reykjavik was still cheaper but they paid for a direct flight instead.